# THE SWOF

## (Joe Hawke #9)

## Rob Jones

ISBN: 9798686693692

## Other Books by Rob Jones

### The Joe Hawke Series
The Vault of Poseidon (Joe Hawke #1)
Thunder God (Joe Hawke #2)
The Tomb of Eternity (Joe Hawke #3)
The Curse of Medusa (Joe Hawke #4)
Valhalla Gold (Joe Hawke #5)
The Aztec Prophecy (Joe Hawke #6)
The Secret of Atlantis (Joe Hawke #7)
The Lost City (Joe Hawke #8)
The Sword of Fire (Joe Hawke #9)
The King's Tomb (Joe Hawke #10)
Land of the Gods (Joe Hawke #11)
The Orpheus Legacy (Joe Hawke #12)
Hell's Inferno (Joe Hawke #13)
Day of the Dead (Joe Hawke #14)
Shadow of the Apocalypse (Joe Hawke #15)
Gold Train (Joe Hawke #16)
The Last Warlord (Joe Hawke #17)

### The Avalon Adventure Series
The Hunt for Shambhala (Avalon Adventure #1)
Treasure of Babylon (Avalon Adventure #2)
The Doomsday Cipher (Avalon Adventure #3)

### The Hunter Files
The Atlantis Covenant (Hunter Files #1)
The Revelation Relic (Hunter Files #2)
The Titanic Legacy (Hunter Files #3)

### The Cairo Sloane Series
Plagues of the Seven Angels (Cairo Sloane #1)

# DEDICATION

*For My Children*

# THE SWORD OF FIRE

# CHAPTER ONE

## Washington DC

Joe Hawke looked at the ring for the third time in an hour and snapped the tiny box shut with his fingers. If anyone had told him he would ask another woman to marry him after the devastation caused by his first wife's brutal murder he would have told them they were insane, and yet he had an engagement ring in his hand. He just hoped Lea Donovan would say yes – if he found the courage to ask her.

He slipped the box in his pocket, gave the two secret service agents a brief nod, and pushed open the heavy door. He hated hospitals and the sooner he was out of here, the better. They had some serious rebuilding work to do if they were to make their home on the island of Elysium secure again, and he couldn't wait to start.

Inside, the room was bright and sunlight flooded in through the slats of a metal Venetian blind. Sitting on the bed, Alex Reeve turned and smiled.

"You're late." She frowned and tapped her wristwatch.

"I had to buy something," he said, returning the smile. Subconsciously, he put his hand in his pocket and turned the small box over.

1

Alex glanced down at the little bulge in his pocket. "Woah, you *are* pleased to see me."

"Funny," Hawke said, but quickly changed the subject. "Ready to go?"

"Sure."

He helped her off the bed and into her wheelchair. She had lost the ability to walk while on a covert CIA mission many years ago, but for a brief, shining moment she had walked again after consuming the strange elixir Hawke had found in the Tomb of Eternity.

He knew how much it had transformed her life, but then her newfound freedom had been brutally snatched away again when the elixir's power faded and her legs had collapsed from under her. She was storming Alcatraz at the time; it was during what they had come to call Operation Aztec Prophecy, and ever since that terrible day she had once again been confined to her wheelchair.

Seeing her like this ripped Hawke in two, and in many ways, he felt offering her the elixir was a mistake. Not only had they been unable to work out exactly how it worked, but in drinking the strange, sparkling liquid, Alex had been given a sharp reminder of what it was like to walk again. When its mystical power drifted away and she had lost the ability to use her legs all over again, the pain she must have felt would have been unbearable, and he knew that was his fault.

And yet she had never once complained about it or blamed him. Now, she looked up at him and gave him that famous smile of hers – curious, knowing, and intelligent.

She looked around the room. The smell of industrial disinfectant drifted through the dust motes. "Just checking I have everything."

Hawke nodded. "What about your suitcase?"

"With the agents outside."

"What were their names again?"

"Brandon and Justin."

Hawke sighed. "Remind me again – which one's your new shadow?"

"Brandon."

"Which one's he – little or large?"

"Large."

"I thought they were supposed to blend in? He's ten feet tall."

Alex rolled her eyes. "He's six foot six – one inch taller than his father."

"He told you that?"

"No, I read it in his tea leaves."

"I thought you said you'd convinced your dad that this wasn't necessary?" he said, and paused to consider the casual way he referred to the President of the United States as "your dad". He couldn't believe how much his life had changed since he had left the Special Boat Service just a couple of short years ago. Meeting Lea Donovan in the British Museum and being drawn into the hunt for Poseidon's trident was incredible enough, but now he was on first names with President Brooke and his daughter.

"Hey – I'm lucky I got them to agree to one. The original plan was for two."

"I still think it's overkill. You've got the ECHO team."

"Not personally assigned to me day and night, Joe. My father's the President of the United States. It was that or they'd never let me out of the White House. Just accept it."

"If you say so."

"I *do* say so," she said firmly. Softening her voice, she turned once again to look at the Englishman. "Any news on Rich?"

She meant Sir Richard Eden, the founder of the ECHO team. He had been blasted into a coma when the man they knew as the Oracle had attacked Elysium.

Hawke shook his head. "Sorry, no change. Lea's with him at the hospital in London. She's staying at my flat."

"All right," she said, sounding resigned. "Let's get the hell out of here."

Hawke thought this sounded like a great idea. This was the third operation on Alex's shoulder since she was shot back on Elysium, and he guessed she had seen enough of Fort Belvoir Community Hospital to last her several lifetimes. This latest operation was some plastic surgery to conceal the wound, and it was the end of the whole business.

As he held open the door for her, the two agents exchanged a few short words and then shook hands. Brandon McGee spoke into his palm mic, collected a small Samsonite case, and began to follow them along the corridor. Hawke felt his presence a few feet behind him and knew this was going to be a problem.

He turned to Alex. "Doesn't it bother you?"

"What?"

He nodded over his shoulder. "Lurch."

"No, and keep your voice down. He's actually a pretty cool guy. Got a lot of experience."

"Last time I checked, ECHO had almost no need at all for a basketball player."

"He's not in ECHO, Joe. Don't make that mistake. He's US Secret Service."

They reached their car and Hawke blipped open the locks. He opened the door and took Alex's suitcase. "In you go."

"Wait," Brandon said flatly.

"For what?" Hawke said.

Brandon pulled a small extendable vehicle inspection mirror from his case and began to check under the car. "Bomb checking protocol."

Hawke sighed. "Oh, for *fu-*."

"Joe," Alex said. "Let Agent McGee do his job."

"Of course."

McGee snapped the mirror away and put it in the case. "Clear."

They climbed into the chunky Escalade, with Hawke at the wheel and Alex beside him. After folding Alex's wheelchair into the trunk, McGee sat in the back with his shaved head pushing up into the headlining velour on the car's roof.

"Couldn't move across a few inches, could you, Brandon?" Hawke said. "You're blocking my mirror."

"Sure thing."

The entire SUV rocked as Brandon shifted across and then Hawke fired up the engine and started on the twenty-mile journey to the White House. Alex's father, Jack Brooke, had been elected as America's Commander-in-Chief the previous autumn and sworn in during his inauguration a few months ago. The press claimed he'd drawn record crowds to Washington that day but Brooke never mentioned it once.

Hawke watched the Virginian suburbs drift by as they cruised along I-395 north to the nation's capital and tried to put the chaos of his life into some kind of perspective. Formerly, Major Hawke of the Royal Marines Commandos and Sergeant Hawke of the Special Boat Service, he was now plain and simple Mr. Hawke of the ECHO team. He was in love with Lea Donovan and ready to ask her to marry him, so life was good, but like the others, he felt the long, cold shadow of the Oracle and his Athanatoi cult looming over his every waking moment.

He glanced at Alex and they exchanged a smile. They knew each other well enough to share a comfortable silence. He pushed the car over the Arlington Memorial

5

Bridge, crossed the Potomac River, and vowed never to stop until he had tracked down more of the elixir.

They drove around the Lincoln Memorial on their way north. It was covered in scaffolding. After Klaus Kiefel had blown half the north side of it to pieces with a Hellfire missile the city's authorities had ordered a major rebuilding project to bring it back to life again.

"They're nearly done with the repairs," Alex said, pointing at the impressive memorial. "I still can't believe what happened to it."

"Bastards," McGee said.

"We got the bastards, though," Hawke said.

He thought about Kiefel and his obsession with the Curse of Medusa that had nearly destroyed America. Today seemed to be the day for old memories to claw their way to the surface of his mind. If there was one thing Joe Hawke hated it was dwelling on the past, so he shook it all from his mind, grateful that they had now arrived at the White House.

Having Brandon 'Lurch' McGee on board had its advantages. Among these was being waved through the northwest gate of one of America's most secure government buildings and then directed to park right outside the West Wing. Another was being whisked through security at high-speed and finding yourself inside the Oval Office with the minimum of fuss. He had never been in the world's most famous office before, and the first thing that struck him was how it seemed much smaller than the one he had seen in the movies.

"Darling!" President Jack Brooke rose from the Resolute Desk.

"It's great to see you too, Mr. President," Hawke said.

Alex rolled her eyes as her father kissed her on the cheek. "You doing okay, kid?"

"Sure."

Brooke locked eyes with Hawke and the two men shared a strong handshake. "You still looking after my little girl, Joe?"

Alex sighed and pushed the chair over to the coffee table. "Dad, don't call me that."

"Most of the time she looks after me, Mr. President," Hawke said, trying to defuse the tension. He knew Alex had serious issues with her father and clearly, his new job as president had changed none of that.

There was a tap on the door and then a friendly face stepped into the office. "We have an update on the Korean situation, sir, plus there's the UK state visit schedule and..." Special Agent Kim Taylor stopped when she saw Hawke and Alex. "I didn't know you were out of the hospital. It's good to see you Alex, and you too, Joe."

"Just got out today," Alex said.

"You're working here now?" Hawke asked.

"That's right. I transferred into the Secret Service."

"And she's great," Brooke said. He walked over to them and sat on the couch beside Alex. "So here's the plan. With me behind that desk and you in this damned wheelchair, I want you to stay in DC for a while. You can work from the White House – I had an office prepared in the Residence." He looked at his daughter intently. This time there was no trace of the now world-famous crooked Brooke grin, just a serious look of concern for a beloved daughter. "What do you say, Alex?"

She hesitated and looked at Hawke.

The Englishman looked from Brooke to Alex and gave a resigned smile. "We can't go back to Elysium, Alex. It's not safe yet."

"Joe's right," Kim said.

Alex gave a reticent shrug. "I guess..."

"Good job, darling," Brooke said. "You and I have a

lot of catching up to do. You're coming with me to London, right?"

Alex scrunched her mouth up a little and frowned. "Do I have to?"

Brooke laughed. "Of course not, but I'd love your company. You'd be strictly behind the scenes."

"I'll think about it."

"Sure."

Hawke looked at her. "You get to fly on Air Force One and you have to think about it?"

"All right, all right," she said, bowing to the pressure. "I'll go – but no press."

Brooke clapped his hands together. "You got it – anyone want coffee? They make great coffee here."

Hawke declined. "No thanks, Mr. President."

Alex shook her head. "I'm good, Dad."

Hawke started to talk when his phone rang. He excused himself and walked away for a moment. When he returned he looked anxious.

"What is it?" Brooke said.

"That was Ryan," said Hawke. "He says we might have a problem."

"What sort of problem?" Alex asked.

"Something about an old manuscript he's located. It could be critical to our mission. He's going to call me back in a minute."

"Where is this manuscript?" Brooke asked.

"Boston."

"Take Agent Taylor. You're in the US now and this is her jurisdiction. No maverick bullshit, Hawke."

"Naturally," he said, and caught a passing look of disappointment in Kim's eyes. He guessed the last thing she wanted to do was leave the nerve center of power to go on a wild goose chase in Boston, but then she said, "Yes, sir, Mr. President."

He also guessed she had no business refusing an order from the Commander-in-Chief.

Mike Clark, Brooke's Chief of Staff, tapped on the other door and stepped into the office. "We have the Vice President on Line 2, sir."

Brooke cracked his knuckles and sat down behind his desk. He picked up the phone and waved a silent goodbye to Hawke and Kim. Alex mouthed *see ya* and then they turned to go.

As Hawke and Kim stepped outside the office, the Englishman just caught the start of Brooke's conversation with his Vice President, Davis Faulkner. "Hey, Davis," Brooke said heartily. "How're tricks?"

And then the President's Body Man gave them a reluctant smile and closed the Oval Office door.

# CHAPTER TWO

## London

Lea Donovan looked down at the man in the hospital bed and clenched her jaw with anger. She had known Richard Eden since she was a child. He had been there when her father was killed and helped her navigate through some rocky teenage years. Now, he needed her help more than ever but she could do nothing except wait and pray and then wait some more.

Beside her stood Ryan Bale, a man changed forever by the cold-blooded murder of his girlfriend, Maria Kurikova. He respected the same grim silence as his former wife as he placed an unlit cigarette in his hand and collapsed into a chair beside the bed. In Ryan, she saw a different man now – harder, colder, and maybe even a little reckless.

The door opened and Lexi Zhang walked in. She was holding three coffees and after handing them around she sat at the foot of the bed and shared the tense atmosphere with her three friends. After a sip of her drink, she finally broke the silence.

"Any change?"

Several seconds passed before Lea replied. "Nothing."

The EKG machine measuring their boss's heart rate sounded a low alarm they had all heard before. A nurse scuttled in and made a few adjustments. She checked the ventilator and the IV drip smiled at them and left again.

Lea sighed. "How the hell did this happen?"

"The fucking Oracle is how it happened," Ryan said.

"And don't think for a second that he won't pay for it with his life," said Lexi.

The anger on her face was met with the sound of a fresh wave of rain lashing on the window and a burst of lightning. For a second or two, Lea saw the London skyline illuminated in stark black and white and then a deep roar of thunder echoed over the city and made the hospital shake.

"That's easy to say," she said, "but all I care about right now is getting Rich back."

"That's what we all want," Lexi said. "I'd be nothing without him. He gave me hope and I owe him everything."

"He gave us all hope," Ryan said. "He gave me ECHO, and that's the only family I've ever really known."

Lea barely heard their words. Her eyes were following the path of the IV tube as it snaked toward the hideous cannula in Eden's bruised hand. Looking at his face – thin now, sunken cheeks and light silver stubble – she saw his eyelids flicker and a moment of hope danced through her mind even though she had seen it so many times before. Soon, he was still once again, as quiet and motionless as the dead.

The heart rate machine beeped gently in the background.

Another bolt of lightning.

Another growl of thunder.

Everything was spinning out of control and she felt like screaming.

The team had split up in Rio with Hawke flying to America to help Alex while Reaper returned to his family in the south of France. Scarlet and Camacho had hooked up and gone to Vegas, and the rest of the team flew to London to be with Eden. Now Lea felt like everything was falling apart. Their home, the secret Caribbean island called Elysium was still nothing more than smoldering ruins since the attack which had almost claimed Eden's life.

ECHO was without a leader and a base and now she and Hawke were split up and separated by an ocean. Not for the first time, she wondered if it was all worth it, but at the center of her soul was the brutal murder of her father. That was the dynamo that would never stop powering her forward until she had gotten her revenge and laid every last ghost to rest. The only way to do that was with ECHO at her back.

"He'll be all right, Lea," Ryan said from the other side of the room.

She looked up and saw he had now moved the unlit cigarette to his lips and it was bouncing around as he spoke.

"I hope so."

Lexi finished her coffee and tried to change the subject. "Ryan, what did Joe say when you called him about – what was it now?"

"An ancient manuscript belonging to the Welsh triads."

"Oh, yeah I forgot about that," Lea said, absent-mindedly. She moved her eyes away from Eden and looked at herself for a moment in the reflection of the hospital window. Then she turned to Ryan. "You asked for money to buy it, right?"

"Yes."

"So what's the deal again?"

"It just turned up in a museum in Boston," Ryan said. "The reason I think we should take an interest is that when I was looking at pictures of it on their website I saw several of the same symbols that we saw on the idol in Mexico. I haven't told Joe that bit yet."

"The exact same symbols?" Lexi said.

Ryan nodded. "Right, which is very odd. If you ask me

whoever wrote that manuscript had seen the symbols somewhere and copied them down. The question is – where did the scribe see them?"

"Another idol?" Lexi said, her eyes almost sparkling.

"Possibly," Ryan said. "That's why I want to see the manuscript more closely. I asked Hawke to buy it from the museum – or at least make an offer. Its market value is well within ECHO's budget for this sort of thing, right Lea?"

Lea was thinking back to her first mission with Eden when they had stormed a facility in northern Russia and killed a rogue colonel. It seemed like a lifetime ago. Now she was dimly aware that someone was asking her a question, but she had missed all the words. "I'm sorry?"

Ryan sighed and fiddled with the cigarette. "I said we can afford to buy it, yes?"

"Oh, yeah... I think so. Rich normally did the numbers."

"But what if they tell us to get lost?" Lexi said.

Ryan shrugged his shoulders. "Then I have to fly to Boston to look through an ancient manuscript or ECHO loses the chance to have another important relic – another important part of this puzzle we're trying to put together."

"Sounds great to me," Lexi said. "Anything that helps us get closer to the truth behind this and take out the Oracle gets my vote. What do you think, Lea?"

No response.

Ryan sighed. "I'm going to call Joe back."

"Lea – did you hear what I just said?"

She flicked her head around. "Sorry, Lex... no – I was miles away."

As Ryan left the room to make the call, he and Lexi shared a concerned glance, but Lea didn't see that either. The truth was she had so much on her mind the stress was blotting out most of the surface stuff in her life.

Eden was the main problem.

What no one knew except Lea was that just this afternoon the doctor heading his care had told her the former Parachute Regiment officer's condition had worsened slightly, and she should start to make preparations in case the worst happened. Doing what Eden himself would do, she had kept the news to herself because there was no point worrying the others unnecessarily.

Not until the unthinkable happened.

Next was the email she had picked up on her phone the day before. It was from her brother, Finn. He hadn't talked to her for ten years, maybe more. That was weird enough, but what she had read in it was playing on her mind. A nursing home in Galway Bay had been in touch about a relative of theirs. Someone named Maggie had died recently.

She didn't recognize the name.

They had a box of things for her and said it was urgent. They couldn't find her, so they had asked Finn to give her the box. He didn't want to deal with it. Not interested. If she wanted to sort it out then she had to come to his place in Dublin and get the box. He was away but he would leave a key for her. The email was typical Finn Donovan – short, blunt, and not even signed.

The message had been bothering her since she read it. She had plenty of relatives over in Galway Bay and all over that part of the country, but she had never heard of that particular nursing home, and as far as she knew she didn't have any relatives in it. Now, someone at the home had told her a loved one had died and left a box of things for her to see. She wasn't sure what to make of it. All she knew was it couldn't have come at a worse time.

It never rains, but it pours.

# CHAPTER THREE

Hawke and Kim Taylor were leaving the West Wing and walking out to their car when Ryan called back. He sounded different these days. He hadn't been the same since the death of Maria Kurikova a few weeks ago. She had been shot by a Russian sniper named Ekel Kvashnin, codename Kamchatka, while Ryan was being kidnapped by an arms dealer named Dirk Kruger. He had been the last to know the terrible truth when Vincent Reno told him on a mountain track in Colombia.

The young hacker from London had reacted by drinking heavily and making erratic and dangerous decisions. He had started smoking again; cigarettes mostly but also cannabis in any format he could get it. Then he had dropped off the radar for weeks. After his absence, the next time anyone from ECHO heard from him was when he texted a picture of his first tattoo – *Маша* – on his upper arm. It meant Masha, the abbreviated form of Maria... what he used to call her.

Hawke climbed into the car as he spoke into the phone. "So what's going on, mate?"

"Definitely something for ECHO."

With Eden in a coma, these calls were now coming to Hawke. There was another man – a mysterious Dane named Magnus Lund who claimed to be part of a far-reaching consortium that owned the island of Elysium. Lund had assumed authority of the ECHO team after Eden's injury, but despite his actions on the Lost City mission, none of the team truly trusted him enough to put

15

their lives in his hands, so for now he was being kept as distant as possible.

Hawke was in the car now and as Kim buckled up he put the phone into the hands-free set and switched to speaker phone. "What is it, Ryan?"

"Do you know anything about the Welsh Triads?"

"Chinese drug-smuggling gangs in Cardiff?"

Ryan gave a heavy sigh. "Please Lord, let that be a joke."

"It was a joke," Kim said. "I think."

"Of *course,* it was a joke," Hawke said with a sideways glance at Kim. "Go on, mate."

"The Welsh Triads are a collection of medieval manuscripts which are centered on everything being brought together in groups of three – a very holy number in ancient Celtic tradition."

"Go on."

"Famous texts include the White Book of Rhydderch and the Red Book of Hergest, but there are others. They were stored all over Wales for hundreds of years but today most of them are in the National Library in Aberystwyth. The manuscripts of the Welsh Triads are almost certainly just the tip of the iceberg, and most scholars agree that there are probably countless missing texts out there."

"Why are you telling me this, Ryan? Do you want ECHO to pay for you to go on holiday to Wales?"

"As I said earlier when you were chilling out in the Oval Office, I'm telling you because one of them has just turned up and I think it could be critical to our mission."

Hawke glanced at Kim and smiled. "Tell me more."

"So this manuscript could be the parent text to both the White Book and Red Book and it's just surfaced in Boston, Massachusetts courtesy of a private collector dying in his sleep and leaving it to the State in his will. It's now in the possession of the Boston Metropolitan

Museum, and they have pictures of it on their website. They're calling it the Gold Book or the Book of Gold. It's very exciting."

"Sounds like it," Hawke said with an eye roll.

"But that's not even the best bit."

"Spit it out, Ryan," Kim said.

"You remember the strange symbols all over the idol we found in Mexico?"

"Sure."

"Well, they're all over this manuscript as well."

Hawke and Kim shared a glance. The symbols they had found in Mexico were very similar to those they had seen on the Valhalla idol, and they had been struggling to understand their connection ever since. How ancient relics from places as far away from one another as Lapland and Mexico could share the same symbols had mystified the entire team, including Ryan and Alex.

"Are you absolutely sure about this, mate?" he asked.

"It's me, Joe; of course, I'm absolutely sure. The problem is, the picture on the museum's website is only giving me a partial image of the symbols and by the looks of the way they taper off the edge of the page, I'm guessing there are more that are totally out of sight. That's why I have to get my hands on the actual manuscript. I could fly to Boston or you could pick it up on your way back to London."

London. Hawke's hometown. A place he loved to visit. A place he loved to avoid. Today he was due to fly back and meet Lea. They were supposed to talk to the doctors about Sir Richard Eden, and he guessed that meant his condition was slipping.

"Where are you, Ryan? The latest picture on your Facebook page is of you in Paris."

A long pause. Hawke knew Ryan was still trying to

17

come to terms with his loss and presumed he'd been on a colossal bender in the City of Light.

"I'm in London now, at the hospital."

"Any change?"

"None."

Kim gave Hawke a look of consolation.

Hawke changed the subject. "How much are we paying for it?"

"That's up to you now, Joe."

"*For* now," Hawke corrected him. "What does Lea say?"

"She says just buy it. She's drifting a bit. She needs you – we all do. You're the acting head of ECHO as far as the rest of us are concerned. This is important, Joe. We all know in our blood that the idols are central to all this, and now a thousand-year-old Welsh manuscript turns up with almost identical symbols on it to the Mexican and Valhalla idols. I have to get a closer look inside it if I'm going to see all of its secrets."

Hawke sighed. "In that case, we'd better get our arses up to Boston."

# CHAPTER FOUR

## Boston

After stopping in Manhattan for coffee and switching seats, Kim Taylor was at the wheel as they entered Boston. This meant a measured and slow journey over the bridge and into North End before finally driving into the Seaport District.

"Take note, Limey," she said with a feigned scowl. "This is where we kicked your asses."

"Why, oh why, would you abuse helpless donkeys?"

"Not funny, but seriously – this is where we beat you once and for good."

"Not really."

"How'd you figure that out?"

"The way I see it," he said trying to suppress a grin, "you weren't technically independent until 1776, so those guys throwing tea into the harbor in 1774..."

"16 December 1773."

"Exactly – they were technically British."

"You can't be serious!"

"Afraid so – technically we were beaten by ourselves, so in a weird sort of way the British won the War of Independence and then decided to become American afterward."

Kim shifted a little in her seat and cleared her throat to speak as she slapped his shoulder. "You know, talk like that might technically be treason."

Hawke laughed for the first time since they had started

their journey.

As they finally reached the Boston Metropolitan Museum the sky had darkened and was threatening a heavy downpour. Not unusual for Boston at this time of year, and Kim had dressed for it back in DC. Now, she snuggled down into her scarf as they crossed the road and walked up the steps to the main entrance.

The museum was large and popular, but it was midweek and the place was relatively quiet. They walked to the front desk where a woman with short blonde hair met them with a smile and a brief introduction. "I'm Melissa Miller," she began. "I'm the Curator of the Celtic Studies section. I gather you're interested in seeing the new medieval Welsh manuscript?"

"That's right," Kim said.

Melissa stopped for a moment and cocked her head a little, staring at Kim. "Have we met?"

"I don't think so."

"You look sort of familiar," the woman said.

Kim sighed inwardly. As part of his personal security detail, she had been photographed with the President on countless occasions, and just a few hours ago she had been standing behind him when he gave a short press conference on the peace talks with Korea that he was trying to get off the ground. The last thing on Earth that she wanted to do was tell this woman she had probably seen her last at the inauguration of the US President – when she had stood a few feet behind him and seven million people were tuned into every second of it on their TVs and iPads.

"She was a child actress," Hawke said in a flash.

"Ah!" A look or recognition appeared on the curator's face. "That must be it."

"Thanks, Joe," Kim said quietly.

"She mostly did toilet roll commercials," he said.

"Oh..."

Kim spoke through gritted teeth. "I said *thanks, Joe.*"

"And who could forget that one about the drain cleaner?"

Kim elbowed him hard in the ribs and Hawke stifled a grunt of pain, but Melissa Miller had already turned and was on her way toward a long corridor.

"If you'll just follow me," she said over her shoulder, "the item you wish to see is right along here."

"I thought it was on display?" Kim said.

"No, not yet. We're very grateful to the previous owner's estate for making it available to us – but at a price." She said this last word with a weary sigh.

"And who was the previous owner?" Hawke said.

"I'm not at liberty to divulge information about our donors or their estates."

Hawke and Kim exchanged a glance – that was them told.

Melissa opened a door leading to the archives and after shuffling down a short series of steps they reached a locked room. The curator deftly turned the key in the lock and then opened the door. They were met with the smell of musty books. "It's right here in this case."

She opened the case and revealed what Hawke and Kim had both expected – a worn-out, battered-looking old manuscript with a hefty leather cover, crumbling at the edges. On its front cover was a beveled Celtic triptych, scuffed and worn and showing its incredible age.

The former commando stared at the manuscript and was massively unimpressed. It wasn't much bigger than a hardback and appeared to be in three parts, held together with twine. "That's it?"

"But of course," Melissa said. "Why do you ask?"

"Looks like a manky old pile of newspaper."

21

Melissa Miller's eyebrows did the talking but then Kim stepped in. "We're *very* grateful for this, Dr. Miller, and I think it looks absolutely amazing. To think of all that history!"

Melissa looked down her nose at Kim Taylor. "Quite."

"I thought it was the Book of Gold," Hawke said, not the *Books* of Gold. Why are there three of them?"

"It's a triad. It was written in three parts over many years, but sadly some of the final section has been lost to history," she said. "Now, as I understand it you wish to view this manuscript before it goes on display here at the museum." She looked at Kim. "Are you an academic researcher of some kind?"

"No, I'm not."

Melissa looked Hawke up and down, dwelling for a moment on his scuffed boots. "I presume you're not either then?"

"Not exactly..."

"Please don't be offended," she said haughtily.

"Offended?" Hawke said cheerily. "Hardly, I'd have been offended if you *had* presumed I was an academic."

"Well, I..."

Hawke broke in before she could finish her sentence. "But I think there's been some kind of misunderstanding. We're not here simply to view the manuscript, but to make an offer to purchase it from the museum."

"Oh goodness, *no*," she said. It was the longest 'no' Hawke had ever heard. "This isn't for sale to the... *public*."

"You might be pleasantly surprised by the price we can offer," he said.

"No, I'm afraid it's not for sale."

As she spoke, Kim picked up the manuscript, and instantly all three books fell apart from one another. "I'm so sorry!" Kim picked one of them up and held it in her hands.

"My goodness, what have you done?" Dr. Miller said, fussing around and picking up the other two books. I'm going to have to ask you to leave or..."

Hawke heard the sound of gunfire coming from above them in the museum. He looked from Kim to a terrified Melissa Miller. "I know you want us to leave but setting gunmen on us is a bit over the top, don't you think?"

"What's going on?" Melissa said, clutching the manuscripts to her chest and starting to hyperventilate. "Is this some kind of robbery?"

"Looks that way," Kim said. "I'd bet my last dollar on them wanting that manuscript as well."

"Over my dead body!" she snapped.

"This way," Hawke said. "We're fish in a barrel while we're down here in the archives."

Kim, who was still holding one crumbling part of the manuscript in her hands, nodded in agreement.

Hawke moved to the door and after checking it was clear they jogged up the steps and returned to the main museum. The first thing he saw was a security guard across the lobby raising his handgun and ordering the attackers to lower their guns. Their response was to open fire on him with what sounded like at least three automatic weapons and perforate him like a teabag. His shredded body slammed back into the front desk and slid down into a bloody heap on the floor.

"Richards!" Melissa screamed. "Oh my *God!*"

She dashed over to him with the manuscripts still clutched against her body.

"Get down!" Hawke yelled.

Diving down beside the guard, Melissa tried pathetically to revive him, but Hawke and Kim had both seen enough gunshot wounds to know he'd have been dead before he hit the deck.

"She's got the Book of Gold!" one of the men yelled and pointed at Melissa.

Hawke saw the man first – slicked-back, black hair, a lean, tanned face, aquiline nose, and dark eyes like sparkling, polished obsidian. He was holding a Beretta M12 submachine gun and without giving any warning he fired on the museum curator.

"No!" Kim shouted.

The rounds tore Melissa Miller to pieces and she released the manuscripts before collapsing on top of them. Before either Hawke or Kim could move, the man with the submachine gun ordered two more men forward. One of them booted the curator's dead body over while the other snatched up the bloodied manuscripts. The man with the M12 fired short bursts over their heads to keep Hawke and Kim pinned down in the archive room stairwell.

"Who are they?" Kim said.

"Hard to tell," Hawke said. "The M12s are used by over twenty countries, including the US."

Another guard ran forward and fired on the gunmen. He killed one of them before the others turned their guns on him. The guard was faster than his colleague and returned fire while diving for cover behind the front desk. The robbers' bullets streaked along his right leg just as he vanished behind the desk.

Hawke pointed at the gunmen. "Heads up – they're pulling out!"

The men blasted a hole in a large window at the front of the museum and leaped through it. After jogging down the steps leading to the street they turned north and started to sprint away from the destruction.

Kim, who was still holding the first section of the ancient text in her hands, gave Hawke a concerned glance. "They have the other two parts of the manuscript, Joe!"

"In that case, it looks like the chase is on!" he said.

# CHAPTER FIVE

"Are you crazy?" Kim said. She stared at the dead bodies strewn over the museum lobby before facing the Englishman. The wounded guard behind the desk called out for help. "Let the cops deal with it, Joe!"

"I don't think so. This was no ordinary museum robbery – those guys wanted the manuscript specifically and they killed to get it."

"So you're just going to chase them all over Boston?"

Hawke looked at her like she was insane. "Of course."

She shook her head. "Do you even know the city?"

"Of course *not*, but that's never stopped me before," he said, snatching up the dead guard's gun. "You stay here. Keep those papers safe, help the wounded guard and try and keep this thing quiet if you can. I'm going to make sure those bastards don't slip away."

"Just hang on a minute, Hawke. You heard what the President said back in the Oval Office. While we're in the US, I'm the ranking officer in charge of... *dammit!*"

Before she finished her sentence he was gone. He knew this was definitely what President Brooke meant by *maverick bullshit* but he had no choice. Checking the guard's gun as he charged out of the museum, he emerged into a flat day of low, gray cloud and a thin drizzle. The subdued hum of late morning traffic drifted on the air. Buses and cars shuffled forward in the rain.

He scanned the scene for any sign of the men, and then caught sight of three of them as they weaved in between some buses. Their next move was to dart behind the enormous IMAX theatre.

Hawke dashed down the steps of the museum with the dead man's gun gripped tight in his right hand. A woman in a heavy red coat and wooly hat saw him and gasped. She ducked inside the Harbor Garage and pulled a phone from her pocket.

*Great,* Hawke thought. *And now the place will be crawling with cops too...*

Sprinting behind the IMAX he raised his gun and prepared to fire, but there was no sign of the men. He saw a fire exit door swinging in the damp breeze and ran to it. Slick with rain on the outside but dry on the inside, it was clear the door had been open only a few seconds.

Stepping inside, the world changed again. The cold air of the day was replaced by the gentle warmth of the theatre heating system, and the low hum of the cars and buses was now replaced by the sound of an orchestral score and people enjoying themselves.

Gun raised in the aim, he moved swiftly inside the theatre until he was immersed in the Amazon rainforest, which now loomed high above him in magnificent 3D on the massive screen. The IMAX customers were flying over the lush jungle in a helicopter, whooping with joy as the chopper swooped over a cliff and dived into a valley. Color splashed all over the screen as dozens of parrots burst through the canopy and flew toward them, but the former SBS man down in the shadows of the aisle was focused on the enemy right here in Boston.

He heard a scream – and this time one of fear. He had reached the end of the aisle and was now right beneath the screen. He saw the men moving stealthily across the apron at the base of the giant screen on their way to the northern exit, but their plan to evade him had backfired when one of the ushers had seen their guns.

Their response was savage. The lead man raised his

M12 and fired at the usher; the muzzle violently flashed in the darkness. The young woman screamed again and then clutched her stomach and collapsed.

Hawke fired on the men and the entire audience started to panic. Innocent people trapped in a confined space with a danger like these men was the scenario he feared most. He had to push the gunmen out of the IMAX and away from the public as safely and fast as he could.

He returned fire knowing he had no chance of hitting them, but the attack forced them to retreat further into the back of the theatre. Now, fearing a terrorist attack, the IMAX management ended the film and slammed on the houselights just in time for Hawke to see the men slipping into the folds of the massive safety curtain and disappearing behind the screen.

A voice boomed over the in-house public address system. "Do not panic. Everyone, please move to the nearest exit calmly and safely."

No one listened. Scarred by the recent terrorist attacks in so many cities, the men, women, and children in the IMAX now stampeded for any exit they could find and a chorus of terrified, panicked screams echoed up to the roof of the cinema. Luckily, they were all bundling toward exits in the opposite direction to the one the gunmen had taken, so Hawke had a clear path to pursue his quarry. He checked how many rounds were left in the guard's pistol, smacked the magazine back into the grip, and continued the chase.

He ran across the apron and leaped up onto the stage area in front of the screen. Behind him, the audience was now yelling and pushing each other out of the way even more aggressively than before as they fought to reach the exits, but the Englishman slid into the curtains and vanished from the disarray unfolding in the main screening room.

Gun raised, Hawke ran backstage away from the bedlam behind him. Quiet now – deadly quiet. A gust of cold air emanated from a narrow corridor to his left. He ran along it and then jogged down a flight of concrete steps until he reached the northern exit. He moved swiftly outside and was met by the sound of police sirens as they slowly closed in on the Wharf District Park.

"There he is!" a woman shouted.

Hawke turned and saw the woman in the red coat who had seen him earlier. She was now ducking down behind a parked taxi cab.

He shook his head and sighed. *You see me, but not the three goons with machine pistols...*

He searched for the fleeing men, but there was no sign of them so he jumped on the hood of a Ford E-350 to get a better view. There they were – moving back in a defensive formation on their way north.

A few moments ago the Ford had been a bagel van but now it was turned rapidly into a sieve as the goons fired on Hawke with their M12s and drilled the vehicle full of hot lead.

He dived off the roof of the Ford and crashed into the sidewalk. He raised the pistol and returned fire. The men were still trying to move north along Old Atlantic Avenue, but Hawke's fire had forced them east. Now they were sprinting along Harborwalk toward the New England Aquarium.

A dead end.

He scrambled to his feet and dashed down the Central Wharf through the drizzle. A fog was blowing in from the ocean and ahead of him the postmodern architecture of the aquarium was shrouded in gloom.

He followed the men inside the aquarium, determined they would not get away with the other sections of the manuscript. If Ryan Bale said it was significant and ECHO needed it, then it was significant, and ECHO needed it. He had learned never to doubt the young hacker and he wasn't about to start now.

He burst into the lobby area and scanned the darkened space for the gunmen. Screams came from somewhere up ahead to his right. He jogged forward, gun raised into the aim once again. He slowed his breathing and steadied his hands. Relaxed his trigger finger. The guard's gun had a heavier trigger pull than he liked – maybe a little over two pounds, but he was used to it by now and knew how it would react when he fired it.

He reached a room several stories high. At the bottom of it was a large pool full of truck-sized rocky islands covered in penguins. Hanging above one of the islands was the reconstructed skeleton of a whale, and through its enormous ribcage, the former British commando just caught sight of the men as they moved through the shadows of a viewing gantry to the east of the penguin enclosure.

One of the men stopped to fire on Hawke and the M12 filled the silent enclosure like a Howitzer in an elevator. The sound of the bullets tore through the peace and quiet and sent the visitors into a frenzy. The penguins honked and dived into the water for safety.

Hawke desperately scanned the enclosure for a way to the men but the only option involved going all the way around the information desk. By the time he made the trip the men would be long gone.

Unless...

He leaped over the wall and crashed down on the first rocky island in the center of the pool. Without stopping, he jumped from the first island to the second island and then launched himself at the whale skeleton. Swinging on the skeleton, like Tarzan on a vine, he cleared the last part of the pool and landed with a smooth parkour roll on the viewing gantry.

Following the sounds of terrified people and automatic fire, he soon reached the tropical gallery. The men saw him close on their tails and loosed a savage fusillade of fire on him to keep him back.

Their bullets raked across the tropical tanks and exploded one of the glass walls. Water burst out of the tank and flooded the gallery with countless fish – catfish, rainbowfish, swordtails...

Hawke leaped over a puddle of Siamese fighting fish and charged toward the men. They had obviously decided that getting rid of the insane Englishman was harder than they had initially thought, and the leader ordered their retreat. Now they were clattering down a narrow flight of steel stairs beyond the tropical gallery's fire door.

By the time he got to the bottom of the steps they were outside again, and this time he emerged to see them climbing into a small boat on the north side of the aquarium. A dead man was lying on the wharf and Hawke knew at once how the men had secured their transport.

With desperate, angry eyes, he watched them as they moved out into the harbor. One was holding the manuscript under his arm while the other steered the boat to the east. The third man smacked a fresh magazine into his M12 and then fired on Hawke. Sweeping the gun from side to side, he blasted holes in the wooden wharf poles and the rounds gradually snaked their way toward the Englishman.

Hawke dived for cover inside another boat and leaned over the portside to return fire. The men were getting away, and he had seconds to get the boat started or it was all for nothing.

# CHAPTER SIX

He yanked the pull cord on the four-stroke Yamaha but it tore off in his hand and he nearly toppled out of the boat. Cursing, he removed the engine cowling and the choke linkage. The bolts holding the top assembly were loose enough for him to undo with his fingers and then he pulled off his belt and wrapped it around the assembly.

He pulled the belt and the engine spluttered to life. Lowering the outboard into the water he started across the foggy harbor in pursuit of the men. They were now no more than ghostly shrouds in the sea mist, but he knew where they were headed. Their boat was too small to go out to sea and their direction of travel was pointing them to Boston Logan International Airport. They had somewhere they would rather be.

Hawke increased speed and slipped his belt back on. Looking up, he was getting closer. With three of them in their boat, the gunmen were heavier and slower in the water, but Hawke was alone and faster. Now, he raised his gun and aimed at the outboard motor on the rear of their boat. One good shot ought to do it, but shooting from one boat to another on restless water wasn't exactly the easiest thing in the world to do so he slowed his breathing and squinted down the sights.

His shots crackled in the gloomy fog and then he heard the reassuring sound of a ricochet. He fired again and this time he saw a small explosion on their stern. One of the men leaped over to put the fire out and check the damage and this time Hawke got him with a single shot. He fell silently into the black water and after a subdued splash he was gone. The men made no effort to stop for their fallen comrade and pushed on into the mist as fast as they could with their damaged vessel.

But his attack on the boat had been successful, and now they were slowing down. Hawke smiled but his celebration was too soon. The men had changed direction and now ahead of their boat he saw the outline of Long Wharf North rise into view in the fog. They hadn't given up yet and had changed their escape plans.

The two surviving gunmen clambered up over some mooring poles and as Hawke's eyes followed them along the wharf he suddenly knew what those plans were: the ferry.

He cursed as his boat plowed through the icy water yard by yard. It seemed to take forever and now the ferry was pulling out into the harbor on its way across to the airport. Soon they would be on board and crossing the harbor on their way to the airport while he was still buggering about in this tiny little boat.

He changed plans too and pushed the tiller hard to change the direction of the boat's travel. The little boat tipped gracefully to starboard in the water and now he was slowly coming up behind the much larger vessel. On the stern, he could see some young people holding coffees and pointing at all the police lights illuminating the wharf district in impressive blue and red strobes behind him.

He was almost at the ferry now and sliding around all over the place in its wake. Fighting against the force of the ferry's powerful wake, he slowly brought the boat up to the rear of the larger boat and grabbed hold of the portside pontoon ladder. The people at the rear of the boat were watching with amusement as he struggled to get some purchase on the stainless steel ladder's side rail. Slick with the fog and seawater, his hand slipped off several times as he struggled to keep the boat level, but on his third attempt, he finally made it.

He raced up the ladder and reached the stern deck. The coffee drinkers weren't so amused when they saw the Smith & Wesson stuffed into his belt and they fell over each other to get out of his way.

Hawke barely noticed their terror. Pulling the weapon from his belt he stalked forward along the portside wraparound deck and raised the pistol into the aim. With each step he took, he swung his gun's muzzle into every nook and cranny in his search for the two surviving men and the stolen manuscript.

The ferry slowly grumbled through the freezing, fog-filled harbor and now Joe Hawke had reached a door near the bow. He stepped inside into the warm and was met by several alarmed ferry workers. He was inside the wheelhouse and looking directly at the captain.

"Oh, my God!" the old man said, reaching for his radio.

"I'm not here to harm anyone," Hawke said. "So just relax."

"Who are you?" the captain said, still staring at the gun in the Englishman's hands.

"That doesn't matter, but I'm in pursuit of two men who just stole something of great value from the Boston Metropolitan Museum."

"You could be anyone," one of the younger men said.

"True, and you're just going to have to live with that," Hawke said. "If I wanted to hurt you you'd all be dead by now, no?"

The men exchanged a weary glance.

"I guess so," the captain said.

Hawke lowered the gun. "Happy?"

The captain sighed. "Not exactly, but it's better than it being pointed in my face."

"So what now?" the younger man said.

"Turn the ferry around," Hawke said.

"We can't do that."

"Yes, you can. The men are trying to get to the airport. If you look to the stern you might notice Boston's a funny blue color. That's the police lights."

The young man peered outside. "He's right, Hank."

"So if you turn the boat around the thieves are out of luck, right?"

The captain made a call on his radio and then started to turn the ferry around. He made a passenger announcement and then the boat was facing west again and sailing directly toward the enormous bank of flashing blue and red lights all over the wharf.

"So what now?" the captain said to Hawke.

"Now we wait. They could be hiding anywhere on a boat this size, but when we're back on the wharf the police will come aboard and search it."

They waited as the ferry made its way back to the wharf, slowly pushing through the cold water and fog. Hawke saw the chaos through the drizzle-soaked windows of the wheelhouse and hoped knowing the President might just be enough to stop him from being sent to Gitmo Bay for hijacking a ferry.

His thoughts were shattered by the sound of a single gunshot and a blood-curdling scream.

The captain and the younger officer exchanged a grim look. "Sounds like it came from the starboard deck," the older man said and fumbled for his radio. "Al? Come in! Are you reading me, Al?"

The younger man started to turn a green-white color, and Hawke knew it wasn't seasickness. "They shot Al?"

"They've worked out we turned around," Hawke said. "Damn it all! I banked on them laying low below deck." He pulled back the slide on the semi-automatic and put a round in the chamber.

The young ferry worker swallowed hard and took a step back. His eyes were fixed on the gun. "What are you gonna do, man?"

Before the reply came to his lips, Hawke heard more submachine gunfire on the starboard side. Everyone in the wheelhouse shared a worried look, and then Hawke pushed past the captain and stepped out onto the deck. Leaning over the metal rail he saw the men he had pursued climbing down into a police boat that was sailing alongside the ferry.

A number of dead officers lay strewn on the small boat's deck, and one was bobbing up and down in the water behind it. The men had clearly seen the police escort and surprised the officers with their superior firepower, and now they had seized the boat and were taking off into the fog.

They were no longer heading to the airport but out to the coast and he guessed they had changed their plans since the shooting started. He heard a police chopper heading over but it was no use. The stolen police boat had raced away from the ferry and vanished in the heavy sea fog.

Hawke cursed, tightened his right hand into a fist, and punched the side of the lifejacket box as hard as he could.

# CHAPTER SEVEN

## Macau

The man known to the Chinese Ministry of State Security simply as Tiger stepped through the lobby of The Venetian Macau and walked past the reception desk. As luxury hotels and casinos went, you had to go a long way to beat this place, not least because gambling was illegal in the rest of China.

No one batted an eyelid as the government assassin walked smoothly down the carpeted steps and made his way to the top of the escalators. He was dressed the part in a smart suit and tie and gently adjusted the middle button as he made his way forward. The right lens and temple of his Persol glasses flashed in the light as he stepped onto the escalator and slowly descended into the casino's Great Hall.

The whole place was decked out to look like Venice, with gondolas cruising calmly along working canals and Venetian architecture so exquisitely reproduced that you could be forgiven for thinking you were in Italy instead of on the south coast of China. Tourists wandered in and out of expensive Western jewelry franchises and relaxing muzak drifted from concealed speakers in the walls.

Tiger was unimpressed. He was here for business and had only one thing on his mind – locating the man he knew only as Rat.

And he knew where to find him.

He made his way through the Great Hall and passed

various gaming areas – Phoenix, Imperial House, and Golden Fish – until finally reaching the Red Dragon. This was where Rat liked to throw away his life. Slot machines buzzed and flashed, but Rat was above such things and Tiger knew it. Deep in the Red Dragon lounge now he looked across to one of the gaming tables to find his colleague sitting at a blackjack table with a large pile of chips at his elbow.

The diffused amber lighting flashed on Rat's golden cufflinks as Tiger drew closer and made his way through the throng of gamblers and drinkers. Waiters dressed in red delivered dim sum and red dragon noodles to diners seated at candlelit tables and polite laughter danced on the air, but the look on Rat's face when he saw Tiger told him that his pleasant evening had now come to an end.

Rat pushed back from the table and gave Tiger a resigned smile. "Despite my best efforts, I see Zhou has tracked me down once again."

Tiger nodded.

"Who?" Rat asked.

"Dragonfly."

Rat paused a beat, then excused himself from the table. "Let's walk."

The two men strolled slowly through the comforting, brash glow of the casino. Silent for a long time, Rat spoke next. "Pig?"

Tiger offered another solemn businesslike nod. "He says it's his last job before retirement."

"He always says that."

"This time it's true. He's planned out his retirement to the letter. His wife is waiting for him in a new apartment. They have it all worked out. He wants to leave all this behind."

Rat scoffed, and Tiger understood his reaction. No one ever left the Ministry or its good works behind. Being part of a top-level government assassination squad like the Zodiacs was not something you ever walked away from.

As if he had read his thoughts, Rat said, "He can move to the coast physically, but *this* will always be Zhou's." He tapped the side of his head to indicate his mind.

Tiger agreed and turned to watch the punters pouring their money into a bank of never-ending neon slot machines. The clatter of the cheap, nickel-plated steel yuans being greedily fed into the coin slots echoed in the large gaming room. Tiger shook his head as he studied the sad faces of the gamblers, hopelessly addicted to pumping their earnings into the machines and desperately waiting for a payout to tumble down the coin chutes.

"And what about *him?*" Rat said.

Tiger knew who he was talking about.

"I tracked him down to Guangzhou. He's been living in a whorehouse in Tianhe for weeks now. They're too frightened to ask him to leave."

Rat gave an appreciative nod. "I suppose Zhou is insisting he come along?"

"Yes. He is part of the squad."

"But after last time, I wondered if he might re-evaluate his position on the team."

Tiger shook his head. "Monkey's unpredictable savagery is an essential part of our work. He can make even the most steadfast person give up all their secrets with his *methods.*"

Both men were quiet now. They both knew what the great philosopher Lao Tzu meant when he wrote that silence is a source of great strength.

Tiger imagined how Agent Dragonfly would react to some quality alone time in a Chinese torture chamber with just Monkey for company. That would be a show worth watching, he considered. Unfortunately, their orders were the immediate execution of the traitor – not that he would tell Monkey that. A man like that needed the proper motivation.

"I presume we're leaving at once?" Rat asked.

"Yes," Tiger said. Everything Zhou wanted to be done was always done at once. He was that kind of boss.

Rat nodded pensively and rubbed his nose. Tiger caught him glancing back over at the blackjack tables with a look of longing in his eyes. He sniffed hard and turned his eyes back to Tiger. "And how are we to trap our dragonfly?"

"The same way you trap anything else," Tiger said quietly. "With high-quality bait."

# CHAPTER EIGHT

## Dublin

Lea Donovan tipped up the potted hydrangea under her brother's kitchen window and slid out the back door key. Finn had left it there when they had arranged for her to collect the box of personal effects the Haven Bay Nursing Home had sent. He was on holiday with his wife and kids and didn't give a damn about any box of junk left by some little old lady no one had ever heard of. Besides – the box was addressed to Lea and that was just fine with him.

"I'm not sure I'm ready for this," she said, turning the key in the lock and pushing open the kitchen door.

"Whatever it is, we'll deal with it together," Hawke said. "We're a team... a family, and we're all here with you."

She stood on her tiptoes and kissed him. He and Kim had met them in Dublin Airport an hour ago after their flight from Boston less than twenty minutes before her flight from London. She was glad he was here at her side, but even having Joe Hawke beside her hadn't taken away the nerves she felt when she thought about the mysterious box that was waiting for her on the dining room table.

She walked into the house and was met with various pictures of her brother and his young family – but not one picture of her. As if he had read her mind, Hawke put his arm around her shoulder. "Let's have a look at this box and get out of here. We still have that manuscript to track down."

41

"Sure," she said and gave him her best fake smile.

She felt sad, but then the rest of the team traipsed into the small Dublin semi and looked so out of place a genuine smile soon replaced the fake one. If Finn Bloody Donovan could see these guys huddled around in his kitchen he'd have a proper fit.

She turned her attention to the box on the table. It was just a normal, small packing box. She opened it up and was met by an array of old junk, just as Finn had described it – old, dog-eared paperbacks, some well-worn reading glasses, and a plastic hearing aid. She searched through the box, growing more confused with each passing second. "Finn was right – this is all just crap."

"Aren't any fags in it, are there?" Ryan said, leaning in.

Scarlet Sloane, who had also met them at the airport, looked at Ryan in horror. "Scrounging cigarettes," she said with disgust. "How very *you*."

"You get off a plane from Vegas less than an hour ago and you're already as obnoxious as ever," Kim said. "No wonder Camacho stayed in the States."

"I was not being obnoxious, and Jack's on a mission for the CIA," Scarlet said. "Besides, it doesn't count if you insult the help."

Ryan moved to give some back, but he was stopped by Lea gasping.

"What have you found?" Lexi said, taking an interest for the first time since they'd landed in Ireland. "If it's the Mona Lisa we can all retire."

"It's not the Mona Lisa," Lea said, her voice almost trembling with shock. "It's this."

She pulled a sleek, but dusty golden idol from the box and held it up for the rest of the team to see. It was the same dimensions as the other idols they had seen, with the same intricate, seven-pointed star shape in the base and an identical inverted ziggurat receding inside the bottom of it.

A long, tense silence was broken by Scarlet: "Jesus Holy Christ on a Brontosaurus."

Hawke frowned as he studied the idol. "What the hell?"

Lea looked almost distraught. "What's going on, Joe? What the hell is all this about?"

Scarlet snapped her fingers. "Nerd needed! Code red emergency! Ryan, get that skinny little arse over here right now or I'm going to beat it with a Runic cursing pole."

Ryan scowled at her as he walked to the table. "I'm impressed you've heard of one, to be honest."

Scarlet tipped her head and blew him a kiss.

"Any ideas?" Hawke said.

"Looks like Tinia to me," Ryan said.

"And now in English, boy."

He turned to face her. "Tinia is a primordial god of the ancient Etruscan religion. A sky god... a chief deity of that belief system."

"Isn't that what you said about the other idols?" Lexi asked.

He nodded. "It is, yes. The idol of Tanit that we found in Mexico was one of the chief deities of the Carthage civilization, which we now know included Atlantis, and the one of Bórr we found in Valhalla was at the top of the divinity tree for Norse culture as well."

"So this is yet another golden idol of a head god," Hawke said.

"Seems that way," said Ryan.

"And covered in more of these sodding symbols," Lea said.

Kim ran a hand through her hair and stared at the team with a confused expression on her face. "Please, will someone remind me how statues from so many different places can all have the same carvings on them?"

"Ryan, you're up again," Scarlet said.

"Our current, working hypothesis is that the symbols belong to some kind of parent culture, but it's controversial."

"Hey! I know what it is!" Scarlet said, jabbing Ryan in the arm.

"I'm sorry?" he said.

"I know what's different about you – you're not wearing glasses!"

"You only just noticed that?" Ryan said, offended.

"Well, yeah."

"Some witness you'd make," Ryan said. "*Yes, your honor – the thief was definitely wearing glasses...*"

"Sorry, but I just don't spend that long looking at you, boy. I only noticed because right about now you'd be pushing them up the bridge of your nose – doing that *Ryan Thing* you're always doing."

"It's contact lenses from now on," Ryan said firmly.

Hawke smiled, but the truth was he hadn't noticed either. Ryan Bale losing the glasses was just an outward sign of the way he was changing on the inside. To Hawke, these changes could go either way – they could strengthen him or break him.

"You know what I need right about now?" Scarlet asked.

Ryan smirked "Half an hour with Jack Camacho, a bottle of Good ol' Sailor vodka, and some Italian lounge music?"

"Piss off, Bale," she said. "But yes, I do need *one* of those and it's not Jackie boy or the cheesy listening. I want a drink."

"What's new?" Lexi said.

"It helps settle my nerves and concentrate the mind,"

Scarlet said. "You should try some – it might improve your personality."

"That's fighting talk, Cairo," Lexi said.

"Seriously though," Ryan said. "How was Vegas?"

Scarlet pulled out her phone and showed them all a picture of her and Camacho with their arms around each other's shoulders outside the Mandalay Bay Casino.

"Looks great," Ryan said.

Scarlet sighed. "And Jack's still there, the lucky bastard."

"Say, I hope Camacho's all right," Kim said. "Vegas is a tough town – guns, knives, drugs, smuggling, punishment beatings, blackmail..."

"But enough about Cairo," Ryan said. "Tell us about the Mafia."

"Hey!" Lexi said, slapping his arm. " I was going to make that joke!"

"You gotta get to the punchline faster than that to beat a wit as razor-sharp as mine," he said.

"So what about that drink, darling?" Scarlet repeated. "I was being serious."

"Over there," said Lea, pointing her chin in the direction of a wooden cabinet on the opposite wall.

Scarlet rummaged through it for a few seconds before hauling a half-empty bottle of Jameson's Irish Whiskey over and plonking it on the table. "Anyone else?"

"Any glasses?" Ryan said.

"Nope," Scarlet said. "Stop being such a girl."

"Glasses in the kitchen, Ry. Don't bother bringing one for me."

"Anything else in there?" Hawke said.

Scarlet shook her head. "No, just some warm cans of Heineken."

"I was talking about the box."

Scarlet winked. "I knew that, sugar cube."

Lea shook her head. "No, just bits and bobs... wait – there's something under one of the flaps down at the bottom."

"What is it?" Hawke asked.

She sighed, long and deep. "It's a letter."

Scarlet leaned in. "A letter?"

"Nothing wrong with your hearing, that's for sure," Kim said.

Lea pulled a cream envelope out of the pile of Maggie's knick-knacks and stared at it for a few moments. "It's addressed to me – look."

She held the envelope up and written on the front in blue ink were the words: *For Lea Donovan.*

Now Ryan leaned in for a closer look. "Are you sure? The handwriting is so weak and trembly I can hardly read it."

"It says her name clear enough," Hawke said. He was looking at her now, and she saw a flash of uncertainty in his eyes.

"So get the thing open!" Lexi said. "The letter inside that envelope could tell us where the Mona Lisa is!"

"Sorry, but am I missing something here?" Kim asked. "I thought the Mona Lisa was in the Louvre."

"It *is* in the Louvre," Lea said. "This is Lexi's way of trying to be funny."

"But you know what I *mean*, right guys?" Lexi protested. "The contents of that letter could be truly mind-blowing. She had one of the idols!"

"Remember, these people are Lea's family, Lexi," Hawke said. "This isn't just another treasure hunt, all right?"

"It's fine, Joe," Lea said, stuffing the cream envelope inside her jacket pocket. "I'll read it later. I need time to process *this*." She pointed at the idol. "And the truth is

I'm terrified about what might be in the letter."

"Whatever's going on, we're going to get to the bottom of it," Hawke said. "Did you speak with Lund about finding out who was behind the Boston raid?"

She nodded. "He's looking into it." Her phone rang, and she pulled it from her pocket to see a short text message.

"Who is it?" Hawke said. "Lund?"

"No. It's Danny. Danny Devlin."

"Ah." He knew who Devlin was. He had heard plenty of good and bad stories about him – the good ones mostly from Lea and the bad ones from Richard Eden. Lea had contacted him when they found out Camacho was unavailable for the mission with the hope he could provide another pair of hands. "What does he say?"

Ryan smirked. "He says that if the guy he's replacing has got third-degree carpet burns on his arse he's not teaming up with Cairo Sloane under any circumstances."

"Stop talking bullshit," Scarlet said. "They weren't on his arse."

"I don't even want to think about that," Kim said.

Lea sighed. "He says he's ready to go as soon as we pick him up."

"And where is he?"

"Flynn's on Harry Street."

"So what are we waiting for?" Scarlet said.

# CHAPTER NINE

Flynn's Bar on Harry Street was in a shroud of drizzle, and the intricate graphics on its front window shone in the lights of their hired Ford Explorer as Hawke parked up outside. When Lea emerged from the SUV she pulled up her jacket collars and tried to keep the Irish weather at bay.

"Good job Camacho isn't here," Scarlet said. "He hates shitty weather like this."

"Why isn't he here again?" Ryan said as he pushed inside the pub. "Something about a serious penile fracture sustained in an attempt to reproduce the Kama Sutra's notoriously demanding Overpass position?"

Scarlet stared at him. "To say I worry about you would suggest I give a damn, but let's just say I have my concerns."

"We *all* have our concerns about him," Lea said, turning to Ryan. "And where was the friggin' Kama Sutra when we were married, you big gobdaw?"

"Still can't believe you two were married," Kim said. "Talk about opposites attracting."

"We don't like to talk about it," Lea said. She glared at her ex-husband. "Do we, Ry?"

"No," he said meekly. "Apparently not."

The chit-chat was interrupted by the booming voice of Danny Devlin as he crossed over from the bar to the door. "Well, if it isn't Lea Donovan!" He squeezed her and kissed her on the cheek. Taking a step back he looked at the rest of the team. "And this time she's brought the cavalry! So this is the famous ECHO team?"

"It is, Danny," Lea said.

"And you're the famous Josiah Hawke?"

Hawke saw a flash of concern in Lea's eyes at the use of his full name, but he didn't mind and fixed Devlin in the eye as he shook his hand. He was a few years older than the Englishman and looked slightly the worse for wear. Lea had told him that her former Commandant liked a few drinks and a good time and it looked like it, but the hand grip was strong. Devlin wanted to show him he was no pushover, and both men knew a handshake like a wet fish would certainly give that impression.

"Lea's told me a lot about you," Hawke said.

"Not all bad, I hope."

"No," Hawke said, ending the world's most awkward handshake. "Not all."

"So, a former Royal Marines Commando, huh?" Devlin said. "The real thing or a rubber dagger?"

"Rubber what?" Ryan said.

"Reserve commando," Hawke said, turning from the young man to Devlin. "I was in the regulars."

"I heard that because a woman passed the All Arms Commando Course the Paras started calling you guys the Royal Maureens."

Hawke paused a beat before replying, not sure how Lea expected him to behave around her old boss and former lover. "Not to my face they haven't."

"And after that, he was in the SBS," Lea said.

Hawke sighed inwardly. He could see what she was doing, but he hated it when people made a big show of his Special Forces background.

"Was that you guys who raided the Iranian Embassy?" Devlin said with a devilish grin on his face.

"You know damn well it was the SAS, Danny," Lea said. "Stop being a fool."

"It was the SAS," Hawke said. "Tell me, when was the

49

last time you guys got a mission in the Irish Rangers? Wasn't it when a cat got stuck up a tree in Cork?"

Devlin's grin grew wider and he nodded his head. "This man of yours isn't just an ugly face, Lea!"

She slapped his shoulder. "I told you that!"

Hawke wasn't sure if this was a compliment or not and didn't have time to consider it, either. He knew Lea and Danny Devlin were old friends but he could already see they had their own little dynamic going on. Truth was, he wasn't sure where to file Danny Devlin, but Lea said he was a good man and he knew he'd helped save her life in Ireland. He respected Lea, and so he decided to give Devlin the benefit of the doubt.

Lexi stepped up and jabbed Devlin in the chest with her forefinger. "And what the *hell*," she said, "is wrong with a woman passing the commando course?"

Devlin looked surprised but then laughed. "Nothing at all."

"Good. I could pass it with you on my back, Mr. Devlin," she said.

"From what I heard," Hawke said, "the only woman to pass the AACC did it in different sessions, not in one go."

"Don't *you* start," Lexi said, putting her hands on her hips. "Have I got to do this damned course carrying *both* of you on my back?"

They laughed and it was over, but then Devlin said, "No woman ever passed P Company."

Hawke's patience was wearing thin. Devlin was an army man and knew the rivalry between the Paras and the Marines. He was deliberately trying to get a rise out of him but he wasn't going to let it happen.

"We need drinks," Scarlet said. "And then we talk business."

Devlin introduced them to Jake O'Hara, the publican. "Finally got the place fixed up," Jake said, polishing a pint glass. He looked briefly at Devlin and then back to Lea. "The last time you came in here I ended up spending thousands of euros getting the place back together. I hope nothing like that's gonna happen again?"

"Don't be silly," Lea said. "What do you think – that I spend my whole life getting shot at?"

Hawke and the rest of the team produced a fake laugh and Jake put the pint glass under the Guinness tap.

"Good," Jake said as the glass slowly filled up. He pushed it over to Devlin who paid for it and they all walked back over to a table in the corner.

"So what's this all about?" the Irishman said. He glanced at each of them in turn before his eyes settled on his former lover. "I don't hear from you for months and then you send a text saying you need me."

"We're a man down," Hawke said.

"Dead?" Devlin asked.

"Worse," said Ryan, pausing a beat for effect. "He's in traction after a debauched weekend in Vegas with Cairo."

Scarlet's elbow swiftly connected with the young man's ribs and he spat out a mouthful of Guinness in response. "He's engaged on a CIA mission," she said over the top of his gasps.

"And since we were in Ireland," Lea said. "I thought – why not?"

"I did save your backside when those French nutjobs came over to trash your father's cottage. Anyway – you look prettier than ever," he said. "You're a lucky man, Joe Hawke."

Before he could reply, Devlin said, "So, is anyone going to tell me what's going on or not?"

Lea said, "I came here to collect some things from a relative of mine who I never even knew existed. Judging from the pictures we found in her box I guess she was a

51

great aunt or something. We also found some other things."

Lea pulled the canvas bag off her shoulder and opened the top a few inches to reveal the section of the manuscript they had saved and the golden idol. "And yes, before you ask – it's real gold."

"Jesus! That thing must be worth a bomb!"

"Keep your voice down," Hawke said firmly.

"It's priceless," Ryan said. "And its value is not in the gold. We don't know what the deal with these idols is yet, but that's where the real fireworks are – not a few thousand quid in gold."

Devlin reached in to touch the idol but Lea pulled the bag shut and shouldered it once more. It felt safe there, on her back – somewhere it would stay safe if she ever had to run for her life. "We also found a manuscript that might help us, but some of it was stolen in a raid in Boston."

"And we need the whole thing to make sense of it," Ryan said. "The section we have only has a few references to a god called Arianrhod, which is great as far it goes, but it's incomplete."

Devlin took a sip of his beer. "So that means the bastards that took the rest of the thing in the raid need this one, right?"

"Correct," Ryan said.

"Has this got something to do with your father's research?" Devlin asked.

Lea was silent for a moment. She wasn't sure how to answer the question, but then she decided on pure, old-fashioned honesty. "It just *has* to be connected, Danny. Especially now this whole thing with Maggie has come up."

"So what's our next move?" Devlin said.

"We have another idol," Scarlet said. "But we need to get the manuscript back. Ryan's convinced it holds more answers to this whole nightmare, and there's a reason why those guys went to such an effort to get hold of it."

"And where is this manuscript?"

Lea said, "On the way to meet you, Danny, I talked to a man who works with Richard Eden. His name's Lund. He told me the men who stole the manuscript and slipped away into the Boston fog eventually ended up in a private airfield north of Salem. They took off in a Citation aimed for Naples."

"So what are we waiting for?" Devlin said, slurping the last of his pint down. "Let's get moving! You've got wheels, I take it?"

"We do," Hawke said, "but there's a problem. We're in an Explorer – a six-seater. Now you're with us we're seven."

"So we get a cab and meet at the airport," Devlin said.

When the cab arrived, Lea decided to keep Devlin company and ride with him while the rest of the team took the Ford, and they pulled away into the Irish rain on their way to the airport.

She sat in the back and closed her eyes as Devlin and the driver shared the usual small talk. In the background, behind their voices, she could hear the wipers beating slowly against the rain. It was nice to be home – to hear the familiar accent and listen to the rain. It never rained enough on Elysium.

She opened her eyes and watched the brake lights of the Explorer in front through the rain as they approached some traffic lights. She saw the lights flick to red but Scarlet piled through all the same. The cab driver tutted and moaned about dangerous driving and pulled up safely behind the line.

"It's tossers like that who cause pile-ups," he said with a shake of his head.

Lea made a mental note to pass his views along to the former SAS officer when they were safely on board the Gulfstream.

The lights changed and they pulled over the line, and then it hit them. Hard.

A Range Rover had been parked up on the road to their right and when the lights changed it swerved forward and piled into the cab, crushing the right side and killing the cab driver instantly in a storm of crumpled door panels and shattered safety glass.

Lea screamed.

Devlin turned his head and cradled it in his arms to protect himself from the flying glass. "What the fuck?" the Irishman yelled. "He must be more pissed than I am!"

"It's not that Danny... we're under attack!"

Looking ahead, the Explorer and her friends were long gone, and there was no time to call them on her phone: armed men were already piling out of the Range Rover and forcing the cab's doors open.

Lea struggled to pop her belt open and reached out for her bag. She knew what they wanted – the other section to the manuscript, and now they were going to get Maggie's idol as well.

One of the men wrenched open Devlin's door and the Irishman twisted around to get a punch in but his movement was restricted by the dead taxi driver now slumped over the handbrake.

"Shit!" Lea said, freeing herself from the seatbelt at last and trying to shift forward in her seat to help her old friend. "Danny, look out!"

Devlin turned but the other man landed the first blow. He knocked him out with a clean, hard punch, but Lea had no time to feel concerned: someone was opening her door and pulling her out of the car.

She fought against it but then her masked assailant

pointed the barrel of a gun in her face and hushed her with his finger. "Into the Range Rover. Don't make me kill you – and bring your bag, please."

"You son of a bitch!" Lea said. "You killed this cab driver and knocked out my friend!"

The man ignored her and shouted a string of commands in Italian to the other men who were standing around in the rain. Somewhere in the distance, she heard the sound of sirens. The Garda were on their way to attend the carnage, but she knew they would be long gone by the time they arrived.

"Why are you doing this?"

The man pulled the hammer back on the pistol and stared at her with the cold, dead eyes of a professional killer. "Because I am paid to do it. Now get into the Range Rover. You have a meeting with a very important man and he doesn't like to be kept waiting."

# CHAPTER TEN

## Isola Pacifica

Hidden from public view in a deep cove on Italy's Amalfi Coast, the Isola Pacifica sparkled like an emerald in the bright blue water. Here in this paradise, anyone with five million dollars could buy their very own private island, but the Isola Pacifica was definitely not on the market. Men like Giancarlo Zito didn't trade on the open market.

"Did you know," Zito told the man cowering before him, "that the Roman writer Lucius describes how a favorite torture method of those glorious days involved sewing people inside dead donkeys, with only their heads remaining outside the animal? The whole sorry business was dragged into the hot sun and left there until the maggots inside the donkey finally dispatched the victim."

"Please... Signor Zito!" Stefano Marchesi was panting with fear.

"This pleases me, but of course where am I going to find a donkey on this island?"

"I only took a few grams, signore! I will pay it back in full!"

"Another method involved nothing more than a cauldron and a simple fire. The torturer would drop some rats inside the cauldron, strap the open end of the cauldron to the victim's stomach and then light a fire at the closed end. As the cauldron got hotter and hotter, the rats were driven by instinct to survive and that meant getting away from the rising heat. Naturally, the rats were unable to gnaw and claw their way through the metal cauldron so they dug their way out through the victim's stomach. His flesh was so much easier to gnaw away and claw through than the metal."

"I needed the money for my son's medical treatment, Signor Zito! It was nothing to you! Nothing... just a few thousand euros. You'll have the money by sunset, I swear, signore."

Zito tapped his fingers on the tabletop and then rose to his feet as he took in the view across the Tyrrhenian Sea. He breathed in the salt air deeply and exhaled with a satisfied sigh. "I do not think we have a cauldron on the island either, and certainly if I found rats on the island I would shoot the man responsible for allowing them to breed here – such filthy creatures. Just like heroin thieves."

"I'm not a thief, sir. I was desperate."

"The ancient Greeks used the wonderful Brazen Bull – a simple bronze bull with a hollow interior in which was placed the victim." Here, Zito paused to pull a cigarette from a solid gold case and light it up. He exhaled the smoke and flicked some ash over the side of the balcony. "They lit a fire under the bull and cooked the victim. Do you know why they shaped the vessel like a bull, Stefano?"

"No..." Stefano sobbed. "I do not."

"Because when the men inside screamed for their lives, the acoustics of the bronze vessel made their screams sound like the bellowing of a terrified bull. The victim inside was roasted until he, or she, was dead. We have such a bull here on the island, but it is so *messy*. Don't you think the ancients were so much more inventive when it comes to methods of torture and execution?"

Now, Stefano was just crying. No more pleading for his life.

"The sad fact is we are just too busy for such fantastic flourishes," Zito continued. "Take the Irish woman I have locked upstairs. She will die the same way as you, I am certain – with a bullet to the brain and then dumped in one of the island's septic tanks."

"You don't have to do this," Stefano said. His words were almost inaudible among the sobs and gasps. "I can find the money by sunset, I swear. Please, Signor Zito! Have mercy!"

"Poor Stefano – how can I show you mercy? Do you know how many men and women I have delivering my products all over Europe? What if word got out that Giancarlo Zito let people steal heroin from him and did nothing about it? Can you imagine what would happen to my empire? My business is not what the authorities call legitimate. If my employees steal from me I cannot go to the police, can I now? If my employees steal from me – as you have done – I have to deal with it myself, and there is only one way to do this. You must be executed."

Stefano's tears stopped now the moment was upon him. His face had turned from one of fear to a pale, frozen dread.

Zito slapped the side of the young man's face almost tenderly. "So you see I have no choice." He turned to a tall man standing just behind Stefano and nodded his head; it was subtle but the man understood what it meant. "Bruno, take Stefano here out to the beach and let him smell the sea one last time before you execute him."

"Si, signore."

The man grabbed Stefano's trembling shoulders and pulled him to his feet. Steering him away from Zito's balcony, the young man began to scream again, almost hysterically now.

"You bastard, Zito!" the man screamed out. "You fucking bastard! Now I'm glad I ripped you off."

"No – wait!"

Bruno stopped dead in his tracks. "What is it, boss?"

Zito walked over to Stefano. "What's that you said? You are *glad* you ripped me off?"

Stefano looked defiant for just a moment, but then started to crumble. "I... you're going to kill me, so I just meant..."

Zito nodded his head. He understood. "The bullet was merciful, Stefano because you showed me remorse. Now, with these new words, you change things."

"I'm sorry... I was so angry, I..."

"Where is the bull, Bruno?"

"On the southern patio."

"Fire it up."

"No!" Stefano screamed. "Please... I'm sorry! I never meant to insult you."

"Goodbye, Stefano."

The young man screamed and tried to lash out as the much stronger and older Bruno dragged down to the southern patio where the Brazen Bull awaited.

Zito's mind drifted away from the moment and turned once again to the Irish woman upstairs and the manuscript on the lid of his grand piano just in the next room.

And that weird golden statue.

*

Richard Eden lay as still as the dead in a small hospital in West London. Outside in the corridor, the two plain clothes police officers were taking turns to get some sleep, but the man they were protecting was unconcerned with their problems. He had plenty of his own, starting with the induced coma he was in and ending with the man they knew as the Oracle.

After getting past the intense security, any visitor to his room who knew the man always responded the same way

– a shallow, polite gasp and then an overwhelming sense of pity as their eyes danced over the tangle of wires and tubes keeping Sir Richard alive for yet another day.

Eden wasn't bothered by any of this. Right now he was sixty feet above the frozen Yorkshire countryside, running as fast as he could over the trainasium. He didn't know how it had happened, but now he was a young man again, in his early twenties, and working his arse off to get through P Company selection. All he had ever wanted was to be an officer in the Parachute Regiment and this was his one shot at making it happen.

Pegasus Company, or P Company as the men knew it, was the toughest selection test in the British Army. Anyone who put themselves up for it faced weeks of punishing beastings and savage physical exertion, not to mention the notorious aerial assault course.

But Eden was in his element.

Reaching the end of the jump illusion he climbed back down to the ground in a hail of abuse from a screeching drill sergeant but he had done it. He would win the world-famous maroon beret and parachute badge. He deserved it. A commissioned officer in the Parachute Regiment.

Now things changed and he was in the back of a C130 by the rear door. It opened to reveal more black. They were ripping over the English countryside in the middle of the night. It was winter. A cold crosswind clawed at the aircraft and it descended to six hundred feet.

Civilian parachute jumps started high – usually ten thousand feet. The reason was simple – a better view for the money and more time to fix the chute if anything went wrong. This was not how the Parachute Regiment rolled. The Paras were not interested in sightseeing and a jump from that altitude meant giving the enemy enough time to locate you, track you and shoot you dead before your feet hit the ground.

When the Paras jumped out of a plane they did it at low altitude. This meant there was no time for the enemy to track and shoot you, but it also meant you had only five to ten seconds to fix any problems with the chute because after that you were hitting the ground at terminal velocity.

Eden took a breath. He felt the freezing winter air scratching at him from the cavernous black mouth at the rear of the Hercules. He was number one in the door, and that meant a good free jump and then no problems with the chute opening.

When paratroopers jumped from a plane they moved fast. The objective was to get all the troopers out the back gate and into the drop zone in a few seconds and then the aircraft could climb back up to a safe altitude. It also meant keeping the paratroopers together in the battle zone rather than all over the place.

For this reason, the men stood on either side of the aircraft facing the door in two lines and jumped out at half-second intervals. The faster the better, but this meant those at the back had their air stolen by the men at the front. When a parachute opened, it pulled down the air inside its canopy, so when you jumped out right over the top of the man in front of you, there wasn't enough air for your chute to open fully, and it would stay collapsed until it found enough air to open properly.

Tonight, Eden was first and that meant no air thieves.

The go light flicked on.

No time to think.

Out the door a heartbeat later, falling into the black night. The ground raced up to him. Low-level parachute descent at twenty-one feet per second. Three seconds for the chute to deploy. Full equipment and weapons were strapped to him. His mind buzzed. Emergency aircraft exit drill. The ground got closer. The darkness swallowed him whole.

But why couldn't he move anymore? And where had the aircraft gone? Everything was black, and his arms and legs were as heavy as lead. He felt a hideous presence looming behind him in the darkness. Was it the Oracle and his Athanatoi army, hunting him even here in the darkest recesses of his mind?

He felt like he was going mad.

# CHAPTER ELEVEN

## Positano

"So that's where this Zito scumbag is keeping Lea," Ryan said. "An exclusive private island crawling with armed security, and it's up to us save her."

"And the manuscript and idol," Hawke said.

Ryan dragged on his cigarette and blew a thick cloud of smoke toward the parasol over their heads. "Of course, the manuscript and idol."

Hawke peered through the gap in between Lexi and Devlin opposite him and watched a speed boat cutting through the turquoise water in the cove. Beyond it, the sun flashed on the Tyrrhenian Sea. His eyes followed the boat until it vanished behind the cliffs at Laurito, and he was startled back to reality by the sound of Lexi laughing loudly.

Thanks to Magnus Lund and his contacts in Interpol it hadn't taken more than an hour to identify the gunmen who had raided Flynn's and snatched Lea. Jake's CCTV coverage of both inside and outside the bar offered near-total coverage and while the men had worn masks they had been able to follow the car all the way out to a small private airfield just north of the city.

After that it was a matter of tracing the aircraft – a Beechcraft King Air registered to a man named Giancarlo Zito. He described himself as a 'businessman', but Lund's Interpol man had clarified what that meant, and it turned out Zito was a drug-trafficking mobster with tentacles connecting him to the criminal underworld all over

Europe. The intel also hooked up nicely with the manuscript thieves who had been traced to Naples.

And now they were here in Positano studying the mobster's private island. It wasn't the first time Hawke had stormed an island but it would be one of the trickier times – locals warned that the tides around the island were unpredictable and dangerous, and if that wasn't bad enough, Zito was notoriously paranoid about being monitored by the Italian Government and kept a constant guard around the island with several armed men.

"What do you have in mind, Joe?" Kim said.

"From looking at the island on Google Earth, it's impossible to land there unobserved, especially considering how many men Zito has on the island. It's too far out to swim to, even for me, so there's only one option."

"Parachutes?" Ryan said.

Hawke gave him a look. "No, not *parachutes*."

"Was that a stupid question?" Ryan asked.

"He who asks Google a question is a fool for five minutes," Lexi said, lighting a cigarette and exhaling the hot smoke. "But he who does not ask Google a question stays a fool for life. Ancient Chinese proverb."

Hawke watched Scarlet Sloane walking back over to their shaded table. She had been in the bars and restaurants asking locals for information. Reaper, who had made the short flight from Marseille, was walking beside her.

"Anything?" he asked.

She nodded. "Just met a lovely waiter chap named Mario."

Ryan rolled his eyes. "Here we go again. It's not enough to break Jack Camacho – now she's going to shag her way along the Amalfi Coast."

"You're only jealous, tiny," Scarlet said with a wink.

"Who is this person?" Hawke asked.

"Just a barman," Reaper said.

"One of his friends used to work for Zito a long time ago," said Scarlet. "He got on the wrong side of him and ended up in traction for a few weeks."

"Are we still talking about Zito now, or are we back on Camacho?" Ryan asked.

"I'll put you in fucking traction in a minute," Scarlet said.

Ryan opened his arms, cigarette hanging off his lower lip. "I'm right here."

"You'd wet yourself if I came anywhere near you."

"Now you're just being rude," Ryan said.

"What did this *Mario* say?" Hawke said, bringing things back to business.

"Well, according to him, Zito sends a small boat out to the smuggling ships and meets them in the middle of the Med. The heroin shipment is transferred to the boat which then comes back to the Isola Pacifica. The island's private so the authorities aren't interested in the comings and goings of a millionaire's speed boats, so how does he get the heroin onto the mainland?"

Hawke smiled. "This sounds like my territory."

"Exactement," the Frenchman said.

Scarlet lit a cigarette. "Young Mario says he uses a small submarine to bring the dope from the island into Positano, and from here it's loaded onto trucks and transported all over the rest of Italy and even further away to countries like France, Switzerland, and Austria."

"He's got to be using an Aurora," Hawke said.

"This is what I was thinking," Reaper said.

"So the only question is – where does he land the thing when he brings it to the mainland?" Lexi said.

"That cost extra," Scarlet said with a weary smirk. "For a small bribe, Mario told me he uses a quiet cove to the east of the town in a place called Arienzo. He says this is because not only is it away from the town but it's got faster access to the main road leading over to Salerno and Zito has a small villa there."

"Little bastard has it all worked out," Devlin said with a shake of his head. "And here's me thinkin' I should work for a living when all I had to do was get me a minisub and smuggle smack."

"That's *illegal*, Danny," Kim said.

"So it is!"

Kim sipped the last of her beer and set the bottle down on the table. It was getting hot now and she leaned back in her chair. "Do we know when the next shipment is?"

Scarlet shook her head. "All Mario could tell me was they come every few days because that way the quantities are kept small enough for the sub. He said there hasn't been one for at least two nights so chances are good that either tonight or tomorrow night we're on."

"So all we have to do is get a nice little hidey-hole near that cove and wait for the action," Ryan said.

Hawke tapped his fingers on the wooden table. "Nothing's ever that simple, mate."

"Maybe," Ryan said with a tired smile. He stubbed his cigarette out and immediately opened his matchbox to light another. "Maybe not."

Scarlet frowned. "So who draws the short straw?"

"To go and get killed, you mean?" Ryan asked.

"No, the short straw means you have to stay here and do fuck all. Going to the island means shooting and violence."

Ryan cupped his hands around the match to stop the sea breeze from extinguishing the flame. "In that case, count me in."

"The sub in question only has four seats," Hawke said. "I'm the only one who can pilot it, plus I want two others."

"But that's only three," Scarlet said.

Ryan shook his head. "She'll work it out in a second. This is precisely why you shouldn't drink Scotch at this time of the day."

"It's *coffee*," Scarlet said, cuffing Ryan around the back of the head.

Ryan laughed. "That coffee's more Irish than Danny."

"It is not," Scarlet protested. "I'm a professional, and I can count as well. Surely we can get four of us into the sub and still have room to bring Lea back? The only question is – who gets all the excitement?"

Hawke rubbed the stubble on his jaw. "We'll draw straws."

Kim Taylor pulled the straw out of her drink.

"What are you doing?" Lexi asked.

"We're drawing straws, right?"

Lexi rolled her eyes, ejected the magazine from her gun, and put it in the center of the table. She spun it around and it stopped with the muzzle pointing directly at Danny Devlin. "Congratulations," she said. "You're on the mission." She spun it again and this time the muzzle pointed at her. "Looks like you can be my wingman, Devlin."

"In your dreams."

"Not fair," Scarlet said. "She cheated. She must have a magnet stuffed down her bra."

Reaper laughed and shrugged. "I will be forced to stay here and suffer an evening drinking wine on the Amalfi coast. C'est la vie."

Scarlet stubbed out her cigarette and shot a quick, doubtful look at Devlin. "I still want to come."

Hawke gave her a look. "You're staying here, Cairo." As he spoke, he slipped a box of Magtech nine mil rounds from his bag and started to load a magazine for his Glock.

He repeated the process with a spare magazine, and then a third time. The weapon held seventeen nine mil caliber rounds and packing a couple of spares meant he had fifty-one shots for the rescue mission. He put all three loaded mags in his bag with the Magtech box and the weapon and then raised the coffee to his lips for another sip. He fixed his eyes on Scarlet. "Is that all right with you?"

"I suppose so, but what am I supposed to do? Tweaking Ryan's ears can only amuse a girl for so long."

"You call Lund," Hawke said. "And ask him what the hell we're supposed to do when we get the manuscript. As for the rest of us, we're heading out to Zito's island as soon as we can get hold of that sub. Lea's depending on us."

*

Alex Reeve gripped the plush, leather armrests of her seat as the colossal Boeing VC-25 started to descend toward the British clouds. For a while, she tracked the progress of the aircraft's shadow as it danced on the cloud-tops, but then the descent pushed them lower and the plane and its shadow became one as they plowed into the cloudscape. Seconds later a wave of turbulence started to bounce her around in her seat.

Air Force One was almost a flying palace and cost millions of dollars to keep in the air on every flight. It was the safest plane in the world, carrying the most sophisticated anti-missile flares and radar jammers. She knew this thanks to Agent McGee who had bored her with this and a lot more, including how technically any aircraft carrying the President automatically became "Air Force One", but there was one thing that was the same as every other plane she had been on: the turbulence.

At least it wasn't the E-4B NAOC "Doomsday Plane".

NAOC stood for National Alternate Operations Center and was a flying bunker to be used by the President in the event of a serious attack on the United States. That one really freaked her out.

"Buckle up."

She looked up to see Agent McGee looming above her. For once, he wasn't wearing his mirror-shades and she was able to look into his eyes. With the glasses on he looked like any of the other agents, but now he had become human again, and he looked kind. "Consider it done," she said with a half-smile.

He gave a brief nod and then sat down opposite her, buckling himself in. "We're on the ground in five minutes," he said. "Then it's straight to the hotel. In the morning we go to the G8 summit. After that, we're at Buckingham Palace to meet the Queen and have dinner and then the next day the President will meet the Prime Minister in Downing Street. After that, he's going to address both Houses of Parliament in Westminster Hall, and then it's wheels up. All set?"

Alex nodded. "Sure."

"We'll keep away from the press as much as we can, but they always get something, okay?"

Another nod. *They always get something*, she thought. Pictures of the poor wheelchair-bound President's daughter splashed across the tabloids; column inches devoted to what had happened to her, what life she led, what she was wearing, her hairstyle. "Thanks, Brandon," she said quietly.

"No problem. It's my job. I'm on your security detail, not the President's, and I'll do my best to make sure you're protected at all times."

A sense of politeness made her give him another brief smile, but the truth was she still had not come to terms with her father's new role as the world's most powerful man, and that coupled with a sense of her own vulnerability made her uneasy. Now, glancing out the window she saw the green fields of England's rural south as Air Force One turned to final approach and its landing at Heathrow Airport. Wondering what Joe Hawke and the rest of ECHO were doing, she closed her eyes and prepared for a whirlwind couple of days.

# CHAPTER TWELVE

Lea Donovan opened her eyes and saw nothing but white. She blinked and noticed an ornate chandelier suspended from the ceiling. The scent of roses and cedar wood drifted over her face. She blinked again and heaved herself up on her elbows.

She was on a large four-poster bed covered in white sheets, and beside her was a small table with a glass of water and a bowl of potpourri. Now she smelled the cinnamon and cloves. It was all very comfortable.

But not safe.

She took a deep breath and swung her legs off the bed. Pushing through some silk voiles. She emerged into a large, expensively furnished bedroom and took in her surroundings. Modern, clean lines and abstract art on the walls. Eclectic tastes.

A scream.

"What the hell was that?" she muttered, walking over to the window.

She heard another horrifying, blood-curdling scream. Was it some kind of animal? It sounded almost like a bull in tremendous pain, but there was a human quality to the agony that gave her the jitters.

The room had two large windows each with its own Juliet balcony. She went around to the other window and pushed it open. The screams were louder now, and coming from behind the house. She considered climbing over the balcony and lowering herself down to the ground. Leaning over the top rail of the balcony she counted the windows down the ground and realized she was three floors up: no dice on the escape plan.

With the hideous bellowing gradually fading out, she turned back into the room and saw a short man with slicked-back hair and deep, cavernous eyes standing in the doorway. He was leaning on the door jamb with his arms casually crossed over his chest. He stared at her intensely, and she recognized the eyes at once: this was the man who had kidnapped her in Dublin.

"Ciao, bella."

Lea took a step back and returned his gaze. She didn't want to break eye contact and show fear or weakness, but she searched the room with her peripheral vision for anything she could use as a weapon. The only thing that came to mind was the crystal potpourri bowl. She reckoned it was heavy enough to knock the man out if she got a good enough swipe at him, but she had no way of knowing what sort of hand-to-hand combat skills he could bring to bear on her during a struggle.

She took a step toward the small table with the lamp and the potpourri. "Who are you?"

"I am Toscano. I work here."

"And where is *here*?"

The man smiled grimly and pushed himself off the door jamb. He moved into the room and pulled a Beretta Neos from a shoulder holster beneath his jacket. "Hands in the air and step away from the table."

Damn. He had figured her out. It was pretty obvious when you thought about it, she considered.

She did as he instructed and raised her hands. The man took a step away from her to increase the distance between them and raised the gun to point at her chest. "We're going for a little walk."

He waved the gun in the direction of the door and took another step back so there were at least six feet between them as she stepped out into the corridor. To say Toscano was giving off a bad vibe was the understatement of the century, so Lea was only too happy with the large space he was putting between them.

"So where are we going?" she asked.

"You will see soon enough."

He ordered her along the corridor and then down a broad, sweeping staircase rendered in polished white marble. "So what was that screaming noise?" she said.

"I heard no screams," Toscano said quietly. He sounded a little less cocky now.

They came to a set of heavy double doors and Toscano ordered her to stand still. She obeyed and then he stepped forward and knocked three times. A short pause, pregnant with serious tension, was ended when a deep, fat voice told them to come in.

Toscano straightened his tie and pushed open the door to reveal a large dining room. A long wooden table stretched away to the other end of the room. At the far end of the table, a heavy-set man in a suit was fiddling with a large sauce-stained buttonhole napkin that was hanging down from his collar.

With a mouth full of food, he sloppily waved Toscano and Lea into the room, as if he were greeting the oldest of friends. "Come closer."

Toscano pushed her forward with a light nudge between her shoulders and she made her way toward the other man. As she drew closer to him she noticed that nestling among the elaborate table décor was a matte black pistol with a wooden grip which she recognized at once as a Pardini GT9. Beside it was the golden idol they had found in Maggie Donovan's things, but no sign of the manuscript.

Closer now she saw he was just about to start eating a

large lobster. It was sitting on a broad silver dinner plate surrounded by a lavish avocado and grapefruit salad. A second plate of lobster was at an empty seat beside him.

"Who are you and why have you brought me here?"

The man pulled off one of the lobster's claws and held it in his hand for a moment. "Don't you know?"

"I wouldn't have asked if I knew," she said defensively.

He picked up some metal crackers and broke open the lower part of the claw. "I am Giancarlo Zito." He cracked open one of the knuckles and pushed out the meat with a wooden fork before sliding it into his mouth and chewing. He picked up the tail, pushed more meat out, and began to peel it with the fork. Speaking with his mouth full of the lobster meat, he said, "Everyone around here knows my name."

"I'm not from around here."

He stared at her and nodded sagely. Dipping the tail meat into a bowl of hot water beside his dinner plate, he sighed loudly and then ate some more. This time he waited until he had finished before continuing. "You think I don't know where you are from? My men took you off the streets of Dublin. I know where you are from. If you were from here, you wouldn't be so relaxed right now." He leaned forward in his chair and swigged from a generous glass of Viognier. "Are you not going to eat your lobster?"

Lea pushed the plate away. "I don't seem to have an appetite. Being kidnapped by a bunch of hoodlums does that to a girl."

"Such a shame – this is Maine lobster I had flown in just a few hours ago, live. As fresh as it gets."

"Why am I here Mr. Zito?"

Zito stopped eating and set his wine glass down. "You are here because someone wants you to be here."

"You?"

"Not me, no. I couldn't care less about you – no offense."

Lea never broke eye contact. "None taken."

Zito pushed his chair back and rose to his feet. He raised one of his hands and snapped his fingers. "Toscano – bring Miss Donovan the zabaione."

"I already told you, I'm not hungry."

Zito stared out across the sun-drenched Tyrrhenian Sea and admired the view for a few tense moments. "In the mythology of Ancient Greece, it was believed that Aeolus kept the four winds hidden in the cliffs surrounding these waters – the Mistral from the north, the Libeccio from the southwest, and the Ostro and fierce sirocco from the south. This region is steeped in ancient folklore and myth. It is why I choose to live here."

"Who ordered you to steal the manuscript and kidnap me?"

Zito was still studying the rise and fall of the sea. "This is a very big question, and I am not sure you will like the answer."

"Try me."

"Both the manuscript and you are to be delivered tomorrow." He turned and faced her. He offered a sympathetic smile. "Then, you will have your answer."

# CHAPTER THIRTEEN

It was nearly dawn when Hawke saw the headlights. He rubbed his eyes and yawned, and stared along the winding road until it vanished on a bend to the south. The lights swept along the side of the villa and then he heard the grumble of the truck's diesel engine. A moment later it died, and the lights went dark.

"Looks like we're on," he whispered. "They obviously park up here and then walk down to the beach to collect the drugs."

No reply.

He turned and saw both Lexi and Devlin were fast asleep. He shook them by their shoulders and they awoke, startled but silent. "It's on – a truck just pulled up in Zito's villa. Keep an eye out for the sub."

He listened as the cab doors swung open and then slammed shut again. Then he heard the gentle, subdued chatter of men trying to talk on the quiet. He struggled to hear the Italian words with the cicadas chirping all around them.

He turned back to Lexi and Devlin. "Any sign of the Aurora?"

"Not yet," Lexi said.

Devlin leaned forward. "Why don't we whack these guys before the sub turns up?"

Hawke shook his head. "Not a good idea. They'll have a signal for the sub to come ashore and we don't know it."

Devlin moved to respond when Lexi interrupted him. "There – to the south of those cliffs! Do you see it?"

Hawke followed her arm and saw the dim glow of light

around a kilometer or so out at sea. "That could be them."

"Could be?" Devlin said.

"Yes," Hawke said, his voice rising. "*Could* be."

They all watched the light and when it came closer they saw it was a fishing trawler. Hawke gave Devlin a look as the trawler chugged past Arienzo and headed into Positano.

He opened his mouth to say something but then Lexi saw a second light, smaller and fainter. "There!"

"And look," Hawke said, indicating the truck parked up on the cliff at the side of the villa. "Watch the headlights."

One of the men had climbed back inside the truck and was flicking the lights on and off.

"It's Morse code," Hawke said, quick as flash. "Just says: All Clear."

"Well, I'll be *damned*," Devlin said with a grin. "The sub's coming in now, and no mistake."

He was right, and so was Hawke – as it drew closer to the cove's little beach he could now see it was an Aurora, and it looked like it had a crew of one. The other seats were presumably stuffed full of Afghani heroin. This was one particular shipment that wasn't going to hit the streets and destroy the lives of hundreds of innocent people.

"Looks like there's one in the sub and three up at the truck," Hawke said quietly. "Three of us versus four of them doesn't seem like a fair fight," he added with a grin.

"You can say that again," Lexi said.

Devlin nodded. "Let's pan them bastards out up at the truck before their buddies come in."

"Agreed."

"So come on now," Devlin said, rolling up his sleeves. "Let the dog see the rabbit!"

"When I give the order," Hawke said.

But the Irishman was gone. He clambered to his feet, climbed up over the low wall, and moved across the villa's lawn.

"Danny!" Hawke moved to pull him back but Lexi grabbed his arm.

"He's not an idiot, Joe!" she said. "Give him a break – Lea says he's as brave as they come."

"Maybe, it's just that..."

Before he could finish the sentence, they both heard Devlin shouting through the trees. "I'll knock your pan in, you silly twat!"

"Oh, *shit*," Lexi said.

Hawke frowned. "You were saying?"

They climbed the wall and ran along the lawn toward the truck just in time to see Danny Devlin ramming his fist forward into one of the men's chops. He knocked him hard to the ground but the other men were now making a break for it up the villa's narrow drive, and one had a phone in his hand.

"Oh, this is just fantastic!" Hawke said.

"Don't lose your lunch, young man," Devlin said cheerily. "He's not going anywhere."

And with that Devlin took off after the fleeing men.

Hawke looked at Lexi and sighed, but there was no time to discuss Lea's former commandant. They watched as another four men tumbled out the back of the truck and headed over to them.

"This is just great," Hawke said. "We're outnumbered three to one."

"Is that all?" Lexi said.

Zito's men bundled in from every angle, taking them all by surprise. If they'd been able to watch the truck for longer they could have counted how many men were in the back but thanks to Devlin they were now in the thick of it and fighting hard to keep a lid on things. If just one of them made a call to Zito the whole operation would be blown and Lea's life put in greater jeopardy.

Hawke took a punch to the jaw and tumbled backward toward the cliff. His fall to an early and painful death was stopped by the trunk of a large umbrella pine. The man punched him again, aiming right for the nose, but this time Hawke was ready. He dodged his head to the right and the man's fist smashed into the hard tree trunk, splitting his knuckles open and breaking some of his fingers.

Hawke punched the wounded man hard in the face and knocked him down in the gravel. As the man propped himself up on his elbows Hawke booted him in the face and knocked him out. Before he knew what was happening he was pulled sharply backward by another one of the men who had grabbed him by his collar.

He spun around fast and smashed a hefty left-hook into the man's jaw, sending him tumbling over toward the cliff edge. He tottered on the edge of the cliff, eyes wide with fear. Straining to keep himself from falling off, he flailed wildly with his arms, but then a typhoon tore past him.

And its name was Lexi Zhang.

Still fighting with another man, she took a few steps back and spun around to deliver a mighty, spinning hook kick into the middle of his terrified face. Her boot heel slashed across his cheek and powered his head hard to the side, knocking him back off the cliff. He screamed down to the rocks below, but Lexi never heard because she was once again focussing on the fight with the other man.

"Thanks for that, Lex," Hawke said.

"Welcome," she said, smashing a hammer punch into her opponent's nose and knocking him out. He collapsed to the floor beside the man Hawke had belted. "We're starting to get a little collection of scumbags here."

79

"Where's Danny?" Hawke said.

Hearing a grunt of pain, they looked up to see Devlin appear from behind the truck. He was fighting with the last of the men.

"Question asked, question answered," Lexi said.

They rushed over to help him as he brawled with the men and as Lexi kicked one of them in the back, Hawke launched himself at the other. Grabbing him by the shoulders, he hauled him away from Devlin and spun him around so he could plant a hefty smack in his face.

That was the plan, but the reality was different: the man was much faster than Hawke had anticipated and was prepared for the attack. He fired a punch at Hawke and struck him hard in the jaw.

The blow sent Hawke reeling toward the edge of the cliff and before he knew what had happened he felt himself going over, tumbling back in the night with nothing below him but a two hundred foot fall to the rocks below.

# CHAPTER FOURTEEN

He reached out and grabbed anything he could find to save his life. His hands found a wild array of root complexes pushing out the side of the cliff edge from one of the umbrella pines above him. He wrapped his fingers around them as hard as he could to stop his fall, but he was still dangling hundreds of feet above the rocks.

He took a second to get his breath back and realized both Lexi and Devlin were still fighting for their own lives and unaware of his plight. He felt the wind blowing through his hair as he swung off the root complex. His mind raced to come up with anything that would get him out of the situation.

He was too far from the top of the cliff to attempt to climb back over to safety without help, but he was way too high up to consider leaping and aiming for the sea. He'd done enough tomb-stoning in his youth to know he was too far away from the water to guarantee hitting it, and if he landed on the rocks they'd be taking him home in a bucket.

The roots started to break away from the crumbling rocks above his head – slow at first and then more rapidly. He felt something snap and then he slid rapidly down another half-meter. Releasing the handful of dead, broken roots he realized there was now nothing more than half a dozen of them keeping him alive.

He looked up to see a boot flying down toward his hands. The man he had been fighting was now intent on finishing the job and kicking his hands away from the crumbling roots.

The blows rained down, smashing into his fingers. He cried out in pain and every instinct told him to move his hands out of the way, but that meant certain death so he had no choice but to hang on and let the man break his fingers and hands.

But then the kicking stopped and a second later he saw his assailant fly over his head in the night sky and fall into the rocks with a distant crunching sound.

A cloud of root dust and rock chips fell into his face and he blinked his eyes to clear them. "What the..?"

"Give me your hand!"

It was Devlin, leaning dangerously over the cliff to save Hawke's life.

"Don't be an idiot, Danny!" Hawke yelled out.

"It's fine," Devlin said, panting. "I've got me a good hold on one of the boulders."

"You'll kill yourself!" He looked down for a second to relieve the tremendous tension in his neck and saw the smashed bodies of the men down on the rocks.

"Just give me your hand."

Hawke stared up through what was left of the root complex to see the Irishman had wriggled even further forward now. His entire upper body was hanging off the cliff as he strained to extend his arm down to reach him. He knew he had to let go of the roots with one of his hands to reach up to Devlin, and if the roots in his other hand should snap in that second...

He let go of the roots with his weaker, left hand and thrust it up as far as he could toward the Irishman's hand. The two men used all their strength and after a few seconds of struggling, Hawke clambered up over the edge of the cliff and took a deep breath.

"I owe you," Hawke said.

"Think nothing of it," Devlin said, dusting his hands

off.

"I said I owe you," Hawke said. "And I mean it."

"Next time we're in Flynn's you can buy me a pint."

They shook hands. It felt to Hawke like they had crossed a bridge, but he still had his reservations about Danny Devlin. The man's bravery was beyond question, but his judgment was still hanging in the balance.

Lexi Zhang finished heaping up the last unconscious man into her collection and then strolled over. The moonlight shone in her eyes as she looked at Hawke. "I think it's time we picked up that shipment of heroin from the sub, don't you?"

Hawke smiled. "One thing I like about you, Lex – you're always up for it."

"I bet that's what all the lads say, eh?" Devlin said.

Lexi gave him a stern look. "I see you're not overly attached to your balls, Mr. Devlin. Would you like me to kick them over to Zito's island?"

A mischievous grin spread on his face. "Sorry, I was sure you could take a joke."

"Of course, I can," she said, returning the grin. "Where would you like to go?"

"Touché," Devlin said, accepting defeat.

Hawke had already started to walk down the cliff path that led to the pick-up point on the beach below. "Can you leave the foreplay for later, girls?" he called over his shoulder. "We have work to do."

*

Vice President Davis Faulkner was tense as the limousine cruised behind the police escort. They were driving south along Rock Creek and Potomac Parkway on their way to the Capitol building where he was due to break a tie on a vote in the Senate. As ex-officio President of the US Senate, the Constitution gave him the power to make the casting vote when the Senate was tied, and today his vote was required to pass the nomination of the Secretary of Veterans Affairs.

It was not exactly his idea of a good time, but the machinery of the US Government was surprisingly delicate and responsive and he had a role to play in that; a role he would continue to play until he got into the Big Chair.

It was also not why he was tense, and now his eyes crawled over the soft leather seats to the car phone. When it rang, he nearly had a heart attack, then he flashed a tongue over his dry lips and picked up the receiver. "Faulkner."

"Mr. Vice President," the voice said. "I'm so glad you found time to speak to me."

"I serve at your will, sir."

A low chuckle. "Of course... of course."

"Let me start by apologizing for..."

"I'm not interested in apologies or explanations, Davis. You were ordered to destroy Elysium and kill Eden. You failed on both counts. The Valhalla idol is still in their possession and Eden lives."

"Yes, sir. The man I put in charge of the assault failed me."

"The man *I* put in charge of the assault failed *me*."

Faulkner swallowed hard and pulled his pocket square from his breast pocket. He dabbed at sweat beading on his forehead. He was the man the Oracle was referring to, and he didn't like where the conversation was going. "I can make amends, sir."

"You can and you will. Say it."

"Yes – I can and I will."

"Good. We need those idols, Davis. Not just the one

ECHO removed from Valhalla, but every one of them." He paused and Faulkner heard him sucking on a cigar. "The most devastating power you can imagine is locked within the idols, Davis; the secrets they guard will rock this world like nothing that has ever come before and elevate me to my rightful place above all of humanity." Another pause, and a deep, masculine exhalation of thick smoke. "You want to be...*part* of this pilgrimage, don't you, Davis?"

"More than anything, sir."

"This is also good. An obedient servant is a happy servant."

"Yes, sir."

"So let me make this clear: I want ECHO terminated and I will not ask you again."

"Yes sir," Faulkner said. Then, trying to look on the ball, he added, "When do you want me to move against Brooke?"

The Oracle chuckled again. "Assassination of a sitting President is high treason, Davis, and yet you talk about it as if you're playing chess with a man in a park."

"I just want to serve the cause, sir."

"You will be given your orders when I want Brooke removed from the White House and not before. Let's just say his days are numbered."

"Yes, sir. it's just that I can serve the cause better from the Presidency. The Vice President has very limited powers. There's no way I can deploy serious forces against ECHO or anyone else from this office."

"I know the way the system works, Davis. I was in the room when the Constitution was written."

Davis swallowed again but tried to keep his voice straight and level. It wasn't easy when the Oracle said things like this. He had no idea if it could be true; it sounded insane but he had faith in his master and the cause he was leading. Besides, he had seen things... things that had convinced him of the Oracle's claims. How could he dare argue with a man like this? That is, even if he *was* a man. "Please, accept my apologies."

"I don't accept failure, Mr. Vice President."

"No."

"Which way were you thinking of voting today?" the Oracle said.

"For McKinney."

"Wrong. You'll vote for Stafford."

"Yes, sir."

The Oracle cut the call and the line buzzed. The sound of the disconnect tone filled the rear of the limo until it almost felt like it was drilling into his head. He fumbled it down onto the cradle and linked his fingers. As they passed the Lincoln Memorial and turned east toward the Senate he realized his knee was jogging up and down like a jackhammer, but no matter how much he tried to rein it in, it just kept going up and down.

What had he done? People talked about selling your soul to the devil, but he felt like that would almost be a relief compared with what he had gotten himself into. What was it Marlowe said about this? He searched his mind for the words he had learned so many years ago when his mind was still young and his conscience fresh and clear.

*Hell is just a frame of mind.*

Yes, that was it – and it made him feel a little better until he remembered the part where the devils came for Faustus and dragged him down into that hell.

He shuddered but a smile crossed his lips: no devil was dragging an immortal soul into hell, and only the Oracle could offer him this blessed salvation. That is why he would do anything to serve the Man and the Cause.

Anything.

# CHAPTER FIFTEEN

## Tianhe District, Guangzhou

Tiger watched a packed commuter train rattle into the enormous East Railway Station and glanced at his watch as he stepped out of the government car. All around him China's third-biggest city buzzed and vibrated with life. The aroma of beef offal stew and steamed vermicelli drifted over from a nearby street vendor, and an old woman in a surgical face mask brushed his shoulder as she pedaled past him on a three-wheel bike.

Pig and Rat emerged from the car, straightened their ties, and flanked him. Tiger was no fan of Tianhe – at least not this part of the district. To him, some of these back streets represented some of the very lowest forms of human life in China.

And now he was about to meet the absolute lowest of them all.

Monkey.

They turned off the main road and made their way the last few hundred meters without the car. Tiger prided himself on being a total professional, and there was no point in having unnecessary witnesses. Deep in a labyrinth of degraded tower blocks and crumbling asphalt, they finally reached the building they were looking for.

Car horns and bike bells jostled for supremacy in the background as Tiger double-checked the address. He stared up at the colonial-era townhouse. Rotten red shutters hung down at odd angles from the sides of the windows, and a TV aerial cable snaked its way down through broken roof tiles before vanishing through the wall on the upper floor.

"I like it," Pig said, lifting a Zhonghua cigarette to his mouth. He deftly slipped a solid gold Zippo from his jacket pocket and fired up the tobacco. Inhaling deeply, he held the smoke in his lungs for a moment and coughed hard when it came out again. "He has taste."

Rat nodded his head. "He's always liked his whores."

Tiger sighed and checked his watch once again. "The Boss says he's in the team, so he's in the team."

A woman stumbled out of the alley to the left of the decrepit brothel. A second later a man stepped out behind her and kicked her in the stomach. She tumbled over and gasped for air. He pulled her to her feet and slapped her around the face a few times.

Tiger and the other two Zodiacs watched impassively for a few seconds. Men beating women on the streets in a place like this was not uncommon, and only an American tourist outside a nearby laundry looked twice. Everyone else walked past, including Tiger, Pig, and Rat as they stepped off the street and entered the dingy brothel.

They walked into a darkened world of coughing and heavy cigarette smoke laying on the air in blankets. Cheap smoke now – rough, and some menthol in there too. A radio chimed in the background, tinny and distracting.

An elderly woman regarded the men's sharp suits with an avaricious eye. "Good day, gentlemen," she said.

Tiger reached into his inside pocket and pulled out a small black and white photo of Monkey. He held it up to her face. "Where?"

The woman realized they weren't here for the women and her eyebrows dropped. Crestfallen, she pointed up the stairs to her left. "Top floor. Front room. No fighting, no killing!"

Tiger placed his hand on her chest and pushed her firmly away from him as he marched past and began to climb the stairs.

The old wooden steps creaked and whined as the three government men made their way up to the top floor, pausing on the landing for a second to check the fire escape. When they reached the top, they padded along the landing until they were at the door to the front room.

Tiger reached out to the door handle. They heard a shallow thud and a woman screamed.

Pig and Rat exchanged a glance and smirked at one another. "Sounds like him, all right."

Another light thudding sound and another scream.

Tiger turned the handle.

Locked.

Now he raised his boot and put the door in and they all saw what was going on.

A blindfolded woman was tied to the bed and on either side of her head, several Chinese flying darts were embedded in the wooden headboard. The Chinese flying dart was a lethal hand-held throwing weapon used in ancient China both as a range weapon or in the fist. Now, half a dozen of the razor-sharp metal darts were just inches from the sobbing woman's head.

"That's his handiwork, for sure," Pig said.

"Indeed," said Rat as he scanned the room. "But where is the man himself?"

"He heard me try the door," Tiger said. "The three seconds in between my turning that handle and kicking the door down was all he needed."

"Which is why he's on the team," Rat said.

Pig nodded and cast a regretful eye at the woman on the bed. "Sadly, yes."

Tiger walked over to her, took off her blindfold but left

her tied up.

As far as the ropes would allow her to move, she recoiled in fear when she saw the three suited men, but calmed down when Tiger showed her the picture.

"Is this him?"

She nodded and pointed her head toward the bathroom door. "I heard him go in there."

Tiger thanked her and put the blindfold back.

She kicked out and screamed again but he ignored her, turned, and moved toward the bathroom. He drew his weapon as he got closer to the door.

Pig and Rat followed suit and now all three men raised their guns into the aim. It wasn't that they didn't trust Monkey, but more that he was unpredictable and had a dangerous trigger finger. He would shoot first and ask questions much later, so they knew they had to be prepared.

Tiger nudged the door open with the toe of his boot. "Come out, come out wherever you are, Monkey Man," he said. "It's the Tiger and his friends."

A heartbeat later an upside-down head appeared above them.

Tiger took a step back and aimed the gun at the grinning face. The man's long hair was hanging down and his deranged smile looked like a frown because he was still upside-down.

"You mean Pig and Rat?" he said.

Tiger and the others exchanged a look, smiled, and lowered their weapons. "Yes, I mean Pig and Rat."

Monkey swung down from above the door. He had hidden up there like a ninja, using the top of the shower cubicle on one side and the aircon vent on the other to hold himself in place. No one else could have done it, but while Monkey shared the other men's former espionage backgrounds, he had been in a circus when they were in

THE SWORD OF FIRE

the army. This added to his enigmatic character but also gave him incredibly powerful arms and legs.

He landed on the bathroom floor with a gentle, controlled thump and then brushed his hair back over his face to reveal his infamous pock-marked face. He glanced over Tiger's shoulder and grinned. "You really *did* mean Pig and Rat!"

"Monkey, this is business."

"Of course," Monkey said. The smile was gone and now he was scowling. He padded across the room and pulled the darts out of the headboard. He slapped the woman's face and she screamed. "When the Tiger, the Pig, and the Rat come to my playground it is only ever business...but tell me, colleagues – is it a kill job?"

"That's for Zhou to decide, and you will obey him."

Monkey moved toward the door and Tiger stepped in front of it to block his exit. "We can trust you to obey Zhou, can't we, Monkey?"

"Of course."

Tiger nodded, his eyes heavy with uncertainty. "We don't want anything like last time."

Monkey looked offended. "Nothing like last time, I promise."

"Good," Pig said, stubbing his cigarette out on the door frame and dropping the crumpled butt to the floor. "Then let's get out of this dump."

"What's the job?" Monkey said.

Tiger fixed his eyes on the dangerous young man. "Agent Dragonfly."

# CHAPTER SIXTEEN

Hawke, Lexi, and Devlin waited in the shadows as the minisub pilot pulled alongside a small jetty and killed the engine. When he opened the hatch the first and last thing he saw was Hawke's fist as it piled into his face. Devlin dragged the body along the jetty as the Englishman fired the engine back up and then they were away.

It didn't take Hawke long to acquaint himself with the controls and set a course for Zito's island. He submerged the Aurora a few meters beneath the surface so they wouldn't be seen: Zito and his men might not be expecting it to return so soon, so Hawke decided to err on the side of caution.

"If they've hurt her, I'll kill every last one of them," Devlin said.

Hawke and Lexi exchanged a glance. "There's a line for that," Lexi said to the Irishman. "And you're at the back of it."

Hawke noticed the offshore bars gradually rising as they neared the island, and he decided to surface the small vessel. When they broke through the waves they all saw the lights of Isola Pacifica's long northern coast. Behind them, in the center of the island, was some elevated ground. It was partly covered in a large pine forest and perching on the top was Zito's villa complex.

"She's in there somewhere," Hawke said, killing the sub's lights.

"Not for long," said Lexi.

Hawke navigated the sub into Zito's mooring jetty and cut the engine. Now, with only the sound of the waves splashing against the glass cockpit bubble, he opened the hatch and climbed out into the darkness. When Lexi and Devlin joined him, he had already lashed the sub to the jetty with some mooring rope and was now surveying the best way to get up to the villa.

They decided to go to the east and use the forest for cover for as long as they could, but there was still the open ground of the beach to cross first. A few steps into their journey they all heard the sound of engines revving in the darkness.

"What the hell?" Devlin said. "How did they know?"

"Maybe they have a crystal ball?" Lexi said, glancing at the Irishman.

"Here they come," Hawke said. "They're on dirt bikes – back to the sub!"

"And desert Lea?" Devlin said.

"We need a new plan," Lexi said, but Danny Devlin was already on his way. He had split up from Hawke and Lexi and was now sprinting toward the cover of the trees.

"What the hell is he doing?" Lexi said.

Hawke shook his head and cursed. "He's going to get us all killed!"

As they took cover behind the minisub, Lexi raised her hand and pointed at Devlin. "They've already seen him. They're on his tail!"

One of the dirt bikes broke away from the other and swerved hard to the left. It was now headed in the direction of Danny Devlin who was still running up the beach toward the cover of a line of stone pines at the top of the dunes.

The Irishman glanced over his shoulder and saw the threat fast approaching, and then they were all aware of the sound of gunfire.

Hawke saw the third man up on the bluff, hunkered

down behind a sage bush and his eye fixed firmly to the telescopic sights of a sniper's rifle. He cursed and called out to Devlin to warn him of the threat.

The man on the dirt bike was now almost nipping at Devlin's heels. He pulled an MP5 from his belt and began firing at his prey. The bullets ripped through the sand and chased after the former Irish Ranger as he raced toward the cover of the trees.

Hawke opened fire with his Glock. Night shrouded the biker, and he was racing away out of sight, but the rounds slammed into the sand around him and nearly knocked him off his bike.

Under fire now, and struggling to control the bike with one hand and fire the machine pistol with the other, the man raised the weapon and fired on Devlin again. The bullets peppered the sand behind the Irishman, but before they could rip into his back, he dived into the cover of the trees and bushes up on the ridge at the top of the beach.

Lexi breathed a sigh of relief but Hawke cursed at the unnecessary risk Danny Devlin had taken. He could have gotten them all killed and had put the entire operation in jeopardy.

"Holy crap," Lexi said. "That was close!"

"Too close," Hawke grumbled. "He could have got himself killed doing that."

But there was no time to think about right or wrong. With Devlin up inside the cover of Isola Pacifica's small forest, the rider burned off down one of the narrow tracks inside the woods in pursuit. The other rider turned around and headed back in the direction of Hawke and Lexi back on the jetty.

"Oh, crap," Lexi said. "That was predictable."

"Yeah – thanks to Mr. Devlin."

The man racing toward them pulled a machine pistol and began firing. Hawke had used a whole mag trying to save Devlin, so now he needed a new one but there was no time. The rider was so close Hawke could smell the two-stroke exhaust fumes and as the bullets danced their way up the wooden jetty, he scanned for a weapon. Spying a loose board in the jetty, he wrenched it free with a hefty tug.

"Jump!" he yelled, holding onto the board as he leaped off the jetty.

They both dived into the water and swam down under the jetty seeking whatever cover they could find. Looking up to the surface Hawke saw the rider had slowed down and was now taking his dirt bike along to the end of the jetty where the Aurora was moored. He was peering down into the water and pointing the MP5 down at the waves as he went, searching for any sign of them.

Thanks to his extensive SBS training, Hawke could hold his breath for several minutes, but he knew Lexi Zhang would run out of air much faster, so he had to think fast and act even quicker. If she broke the surface to take a breath the rider would rake her full of holes in a heartbeat.

Lexi had swum over to him now but he could barely see her in the dark water. The full moon gave a low light and lit her face a ghostly silver, and her eyes were staring at him with desperation and fear.

The rider fired the MP5 and they both saw the bullets tracing through the water all around them. He had no idea where they were and Hawke knew it. He was firing blind and would soon give up.

Hawke waved at Lexi and gestured she should follow him, and then he turned and swam back along the length of the jetty toward the shore. With the plank of wood still in his hands, he swam up to the surface and sure enough, the final rider turned and headed back to the shore.

Speeding up as he prepared to jump the dirt bike off the jetty and land it back on the sandy beach, Hawke waited until the last second and then rammed the plank up through the gap in between the jetty boards.

The dirt bike rider had no time to react. Half a second later his front tire smashed into the plank and the spinning wheel came to an instant stop, propelling the rider off the bike. He backflipped through the air and landed with a heavy crunch while his bike crashed down on its side and came to a rest at the beach end of the jetty.

Hawke and Lexi clambered up out of the sea and then the Englishman made his way over to the rider. Still soaking wet, and aware of the sniper hiding up on the bluff, he acted fast. Grabbing hold of the disoriented man's helmet he twisted it hard to the right and back again. They both heard his neck snap and then a high-velocity round took the top inch off one of the jetty poles.

"Shit!"

A shower of splintered wood burst into the air between them. They looked at one another and said at the same time, "Night sights!"

Hawke cursed again and grabbed Lexi by the arm, pulling her down off the jetty and into the sand. He knew the direction of the sniper because of the way the round had struck the pole, and now they were tucked down behind the riders's dirt bike.

"This is our only way out of here," he said.

Lexi looked at him. "So what are you waiting for?"

He pushed the dirt bike back up onto its wheels and straddled it. Lexi jumped on behind him and wrapped her arms around his waist. "Just like that night in Hong Kong, remember?"

Yes, he remembered, but when another high-velocity sniper's round thudded into the sand a few millimeters from the front tire he was very much back in the moment.

Revving the bike wildly and releasing the clutch he was soon steering the dirt bike across the dark beach and up toward the same ridge Danny Devlin had used for cover a few moments earlier.

Sniper fire was now spitting all around them as the gunman up on the bluff tracked them along the beach through his night sights. Hawke swerved the bike left and right in an attempt to make them harder to track, but then one of the rounds ripped out the rubber on the rear tire and sent the bike skidding all over the place.

Gunfire from the forest now. He saw a muzzle flash from behind the trunks of the stone pines. For a second Hawke almost turned the dirt bike west and headed away from the ridge but then he realized the shooting inside the pine forest was aimed at the sniper up on the bluff.

"Must be Danny!" he said.

"He's redeemed himself, then," said Lexi.

Hawke aimed the battered dirt bike for the ridge, and seeing a narrow pathway that seemed to lead off to the right, he raced up it as fast as he could intending to jump the last few meters.

With Devlin's cover fire to their left, Hawke now zoomed the bike up the incline and launched into the night air. The engine growled as they flew through the night and then crashed back down on the path leading into the small forest. Gravel chips and pine cones exploded out around them as the bike smashed down to earth.

Lexi pointed to another muzzle flash. 'There!"

Hawke revved the bike and turned the handlebars to the left. Navigating the narrow path for a few seconds they were soon beside Danny Devlin. He was crouching behind one of the pine trunks with a good view of the sniper. A few meters behind him was the other rider – dead in the undergrowth, and his bike was propped up against another trunk.

"Glad you could make it," Devlin said.

Hawke opened his mouth to tell the Irishman his fortune but Lexi grabbed his arm. "Not the time, Joe."

She was right, but he couldn't help it. "You could have killed all of us, Danny!"

He smiled and winked. "Not my fault if you're slow off the mark, Josiah."

Hawke's response was silenced by Devlin turning and firing the stolen rider's weapon at the sniper.

"Now," Devlin said coolly. "I wonder if that third round made the mark?"

They looked over the top of the dark beach at the bluff and then they saw the sniper roll gently away from his position and let go of the rifle. It tumbled off the edge of the bluff and hit the sandy beach below it with a soft thud.

Devlin gave them another of his famous winks. "I thank you..."

"Good shot!" Lexi said.

"Thanks," said Devlin. "I don't think that naughty little monkey's ever going to reload again."

She turned to Hawke. "Wasn't it, Joe?"

"What?"

"A good shot!"

Hawke paused for a second. "Let's get on with it, yeah? We can congratulate ourselves when Lea's safe."

"We'll get her back safe, all right," Devlin said with confidence.

"Maybe," Hawke said flatly. "But thanks to you, the whole world and his wife knows we're here."

The former SBS man pushed past Devlin and padded through the undergrowth toward the treeline closest to the villa. With the two dirt bike riders and the sniper taken out, it was pretty obvious Giancarlo Zito was not going to be in a very good mood when they finally caught up with him.

Worse, thanks to Devlin's crazy call to make a break for it back on the beach, the Italian mobster would be totally prepared for any assault and maybe even making plans to leave the island with Lea and the manuscript before they could reach the villa. He knew Lea spoke very highly of 'the Commandant' but he was starting to ask questions about her judgment of the man.

As they trudged through the forest toward the southern part of the villa compound Hawke turned to Devlin. "This time, you do as I say, when I say it, right?"

Devlin raised his palms in a truce gesture and gently bowed his head. "You're the boss, Joe, you're the boss."

Hawke locked eyes on him and sighed. "On an ECHO operation, in the field, then yes, I am, Danny. If you can't handle it then you can't roll with us, all right?"

Devlin was silent for a few tense seconds, and then smiled and said, "I already told you – you're the boss."

"Joe – leave it, we have to think of Lea," Lexi said.

"I *am* thinking of Lea," Hawke said defiantly. "When we get inside Zito's villa we can't afford another fuckfest like we just had back on the beach, and that happened because the chain of command broke down. Are we all clear?"

Devlin and Lexi nodded. Everyone knew the reprimand had been aimed at the Irishman, but no one mentioned it again as they trudged through the final part of the forest, broke the tree line, and finally emerged face to face with Zito's private villa.

# CHAPTER SEVENTEEN

Crouching in the shade of the perimeter wall, Hawke pushed the magazine release button on his Glock and pulled the slide back. The empty mag dropped to the ground and he quickly smacked the spare into the grip. Wasting an entire mag trying to save Devlin's life on the beach had got his blood up, but now wasn't the time for debates.

The peace didn't last long, and now Zito's men activated a series of security lights around the property. The bright lights lit the perimeter up almost as bright as day, and then the shooting started. The first to open fire was a man on the roof with what sounded like a compact machine pistol.

"Aim's well off," Devlin said.

"He doesn't know where we are," Hawke said. "He's just making a statement."

"I'll give him a statement," Lexi said and raised her gun into the aim.

"You'll never hit him as long as he's behind these damned lights," Devlin said.

Lexi threw him a look. "Thanks for that, *bái chī*." She shook her head and then lined up the first light with the front sight post of her weapon. She pulled the trigger and the light exploded in a shower of sparks. "One down, four to go."

Before the Irishman replied, Lexi Zhang, astonished him by blasting the four remaining security lights to shattered glass in as many seconds. Then she lifted her weapon and fired on the shooter on the roof. He tried to take cover behind a chimney stack but she was too fast for him. She plowed the first round into his left shoulder as he dived for the cover and turned him around like a spinning top. Firing a second time she hit his throat and he crumpled down like an empty suit.

She raised her smoking muzzle to her lips and blew the smoke into Devlin's amazed face. "How was that?"

Devlin laughed. "Pretty damned good, as a matter of fact – but tell me, what does *bái chī* mean?"

"It means you're very rugged."

"Does it now?" he beamed.

"Yes," Hawke said with a withering glance. "*Does* it now?"

Turning her back on Devlin, Lexi winked at Hawke and they turned to face the villa again. With the grounds plunged into darkness, they noticed a flashing light in one of the upstairs windows. "Check it out," he said.

Lexi squinted up at the light. "What is it?"

"Morse code – SOS."

"Lea!" Devlin said.

"Maybe," Hawke muttered. "Or maybe a trap."

"We have to check it out," said Lexi.

Hawke nodded, and the team cut across the blackened lawn until they reached a broad patio and a set of French doors. Trying the doors and finding them locked, Hawke fired at them with his Glock and fractured the safety glass into a thousand pieces. He picked up a heavy bronze patio chair and hurled it at the window. It smashed through the pane and skidded to a halt in a sea of glass splinters all over the floor inside.

"Come on," he said. "We haven't got much time until..."

The lights went out.

"Damn it!" Lexi said. "Now they have the advantage."

"They always had the advantage," Devlin said.

"Not while I'm around," said Hawke.

Lexi looked at him in the darkness. "If there's one thing that always amazes me it's the size of your cock-"

Her words were cut short by the sound of the enemy firing on them. Judging by what the rounds were hitting, Hawke figured they didn't have night vision, but he dived on the floor just as fast. Seconds later Lexi and Devlin were beside him, taking shelter from the gunfire behind a large, antique sofa.

"It's just two guys, I think," Devlin said. "On the landing of the stairs there."

With her eyes now accustomed to the darkness, Lexi peered around the sofa and confirmed what Devlin had said.

"There's another staircase over there in the kitchen," Hawke said quietly. "You keep these clowns company," he said. "I'm going upstairs to get Lea."

With Lexi and Devlin giving him cover fire, he crouch-walked across the sunken living room and hit the stairs. Seconds later he was sprinting down a long central corridor until he found a door that he thought was in approximately the right place. Opening it, he found an empty bathroom with moonlight glinting on the polished silver taps of the bath, so he moved on down the corridor. Lea was up here somewhere and it was up to him to rescue her.

With the sound of gunfire and yelling below him, Hawke sprinted to the next room along the corridor and booted the door open to find Lea Donovan standing in the moonlight beside another man. With his back to the window he was little more than a silhouette to Hawke, but the Englishman could see clearly enough that he was holding a gun to her throat.

"Joe!" Lea cried out. "Behind you!"

Hawke spun around to see another man stepping out from behind the door. With the moonlight shining directly in his face he was able to recognize him at once as one of the men he had fought back in Boston.

"Drop the weapon," Moonlight Man said, calmly lifting a pistol into view. The silvery light shone dully on the weapon's muzzle as he grinned at Hawke. "I'll ask you only one more time, and then I'll..."

Hawke fired his gun at the man before he'd finished the sentence. The round tore through the man's eye and sprayed a misty cloud of blood and brain matter on the wall behind him.

The former commando turned and fired at the man holding Lea before the first man hit the floor. The back of the second man's neck blasted away into pieces and he slumped to the floorboards with a look of terrified realization etched on his now-dead face.

Lea screamed. The sheer speed with which Hawke had despatched the two men holding her at gunpoint had shocked even her. She had expected a wisecrack, an insult, and then for her lover to throw down his gun. Instead, she got a bloodbath, dealt out in less than two seconds. With the gun still smoking, Hawke crossed the room and held her by her shoulders.

"Are you all right?" he said. He noticed the shooting downstairs had stopped.

"Sure... I..." she glanced down at the dead man at her feet. "I'm glad you're here."

"Where's Zito?" Hawke asked, straight to business.

"I'm not sure. He was in here but when you attacked the villa he ran out and started barking orders at his men."

Lexi and Devlin ran into the room. The Irishman approached Lea and smiled warmly. "Are ya alright, girl?"

"I'm fine, Danny. Joe... *handled* it."

103

Devlin looked down at the two dead men and sniffed. "So I can see."

Hawke kissed Lea but then locked his eyes on her. "What about the manuscript and idol?"

"The idol's already gone," she said. "Some guys turned up a few hours ago and took it. Zito told me that finding it on me was an unexpected pleasure. All he was hired to find was the manuscript."

"But the men that took the idol," Lexi said. "They didn't take the manuscript?"

Lea shook her head. "Nope. Zito said that's being delivered to someone else."

"So where's Zito got the manuscript?" Hawke asked.

"How should I know?" Lea said, hands on hips. "He didn't invite me here for a tour of the place, you know!"

"Fantastic," Hawke said. "You're on the island for bugger knows how many hours and you haven't found out where Zito's safe is."

"Give her a break," Devlin said.

Hawke and Lea turned to Devlin and spoke at the same time: "Keep out of it!"

"I was just..."

"I'd keep out of it if I were you," Lexi said.

"So now we've got to track the safe down," Hawke said.

"It's not in the damned safe," Lea said, squeezing her eyes shut as she struggled to remember something. "Wait a minute – he mentioned something about reading it in his observatory. It means nothing to him, anyway – he was hired to take it by someone else like I said."

"Who by?"

She shrugged her shoulders. "He wouldn't let that particular cat out of the bag. He said I'd find out tomorrow."

"Too bad neither you nor the manuscript is going to be

in his possession tomorrow then, isn't it?" Hawke said. "We need to get out of here and in a hurry, but we need the manuscript first. Danny – can you arrange some transport while we go to the observatory?"

Devlin chuckled. "Leave it to me, Joe."

They watched Devlin vanish into the darkness of the corridor and then Hawke turned to Lea. "So, which way to this observatory?"

"I think it's at the far end of the corridor outside this room," Lea said.

They checked the corridor was clear and then made their way hurriedly toward the observatory.

"It's definitely down here, right?" Lexi said.

"I already said that I *think* so," Lea said, "but only from overhearing snatches of their conversation."

They made their way down the final stretch of the corridor and turned a corner to find themselves faced with large double doors. *Osservatorio* was written on one of them in polished gold letters.

"Bingo!" Lexi said.

They entered and found a large, low-lit room with the largest telescope any of them had ever seen in the center of it. It was mounted on a turntable and pointing toward a retracting roof.

"So this is what old Zito spends his time on when he's not giving people the cement shoes?" Lexi said, mesmerized by the enormous telescope.

"There!" Lea shouted. "That's it – on the chair next to the telescope."

Hawke jogged over to the chair and snatched up the manuscript. "All right – we're set. Let's just hope we can get out of here as easily as we got in."

"So what's the plan, Joe Hawke?" Lea asked.

Hawke stuffed the manuscript into his shirt and winked

at her. "Just like usual – we wing it."

They left the room and jogged down the stairs toward the lower part of the villa. "So this winging it..." Lexi said. "Is that an SBS thing?"

"If you mean improvising, then yes," Hawke said with a grin.

They were near the smashed patio doors now and heard raised voices from a room on the other side of the house. "That's Zito," Lea said.

"Sounds pretty pissed off to me," Lexi said with a chuckle.

"Time for us to go," Hawke said. "And pray your Commandant has got us some of those bikes we saw earlier."

Lea gave him an odd look. "Former Commandant, Joe."

Outside in the hot night, it wasn't long before Zito's men located them and opened fire, but they ran from the lethal fusillade with everything they had. Hawke navigated them across the lawns and into the shrubs which formed the border between the villa and the small forest, and they scanned the trees for Devlin.

"Over here, you silly bastards!"

Looking deeper into the trees they saw Danny Devlin half-obscured behind a trunk of a large stone pine. He was waving them over and they ran to him in the relative safety of the small forest.

"I got two of the bikes." Devlin straddled one of them and started it up. "Back to the Aurora, and quick as you like!"

Lexi was giving them cover now, firing at Zito's men as they tried to cross the lawn and reach the forest. Above them, they heard the sound of rotor blades whirring and then a Robinson R44 helicopter rose over the villa. After swooping over the forest it turned hard to port and made for the coast.

"Looks like Zito's out of here," Lea said.

"He must have got what he wanted from the manuscript," said Hawke.

Lexi frowned. "So someone's given his strings a tug."

Hawke thrust the manuscript into Lea's hands. "We'll worry about that later. Right now get this thing out of here!" he yelled. "We're right behind you!"

Lea jumped on the back of Devlin's dirt bike and clung on tight as he raced away into the night.

Hawke kick-started the other dirt bike and Lexi continued to spray hot lead all over the men. "Time to go, Lex!"

She leaped on the back of the bike and wrapped her arms around Hawke's waist.

"Go!"

# CHAPTER EIGHTEEN

Hawke revved the bike and took off down the narrow forest path. Behind them, Zito's men fired into the darkness of the trees but they were firing blind.

"We did it!" Lexi screamed.

"Not yet we didn't," said Hawke.

His eyes were focussing hard on the brake light of Devlin's dirt bike a few hundred meters up ahead. He could see Lea on the back of it, her arms clinging to the Irish soldier for safety as they ripped through the forest.

Then Lexi interrupted his thoughts. "Company!"

Hawke turned and glanced over his shoulder. He saw the bright headlight of another dirt bike bobbing about on the path behind them. "Damn it all!"

They were racing through the heaviest part of the forest now, with the path narrowing every second.

"We have to get them off our tail, Joe!"

"Easier said than done."

Lexi laughed. "Did you never watch Star Wars?"

"Eh?"

"Return of the Jedi? Speeder bikes?"

Hawke zoomed the dirt bike along the track, his headlight flashing on the trunks of the stone pines. "And your point?"

"My point is, you have to take us off the path! They'll follow us and that lets Lea get the manuscript off the island."

Hawke sighed. "I absolutely *knew* you were going to say something as insane as that."

"So, do we have a date, or not?"

With no mirrors on a dirt bike, Hawke twisted in the seat and looked over Lexi's shoulder at the enemy rider behind them. Getting closer now, and then the unmistakable muzzle flash of an automatic weapon. "Fine," he called back. "Star Wars it is!"

He turned the handlebars and raced the bike off the path. They crashed down in a carpet of pine needles and swerved for a few seconds before he brought the bike back under control.

"I know I talk about having a spirit of adventure," he yelled over his shoulder, "but this is pushing it even for me."

They were racing east now, zooming through the pitch-black forest with only their puny headlamp to light their way. Trunks flashed either side of them and they both knew an impact with one would mean a violent and painful death.

The other dirt bike was still behind them and closing fast. The man on their tail fired again and missed by millimeters. The bullets ripped into the bark of one of the stone pines and blasted a cloud of wood splinters and pine sap into their faces.

They burst through it, and then Hawke saw a ditch ahead of them. It approached them rapidly and he slowed the bike to drive down into it. At the bottom, he speeded up and raced up the other bank at an angle to decrease the gradient. The next thing they knew they were launching off the top of the other side of the ditch and flying through the air.

They crashed back down to earth in a raging storm of pine needles, dust, and two-stroke fumes but there was no possibility of stopping. Just a few meters behind them the other bike was driving down into the ditch, still hot on their tail.

"We need to head west again," Hawke said. "Get back to the Aurora before they decide to leave without us."

He revved the bike and skidded away once again just as the enemy behind them was flying up out of the ditch. He raced into the night, his tired eyes squinting now as the trunks flashed past them at an insane speed. As he was weaving the dirt bike through a dense patch of pines, he realized they were fast approaching a deep gorge, at the bottom of which was a river they had seen on the map back in Positano.

There was no way they could jump it and he struggled to see a way across. Turning back wasn't an option, and if they decided to drive along the eastern bank they would be pinned down between the river and the enemy gunman.

"What now?" Lexi said.

"There!"

Up ahead he spied a fallen tree trunk that was spanning the river.

"Can we get across it on this?" Lexi said, sounding mildly anxious.

"Only one way to find out, Agent Dragonfly!"

He turned the bike toward the fallen trunk and sprayed another pile of needles and cones up in a massive arc behind them. Racing toward it, he launched the bike up on the fallen trunk and zoomed over the narrow wooden bridge it formed.

"We're almost there!" Lexi shouted, but then a grenade exploded a few meters to their right.

Hawke, Lexi, and the bike were blasted off the fallen trunk and crashed down into the water below.

The explosion threw Hawke clear but the bike's front wheel had fallen on Lexi's leg. Hawke scrambled through the water and pulled it away from her and then the two of them waded over to the bank.

"They're getting closer – at least two," Lexi said,

rubbing her leg. "I can hear them."

She was right, and when the gunmen opened fire again it was even more ferocious than before. They split up to create two fronts, with Hawke tucking down beneath the fallen trunk spanning the river while Lexi went in the opposite direction and crouched down behind a large cork oak.

Calmly and quickly, Hawke hit the magazine release button, dumped the empty mag, and smacked the last one in the grip. Lexi was still backed up against the tree trunk, using it for cover now as the automatic gunfire ripped the surrounding undergrowth to ribbons. She was holding a sidearm in her right hand but the enemy had her pinned down so tight behind the tree she was unable to return fire.

Hawke knew there was a shooter somewhere east of their current position, but he could hear at least two weapons, so where was the other gunman? Another burst of fire gave away the second gunman's position. To the south of Lexi, he saw the telltale flash of a submachine gun's muzzle as the man opened fire on them once again.

He fired back but missed. He heard something fly through the air and crash into the undergrowth to his left.

Grenade.

Knowing there was no way he could locate it in all the vegetation in time to throw it back, he turned on his heel and dived away as fast and far as he could along the south bank of the river.

The grenade detonated.

He dived into the river for cover as the explosion blasted tiny, lethal fragments of shrapnel out at hundreds of miles per hour. Safe under the water he spun around onto his back and watched the fireball light up the pine trees stretching high above the river as the grenade burned out.

He had missed the shockwave by a fraction of a second but the river offered only a temporary sanctuary, and while the smoke from the grenade blast was still drifting in the air he saw the silhouette of the gunman as he approached his hiding place.

Running out of air, he pulled the slider back on his weapon and hoped the waterlogged gun would still fire but he wasn't hopeful. Just as he twisted in the water to fire the gun he watched as the man crashed over in a heap.

Emerging from the surface of the rushing river, he saw Lexi Zhang standing over the dying man. She fired two more shots into him and killed him stone dead before stuffing the gun into her belt. "I know you frogmen like water, Joe, but do you think this is an appropriate time to go swimming?"

Hawke waded out of the water and joined her on the river bank. "Funny, Lex. The other shooter?"

"Right between the eyes, baby."

"Good job. Let's catch up with Lea and Danny and get out of here."

*

They met up with the others on the tree line dividing the forest from the beach and decided the sub was the only way they could get back without Zito's men finding them again.

Leaving the warzone back in the forest and hitting the beach, they saw the Aurora glinting in the moonlight down on the waterline. The only problem was the sight of a man climbing into it. "Can't be Zito," Hawke said. "He took off in the chopper."

"No," Lea shook her head "Plus Zito's much bigger than that."

Hawke sighed. "In that case, he must have ordered one

of his men to submerge the Aurora to trap us on the island."

"We better get a move on, in that case," Lexi said.

They ran across the beach but as they drew closer to the sub the man heard them and jumped inside. He started to close the bubble cockpit down ready for diving, and Hawke knew if he closed it there was no way to get to him. The glass dome on the sub was designed to withstand tremendous pressure, and he doubted even shooting at it would be enough to stop the man before he dived and took it out of range.

He threw himself inside the submarine just as the man was bringing the bubble down. The heavy dome caught on his back but at least he was inside. He grabbed the man around the throat and pinned him against the seat. Pulling his fist back he powered a hefty punch into his face and knocked his head back into the bulkhead.

The man's skull struck the metal hard and his eyes rolled up inside his head as he tumbled over in his seat. He came to a rest, supine and motionless and with cold, blank eyes staring up at the stars above the open bubble.

"Come on – he's out cold!"

The others stepped off the jetty and climbed inside the Seamagine Aurora as Hawke stuffed the man down in front of the three front passenger seats and then climbed back into the pilot's seat at the back.

Lea leaned over and kissed him on the cheek. "Thanks for coming to get me."

"What else was I going to do?"

"You're lucky we made it," Lexi said, looking at Devlin. "Thanks to the Lone Ranger here who went rogue and nearly got us all killed."

"Is this true, Danny?" Lea said.

"I was just using my initiative."

"Don't get me hepped up again, Danny," Lea said.

"You should have waited for Hawke to give the order to go. He's in charge of this operation, not you. Ya got that?"

Devlin was contrite and offered his most charming Apology Smile. "I'm sorry."

"What are you saying sorry to me for, ya eejit? You owe Joe the apology, not me!"

Devlin glanced at Hawke and offered his hand. "I'm sorry."

A quick handshake and then they all strapped themselves into their seats as Hawke closed the cockpit and fired up the engines.

"This guy makes a handy footrest," Lexi said. "Perhaps they should build an asshole into their next model as standard?"

Hawke turned the Aurora around and piloted it out into deeper water. They all heard the gunfire back on the beach, but now the former commando was diving them under the waves and taking them deep underwater.

After a long silence, Devlin turned to Lexi and said, "So what was that you were saying earlier about the size of Joe's..." he paused a beat. "*Cock*, was it?"

Lea turned sharply. "What's this?"

"I was going to say the size of your cocky attitude," Lexi said with a weary sigh.

"See?" Hawke said with a smile.

"So don't get any ideas," Lexi added.

"I thought you were reminiscing about our little romance in Zambia," Hawke said with a wink.

Lexi nudged Hawke in the ribs and laughed. "Yeah... right."

*

Sitting in the back of Zito's drug trafficking truck, Scarlet lit up a cigarette and watched as Hawke and Devlin dragged the unconscious man up over the tailgate and tied him up with some old rope they'd found.

"Is that what you call a knot?" Scarlet scoffed as she looked at Devlin's work.

"I suppose the SAS do better knots than everyone as well?" Devlin said.

"It wasn't the SAS that taught her knots," Ryan said. "It was her formidable sex life."

Scarlet sighed and exhaled the smoke, unmoved by the attempt to wind her up. "So I take it you got the manuscript, darlings?"

"Indeed we did," Hawke said. "But the idol is long gone."

Scarlet sighed. "Simply fucktastic."

"Who's this?" Reaper asked.

"Submarine pilot," Hawke said.

"Any word from Lund?" asked Lexi.

Scarlet nodded. "He wants us to go to Europol HQ in The Hague. Apparently, he has some contacts there who have been monitoring Zito's European drug empire for some time now and they can help us fill in the dots."

"I'll call the airport and have them refuel the jet," Lea said.

"Already done," Kim said with a wink. "I'm not just a pretty face, you know."

# CHAPTER NINETEEN

## The Hague, Amsterdam

Hawke looked through the one-way mirror and watched the man they had caught back in the Aurora. He was now in an interrogation room deep inside Europol HQ and had been identified as a low-level scumbag named Marco Maroni. Not so tough now, he was sitting handcuffed to the chair and sweat was beading on his forehead.

Besides the former commando, his old friend Vincent Reno was looking at the 'No Smoking' sign above the door with a cigarette on his lips and a frown on his face.

"For me, the world ended when they banned indoor smoking," he said glumly.

Before Hawke could respond, Lea and Danny Devlin joined them with steaming coffees in their hands. Lexi and Ryan were a few steps behind them, carrying more coffees.

"Cairo and Kim?" Hawke said.

"Arguing in the canteen," said Lexi.

"Could get interesting," Ryan said, handing Hawke a coffee. "Want to come down and watch?"

"Not a lot," he said.

Lea gestured toward Maroni. "Got anything out of the bastard?"

"Some, but not much," Hawke said. "Jansen's good but I think Marco needs a little more encouragement to speak than a Europol official is prepared to give."

They all knew what he meant. As a former SBS man, Joe Hawke had undergone extreme interrogation training and he knew what worked and what didn't. Piet Jansen, the lead interviewing officer was doing a good job if they had all week, but they needed answers faster than that.

Jansen came out of the room and gave a regretful sigh. "He's not talking."

"When do we get to talk to him?" Reaper said.

Jansen looked disapprovingly as the cigarette wobbled up and down on the former French legionnaire's lower lip and then cast an unimpressed glance at the tattoo of a burning grenade on his arm. "I just spoke with my superior officer and he says one of you can come in and attend the interview."

Reaper rubbed his hands together and grinned. "Then let's go."

He moved toward the door and Jansen raised his hand. Placing it on the Frenchman's chest he stopped him in his tracks with another heavy sigh. "Not you."

"I don't understand."

"Mr. Hawke will join me in the interview room. The rest of you will wait here and let us get on with our job."

Hawke followed Jansen into the room. There were two wooden chairs against the wall, but only an uncomfortable plastic bucket seat at the desk. He sat in it and fixed his eyes on Maroni. After the fifteen minutes it took for the Dutch official to apprise the prisoner of his various rights, Hawke sighed and said, "Who hired Zito to take the manuscript?"

Maroni looked confused. "What manuscript?"

Hawke smiled. "You want to play games, is that it?"

"He is under no obligation to speak," Jansen said calmly.

There was a knock at the door and a small man in a gray suit shuffled into the room. He had a serious frown on his face.

Jansen stood and shook his hand. "Mr. De Jong, I presume?" He turned to Hawke. "Mr. Maroni's appointed lawyer."

"I am Roland De Jong, yes, and I want to know why this interview has started without me?"

Hawke gave a silent, inward sigh and checked his watch. "This is going to go on all night."

Jansen and De Jong spoke at length about Maroni and the Dutch lawyer informed the Europol man in great detail about all the consequences he would face for breaking so many rules.

Another knock at the door and a young woman entered. She looked alarmed. "Mr. Jansen – your boss is on the telephone. She says it's urgent."

A look of confusion spread over Jansen's face as he looked from Hawke to De Jong. "Please, gentlemen – excuse me."

As soon as Jansen was out of the room, Hawke leaned forward and grabbed Maroni around the throat. "Who's pulling Zito's greasy little strings?"

De Jong gasped in horror and pushed back from the desk so hard he nearly fell out of his chair.

Maroni's tired, bloodshot eyes widened like saucers with the shock of the attack. "You can't do this to me!" he squealed. "I'll sue you for this!"

"How dare you?" De Jong said, dusting himself down. "This a criminal matter now!"

"No need to fill your pants," Hawke said.

Lea and Ryan walked into the interrogation room.

"I take it you're Jansen's boss now?" Hawke asked, smiling at Lea.

"I am, indeed."

Hawke looked at Ryan. "And what was your part in this, mate?"

"Teaching Lea how to say *Get to my office right now*

in Dutch."

Hawke gave an appreciative nod. "Good work. By the way, meet Mr. De Jong."

He turned back to Maroni, whose throat he was still gripping. "Now, I want to know who hired Zito, and I want to know now."

"Let me out of here!" De Jong barked. "I must call the police at once!"

Without warning, Ryan fired a sharp jab at the lawyer and planted one right on his jaw. The strike knocked him clean out and he slumped down on the shiny tile floor like a drunk at the end of a long night. His head lolled lifelessly on his shoulder and some drool rolled over his bloodied lip.

"Bugger me!" Hawke said.

Lea was aghast. "What the actual fuck was that, Ry?"

Ryan shrugged his shoulders and loaded a cigarette onto his lower lip. It was a Gauloises he had cadged off Reaper earlier. "He was getting on my nerves. Anyway, he was getting in the way of getting intel out of this twat." He nudged his chin at Maroni and fired up the cigarette.

Hawke didn't know whether to be impressed or concerned. "Well, good work, Ryan, I suppose," he said, clapping a hand on his shoulder. "Take yesterday off."

"Funny."

Hawke returned his attention to the Italian. "We all get the situation here, Maroni. Zito's the engine driver and you're the greasy rag. I want to know who's the fat controller. Name – now."

Maroni's nervous eyes wandered from Hawke to De Jong's sleeping body and then up to Ryan Bale. The young man took his jacket off and rolled his shirt sleeves up, revealing the Russian tattoo. "Why is it so fucking hot in here?"

"Well?" Hawke said, increasing his grip on the man's throat.

"Kruger. The man who hired Mr. Zito is called Kruger."

\*

Tiger cruised the black government Audi A6 along the Liangmaqiao Road until he reached the next exit and then pulled off into Chaoyang Park. The other Zodiacs were quietly contemplating the job ahead, as was he.

*Hold out baits to entice the enemy, feign disorder and crush him.*

Tiger had studied the great war philosopher Sun Tzu in college and rarely struggled to find a quotation appropriate to any of his missions.

He turned the car through a series of streets, each one a little narrower than the last until they finally reached their destination. Switching off the engine, he checked his gun and knives and then ordered everyone out of the car. He had kept a close eye on Monkey on the drive from the airport and so far so good. None of the usual signs of his many personality disorders had leaked through the young man's concentration, but he knew they were just beneath the surface; they all did.

Tiger led the way into the enormous apartment block and the four suited men waited patiently beside another man for an elevator to arrive. The other man was holding a bag of groceries in each hand. Neon green Chinese celery leaves poked ambitiously from the top of the plastic bag along with some bok choi and a multipack of instant noodles.

He smiled and nodded at the men but they gave no response.

The elevator arrived and a metallic ping filled the lobby. The doors swished open and the Zodiacs stepped inside. Tiger held the door open for the man but he took a step back and let the doors close without him on board.

They rode the elevator in silence for several quiet moments. Each man used the time to process his own thoughts. Tiger didn't know what his associates were thinking, but he was considering his family across the other side of the city. His wife, his daughter – both safe in their little home.

Unlike the Zhangs.

The elevator pinged and the doors opened. Moments later the four men were standing outside the Zhangs' apartment. Tiger looked at Rat and nodded.

Rat pushed the doorbell.

Moments later, Tiger watched a sweet old lady open the door. She reminded him of his grandmother from Chengdu.

Tiger smiled warmly. "Mrs. Zhang?"

The elderly woman nodded. "Yes."

The response was fast and silent. Within a second of her confirming her identity, Tiger pulled his gun from his holster and pushed the muzzle into her forehead. In the same movement, he entered the apartment and pushed her back along the hall with his finger to his lips to indicate she should remain silent. She didn't argue with the command; they never did.

The moment unfolded in seconds. In the living area now, an elderly man brought himself to his feet as they moved closer to him. He looked confused and started to speak, but Monkey darted toward him and powered a mighty left hook into his face.

The old man crumpled like waste paper and fell back unconscious into the cheap sofa that ran along the rear wall. The woman screamed but a well-timed slap from Tiger silenced her fast.

"Who are you?" she said.

"Just do as you're told."

Rat was already tying her unconscious husband up with a roll of duct tape and gagging him. Pig picked up her landline telephone and put it down in front of her.

Tiger said, "Stop looking at the phone and take a look at the clock on your wall."

The old woman obeyed.

"What time does it give?" Tiger said.

"Four minutes to eight."

"Correct. You will telephone your daughter now, and you will tell her that her father is gravely ill and that she must return at once. If you do not do this or try any tricks, neither you nor your husband will live to see eight o'clock. Understand?" He pushed the gun's barrel into her forehead again, hard enough to leave a little red mark.

"I..."

He saw her torment. He had seen it before on the faces of other mothers and fathers. She was torn between the immediate problem of saving her own life, and that of her beloved husband, or using her own daughter as bait. You could see the cogs whirring behind her eyes as she thought the matter over in her head.

Tiger was happy to give her the half-minute she would need to make the choice they always made, and then after a terrified look at her gagged and bound husband she came back to him right on time with the standard reply.

"All right... I'll do what you want but please don't hurt us."

"Make the call."

They always made this decision. It was human nature. Kick the can down the road. If she called her daughter that would give her extra time to live right now; time to think – space to breathe and come up with some kind of strategy. He knew she was going to make this decision before he

122

had even posed it to her – he had read it in her eyes. He studied his victims with an assiduity most people were unable to match, and his hard work and commitment to the job always yielded the results he was seeking.

She picked up the phone and started to push the buttons.

Tiger pulled the slider and pushed a round into the chamber. It was unnecessary but people almost expected it. They had seen it in the movies and knew it meant business – the final step before the lead started flying and things got ugly. "And make it convincing," he whispered. "*Very* convincing, or..." he glanced over at Monkey who was using his fingers to shovel her husband's noodles into his face.

The woman nodded. She understood. "Xiaoli? This is your mother. I have very bad news..."

After she had finished the call he took the receiver from her and placed it gently in the cradle. "You did good today, Mrs. Zhang."

"Why do you want my daughter?" she asked. "Who are you?"

"We are the long shadow of your greatest fears."

# CHAPTER TWENTY

"Dirk Kruger?" Hawke repeated the name with disgust. Lea and Ryan shared a silent glance each knowing what the other was thinking.

Maroni nodded sullenly. "Yes. You know him?"

Hawke turned his head to look back at the mirror. He saw only his own reflection, but he knew the rest of the team were right there, hearing what he was hearing. He glanced over at Ryan, and he could guess what the young man had felt when he heard that name. It was Ryan whom Kruger had kidnapped and beaten and used to help him find the Lost City of the Incas.

Hawke turned to face Maroni. "What's Zito's relationship with Kruger, exactly?"

The Italian shrugged. "How should I know?"

Hawke hit the man hard in the face. He had struck him harder than he needed to, driven by the memories of the Seastead battle.

Maroni's head smacked back on his left shoulder before rolling forward again. Blood frothed and bubbled in his mouth and he looked like he was about to pass out.

Hawke grabbed a tuft of the man's long, raven-black hair in his hand and held his head up straight. "Don't piss me about or you'll get more of that, got it?"

As the Italian mumbled something in reply, Hawke punched him hard in the stomach. He reeled forward, sucking air through his bloodied mouth and coughing wildly.

"I'm a details man, Marco," Hawke said. He kicked the table over and it crashed to the floor upside down.

Then he smashed one of the wooden chairs into pieces, snatched up one of the legs, and held it like a baseball bat. "Give me some details, or I'm going to smash your kneecaps."

Hawke stared at the young man, chained to a chair in an interrogation room. He hoped he had convinced him he could do it, but deep inside he wasn't even sure himself if he could do it anymore. Maroni was a low-level scumbag, working for a medium-level scumbag like Zito. Now he had just found out that the man pulling their strings was none other than Dirk Kruger. It had lit his fuse and he could feel it burning down, creeping ever closer to the dynamite keg that lurked inside him. Suddenly Marco Maroni was everyone who had ever crossed him, and yet could he break the man's knees with this chair leg just to get information about Kruger?

He was about to find out.

Hawke eyed up Maroni's right knee and swung it back ready for the attack, but then the Italian started singing like the proverbial canary.

"No, please, no! Wait! I will tell you what you want to know!"

Inside, Hawke breathed a sigh of relief. Would he have swung the chair leg and crippled the young man? He didn't know, not anymore. "Well, go on then," he said, bringing the smashed chair leg down to his side. "Don't let me stop you."

"You must understand that Zito is a very private man, and he has a large organization around him; many, many people work for Mr. Zito and he keeps them compartmentalized so only he sees the full picture."

"Go on."

"I tell you this so you understand that I only know part of what goes on."

"Let's hope it's a big enough part to save your knees."

Maroni looked at the make-shift baseball bat hanging from Hawke's right arm. "I am employed by Signor Zito to guard the island, that is my job. There are many of us on the island, I am but one."

"Get to the good stuff," Hawke said, glancing at the two-way mirror. Jansen would be back any minute. "I want to know about Kruger's part in all this."

"Zito met with Mr. Kruger several times over the past few weeks. The first few times were in Rome and Naples, and then when he thought he could trust him he invited him back to the Isola Pacifica."

Reaper stepped into the room. His eyes crawled from Marco Maroni's shocked and bloody face up to the Englishman. "Jansen is on his way, mon ami."

"You heard him, Marco. Dish the dirt and make it fast. My friend here can hold that door long enough for me to swing this bat. What did they discuss on the island?"

"Kruger is searching for some kind of ancient relic."

"A relic?"

Maroni nodded. "Si – but not just any relic. The South African was very keen for Zito to understand that this was a special relic, a very ancient and powerful one. He said it had some kind of power that would unlock a great secret. The other guards and I thought it was a joke, but Zito took it seriously enough to take the contract and use his extensive network to locate and snatch the manuscript."

Hawke believed Maroni was telling the truth. "Tell me more about this relic – what's this power Kruger was talking about?"

"He was very vague when he spoke to Signor Zito and I did not hear everything. I am part of Zito's security so when I'm in the room I'm there to protect him, not listen to his private business. If he finds out I have spoken to you he will kill me."

"The relic, Marco," Hawke repeated. "Tell me about what Kruger's looking for."

"As I say, I didn't hear everything they talked about. All I can tell you is that the South African seemed nervous when he talked about it, but also excited. His eyes lit up like diamonds when he described it to Zito."

"And how did he describe it?"

"He said it contained some kind of special property that gave it immense power and that it was priceless in value. He said he wanted it because he has an appreciation of ancient weapons and wanted it in his collection – but he would never explain precisely what it was."

Hawke snorted and looked up at Reaper. The Frenchman returned a similar look of disbelief. Dirk Kruger had zero interest in collecting ancient artifacts and relics and was always about nothing but the money. This was the very same man who had nearly brought a genocidal bacterial plague to the world just for a large payoff from a deranged, rogue Syrian terrorist named Ziad Saqqal.

"So Zito works for Kruger and Kruger wants some kind of ancient relic?" Hawke said, almost to himself.

"Yes."

"And what's his next move?" Hawke asked.

Maroni shrugged his shoulders. "I don't know exactly, but I can tell you that neither Zito nor the South African has a clue what that manuscript says, so they are going to need someone to translate it."

"But we have the manuscript now," Lea said.

Maroni laughed and shook his head. "Zito had the entire thing photographed and emailed to Kruger. That's why he took off without a real fight on the island. Now all he needs is the translator."

"Name."

127

"They found a man named Dr. Henk Kloos. He's some kind of world-famous expert. I have told you all I know, and put the rest of my life in constant danger in the process."

"That's your lookout," Hawke said. "You should be more particular about who you work for."

Maroni gave Hawke a weary glance. "I'm still getting full immunity from prosecution, right?"

"Don't ask me, mate," Hawke said. "That's Jansen's department."

"Talking of which," Reaper said. "We should get out of here before he returns, non?"

*

Lexi Zhang stood beside her friends outside the two-way mirror and watched Hawke interrogate the young Italian man. Ryan was now walking in circles around them as they spoke. He looked different to her now. The nerd had become a man, she supposed, but then nothing was ever as it looked. She knew there would be more to Ryan's transformation than met the eye.

Her thoughts were interrupted by the vibration of her phone. Someone was ringing her.

She fumbled it out of her pocket and saw it was her mother calling. She raised it to her ear and moved a few steps away from the group. "Yes, Mama?"

"Xiaoli? This is your mother. I have very bad news..."

Lexi's eyes narrowed with confusion. Her mother rarely phoned. When they spoke it was when she called her parents back in their Beijing apartment. "Is everything all right?"

"No... no, it's not, Xiaoli..." her mother sighed. "It's so good to hear your voice after all this time."

Lexi swallowed and lowered her voice to a whisper. It

was instinctive; no one standing around her would have been able to follow a conversation in Mandarin. "What's happened?"

"It's your father."

Lexi gasped and felt her heart speed up. "Ba? What's the matter with him?"

"He's very sick, Xiaoli... very ill."

Lexi struggled to hear her mother's voice over the sound of the blood pumping in her ears, and her head started to spin. She had dreaded the day this phone call would come, flying out of the darkness like some vampire bat ready to wrap its leathery wings around her face and smother her until she couldn't even breathe. "Ba?" she repeated dumbly.

"I'm so sorry, Xiaoli," her mother said. Her voice was weak and frightened. She sounded lost and scared. "If you want to see him – if you want to talk to him again, then you must come home at once."

Lexi breathed deeply and turned to her friends in the ECHO team. They were all captivated by the scene unfolding in the interrogation suite where Hawke was grilling the Italian under the cold, greasy strip light.

*If you want to talk to him again*

She knew what that meant. Her father was on the edge, dying but still in this world. He was in that terrible place between life and death and her mother was trying to tell her that he wouldn't stay there for long. It was now or never, and she knew she couldn't live with never.

She turned away from her friends and stared at the corner of the corridor. The blankness of it brought some weird comfort as she processed her mother's terrible words. They had hacked inside her like an ice pick, but she had already made her decision. The mission was critical, but ECHO was capable of doing it without her. On the other hand, her mother needed her now more than ever. She had to go back.

"I'm coming, Mama."

"You are a good girl, Xiaoli."

Lexi bit her lip and cut the call. She slipped the phone back into her pocket, sighed, and closed her eyes. She started to make plans to fly home to China but her thoughts were interrupted by the sound of men shouting at the other end of the corridor.

It was Piet Jansen and he was with two armed security guards.

"Out of my way!" he boomed. "There was no call from my boss. Who's behind this?" The Dutch Europol agent raced over to the two-way mirror and gasped in horror when he saw the carnage inside the interrogation room. Before he could speak, the door opened and Hawke stepped out. Lea, Ryan, and Reaper were right behind him.

"Ah, Mr. Jansen – the prisoner's all yours," Hawke said, and then leaned in closer and lowered his voice. "You might want to rethink using De Jong as an official lawyer – the man's as drunk as a Russian sailor."

Jansen scowled at Hawke, but the Englishman's conscience was clear. Thanks to the interrogation they now knew what they had suspected all along: not only was Giancarlo Zito working for someone else but that person was none other than Dirk Kruger.

Jansen and the Dutch authorities could worry about Marco Maroni later on, and as for De Jong – that was nothing a couple of headache tablets wouldn't sort out. He was already focussing on tracking the South African arms dealer down. They all had a desire to see Kruger caught and brought to justice, but Hawke could see from Ryan's eyes that he wanted more.

"So what now?" Lea said.

Hawke's reply was immediate. "We need to speak with this Dr. Kloos, and fast."

# CHAPTER TWENTY-ONE

## Amsterdam

After they parked up a hired Suburban in the city center, Dr. Kloos was not hard to find. He worked out of an office in the Centrum district not far from the city's main railway station, and when he came to the door he was already expecting them.

"I thought you said there were eight of you?" he asked.

"One of our colleagues was called away to China," Lea said. "Family emergency."

Kloos studied their faces, stepped back, and ushered them inside. "I was surprised when I got your phone call, Miss Donovan," he said, showing them into his office and offering some seats. "Very pleasantly surprised, in fact – but also concerned."

"We understand. Learning about how these men need you to translate the manuscript must have been unsettling," Lea said.

Kloos looked at her with watery eyes. He was a tired man, but he looked like something had breathed new life to him. "Indeed. When I saw the museum in Boston had put the Book of Gold up on their website I could hardly believe it. I have spent my life researching this subject. Now you tell me that this Kruger has worked with a man named Giancarlo Zito to steal it, but that they had unknowingly snatched only parts one and two."

"Correct."

He sighed and rubbed his face. "Then they kidnapped you to obtain the other part?"

"Correct again."

"This is a worrying development. The symbols etched into the full manuscript are a treasure trail leading to something of legendary historical importance and power. If these men are as dangerous as you say, then what they seek will only make them even more so."

"Then we share your concerns, Dr. Kloos," Lea said. "We managed to get the Book of Gold back, but we know Zito scanned the entire thing. For all we know, they've found another translator and they're already well on their way to finding what they're searching for."

Kloos looked at her and gave a mischievous smile. "I wouldn't be sure about that, Miss Donovan."

The team fixed their eyes on the doddery old professor. Each of them felt the same wave of hope. "What do you mean by that?" Scarlet said.

Kloos smiled. "Kruger and Zito only have nine-tenths of the story."

"What do you mean?" Hawke asked him.

He closed his eyes as he considered a response; the old man's chiming clock gently marked the passing of their lives with a solemn ticking sound. "Wait here."

He swiveled in the leather chair and got to his feet. Stepping across his office he opened a small safe and pulled a metal box from it. Placing it on his desk, he then searched his pockets for a key. He opened the box and gently drew out a single piece of paper in an acid-free folder. "This is kept at room temperature at all times, and is never exposed to light."

"What is it?"

He beamed with professional pride. "This is the other piece of the puzzle."

Scarlet made no secret of her frustration and sighed rudely. "An explanation would be nice."

ROB JONES

Kloos held up the paper. "You are looking at a page from the third and final section of the Book of Gold. It's an essential part of the manuscript but was separated from the main text centuries ago. Without this, there is no way Kruger can find the relic he's hunting for, just as there was no way I have ever been able to locate it without the rest of the manuscript that is now in your possession."

"Wait," Lea said, indicating the ragged piece of paper. "That's part of the Gold Book?"

Kloos smiled. "Certainly. I located it in a private collection in England nearly thirty years ago, and for the intervening three decades, it has mocked me by only giving part of the location of the relic. Now we can put these pages together and work out the precise place where the treasure has lain for countless centuries."

"Now we're getting somewhere," Ryan said.

"And the best part is that Kruger and Zito have no idea they don't have all the manuscript, right?" Lea said.

"Almost certainly," Kloos said. "Now, let me return it to its rightful place with the rest of the manuscript and we'll see the symbols when they're put together with one another."

Kloos opened the manuscript to the end and inserted his piece of paper, carefully lining it up in various ways until finally, he gasped with joy.

"What is it?" Lea said.

"I think we have something here!" Kloos said. "Something that will lead us straight to the relic."

Kim sighed and crossed her arms. "Hey, *I* have a question: what sort of goddam relic are we talking about here?"

Hawke smiled. "That was my next question – professor?"

Kloos furrowed his brow. "You mean you don't know?"

"Christ on a giraffe unicycle," Scarlet said. "Does it

sound like we know?"

"She means, please tell us," Reaper said.

"The relic Kruger and Zito are searching for is the Sword of Fire."

Hawke shared a knowing glance with Lea. He turned back to Kloos and fixed his eyes on him. "Tell us about this sword."

Kloos bit his lip while he considered his next words. "Little is known about the sword; this is the first thing to understand about it. Like many ancient Celtic legends, the myths surrounding it simply vanish into the mists of time. What my research has revealed is that the sword has very special properties."

"What sort of properties?"

"In the ancient times they called them magical, but today we might not like to use that word. The sword was called Dyrnwyn, and there are many translations for this, including *White Hilt*, but I use the Sword of Fire. References to the sword are scarce, but most agree on two basic facts – first, its ownership by Rhydderch Hael, one of the rulers of an ancient British kingdom called Alt Clut in the far north of England and southern Scotland."

"And the other?" Lea asked.

Kloos paused a beat. "The magical properties I mentioned a moment ago. Most of the ancient writings describe that the sword becomes enveloped in a bright, blue fire when it is loosened from its sheath. If a man of honor uses the sword he will be given great power, but if a dishonorable man tries to wield it the fire will turn on him and burn him to death."

"Some of this sounds like the legend surrounding King Arthur," Ryan said.

Kloos nodded vehemently. "Yes, and both legends are from the same Celtic background, of course. Some have linked the Sword of Fire to Excalibur through a North Welsh prince named Owain Ddanwyn. It's probably because he was a King of part of Gwynedd in the Fifth Century."

"What's the link?" Kim asked.

"The link is that some have argued that Owain Ddanwyn may even have been King Arthur. Both were from the same region and lived during the same time, and legends state that both were murdered by their grandsons. Both men are also linked to the ancient Roman settlement of Viroconium, or Wroxeter as it's called today, a village in Shropshire. Once, it was the fourth largest city in Roman Britain."

"Do you think Ddanwyn was Arthur?" Lea asked.

Kloos shrugged his shoulders. "I want to believe it, but there is no evidence to suggest that Dyrnwyn is Excalibur. In all honesty, the legends surrounding the Sword of Fire describe it as much more powerful than Excalibur."

"So if it's so much more powerful," Scarlet said, "why has no one ever heard of it?"

Kloos gave a cautious, knowing smile. "There are many things in this world we are not supposed to know about. Dyrnwyn is one of them; an ancient weapon from a time long forgotten."

He paused again and looked at them with uncertainty. "Some call Dyrnwyn the Black Sword because of its terrible power. It was lost to history during the reign of Rhudda, a notorious giant who ruled over Snowdonia. Rhudda is heavily connected to Arthurian legend, so even though Rhydderch lived in the Old North, in northern England, the last the sword was seen was in Snowdonia. This is where Arthur killed Rhudda with Excalibur, after all. Arthur had the giant buried in the mountains, and today we call that burial ground Yr Wyddfa, or Mount Snowdon."

"So that's where we're going?" Kim asked.

Kloose frowned and studied the manuscript again. "No, I don't think so. If my translation is right then it looks like the sword is further to the south in the sub-kingdom of Meirionnydd, in the south of Gwynedd." He paused again removed his glasses and then rubbed his eyes before returning to the faded symbols. "This says that the Sword of Fire slew another giant – Idris Fawr."

Hawke sighed. "Eh?"

"Idris Fawr was another giant and he ruled Meirionnydd in the Fifth Century, exactly when Arthur, Ddanwyn, and the Sword of Fire were in action."

"So you have another location?"

Kloos nodded and pulled an old map out of his drawer. "It means the last place the sword was ever used – or seen – was on the slopes of Cadair Idris. It's a mountain in Meirionnydd and it means Idris's Chair in Welsh. The giant would sit on the top of the mountain and study the stars. It's a very important and magical mountain in ancient Welsh legends. This confirms what I was thinking about its location being further south. There is no way Kruger can know this without seeing this page, no matter who is translating it."

"And you definitely think this is where the sword is today?" Ryan said.

Kloos nodded, but reluctantly. "I think so," he said, pointing to a specific slope on the map. "It says that particular mountain peaks can be seen from the location, and that leaves only this place here. It also seems to hint that the son of Arianrhod will reveal where the Sword of Fire is located, and also something about the heavens lighting the way."

Ryan nodded. "I translated the piece about Arianrhod in Ireland, but it was only a partial translation because at the time Zito had the rest."

A new wave of excitement flashed over the professor's face. "Also of note here is a reference to the old legend about staying the night on the mountain. I think this must be done to pinpoint the final location."

Scarlet sighed. "Christ, more ancient gods, and legends..."

"What legend?" Kim asked.

"It states that whoever spends the night on Cadair Idris will either become a poet or a madman. They must witness dawn from the peak to fulfill the legend. The text here indicates that this is essential to finding the location of the sword."

"Sounds like we're on our way to Wales," Lea said.

"Whoop-de-doo," Scarlet said. She sidled up to Kloos and touched his arm. "Are you *certain* this mountain isn't actually in St. Lucia or somewhere like that?"

The Dutch academic narrowed his eyes and looked at her with confusion. "I don't understand – the mountain is in..."

"We know where the mountain is, Dr. Kloos," Lea said. "Please ignore our colleague. That's what we try and do."

*

Kloos locked his townhouse and they stepped out into Prinsengracht. Birds sang in the trees and a boat full of happy tourists chugged down the canal opposite his front door. He glanced at his watch. "If we hurry, we can get the next train from the Central Station to Schiphol. We can be in Wales in a couple of hours."

They made their way along the street en route to the station. A drizzle had started to fall but the city was still busy with people going about their business. Hawke had visited the city many years ago with Liz. They had strolled along the canals together and shared a long weekend before promising to return one day.

Her murder meant that would never happen. He felt the anger rise in him once more: killing the bastard who had ordered her death had almost closed the book, but the trigger man, Alfredo Lazaro, was still out there somewhere. As far as Hawke was concerned, the Cuban hit man had given up his right to live after he'd murdered his wife, and he had vowed to hunt him down, but so far not even the ECHO machine had managed to find so much as a trace of him. It was as if since the murder he had turned into a ghost.

He quelled the range inside his heart by glancing over at Lea. She was talking quietly to Dr. Kloos and Kim Taylor as they walked along the cobblestones beside the canal on the way to the station. As he watched her smiling and laughing, all the world started to make sense again, and he realized he was holding the box containing the engagement ring. He had put his hand in his pocket without even knowing it and was now turning the small box over in his fingers.

It was time to put the past behind him. Lazaro could wait. He knew in his heart that it was time to move on, and that meant popping the question. The thought of it made him more nervous than the idea of going into battle, but he'd done it before so he could do it again. He made up his mind to ask Lea to marry him as soon as the mission was over and prayed she would say yes.

As they approached the station, Hawke was on edge. Everywhere he looked he saw innocent people – men, women, and children enjoying their day. He was always concerned when members of the public got dragged into the battlefield that the ECHO team spent their lives fighting on and this was no exception.

139

"We should just be in time to get the next train," Kloos said, tapping his watch.

A man beside him was now telling off his daughter in the bustle of the crowd and she was crying in response. With one eye on them, Hawke scanned the crowd for potential problems; the man in a badly-fitting business suit leaning against the station wall, the two men standing just inside the station's entrance... the woman with the briefcase who seemed to be monitoring the crowd.

It happened fast. The man with the crying child had been walking beside Hawke toward the station, but now he leaned into the Englishman and started to speak. "Hand Kloos over or this girl dies."

Hawke was stunned. He looked at the man's face and saw he meant business, and more than that, he now gently lifted the magazine to reveal a semi-automatic Colt beneath it. With calm, steady hands he was pointing it into the girl's back.

Hawke's mind raced. When Maroni had told him that they'd identified Kloos as being able to translate the document he knew Kruger would send men after him, but not this way. From what he had seen so far of Zito's men he'd expected an all-out attack, not something as depraved as using a kidnapped child as a bargaining chip.

"Make a fuss and she's dead," the man repeated.

The others caught on to what was happening, and Devlin fronted up to the man, but Hawke pulled him away and pointed at the magazine. "M1911," he said. "Aimed at the kid."

"Toscano," Lea said. "I recognize him from the island."

Before anyone said another word, a second man slipped out of the crowd behind them and dragged Kloos away from the ECHO team, and then they were gone, both men, Kloos and the crying girl. "The other one's called Bruno," Lea said. "I think maybe they're brothers but I'm not sure."

Hawke watched them as they pulled Kloos and the girl deep into the crowd and headed toward the station.

"What the hell are we going to do?" Kim said.

"They're using the crowd for cover," said Scarlet.

Hawke pulled the Glock from his pocket. "Not for long they're not."

# CHAPTER TWENTY-TWO

Tiger turned the cards and revealed Four of a Kind. He raised his eyes to Pig to see his reaction but the older man was a veteran of poker and simply folded his hand with a weary sigh. "That's the third hand in a row that I have won," he said. "Perhaps you should consider retiring not only from the Ministry but also from the poker circuit."

"Maybe you are right," Pig said, and then looked over Tiger's shoulder, causing the younger man to twist in his chair. He saw Monkey sitting beside Mrs. Zhang. He was running the tip of his switchblade up her inner thigh, but the duct tape over her mouth kept her screams silent to the rest of the world. Mr. Zhang was sitting on the floor with a bag over his head and his hands tied behind his back.

"Stop that," Tiger said. His words were mild, but his tone was sharp and left no room for misunderstanding.

Monkey held the knife in place for a moment, staring into the eyes of his leader as if to judge the man's mettle. Without taking his eyes off Tiger, Monkey pushed the button on the ivory handle and the blade snapped back inside with a metallic click. Mrs. Zhang jumped with fear.

Rat strolled back into the room with a tray full of food from the Zhangs' kitchen cupboards. He glanced at Monkey with disgust. "She's old enough to be your grandmother. This is not professional. Why did Zhou call you Monkey? You're the Pig."

Monkey leaped from the saggy sofa and flicked the knife open again. "What was that?"

"Is there a problem with your ears as well as your mind?" Rat said, lowering the tray of food onto the table and reaching into his jacket.

Tiger grabbed his arm and stopped him from pulling his weapon. He sighed heavily and pushed back from the table. "No fighting in here," he said, and moved his eyes over to the terrified Mrs. Zhang. "And no more of that."

"I was bored," Monkey said. A fiendish smirk crept over his lean face.

"That's part of the job," Pig said, collecting the cards up. "We wait."

"And this brawling stops now." Tiger closed his eyes and started to count to ten. "The next time I see any of you, you will be minding your own business in silence."

He heard a sigh. A shuffle of feet. The tension eased away like sesame oil sliding off a warm spoon. When he opened his eyes, the others had obeyed him and backed down. Pig was shuffling the deck of cards, Rat had moved into the kitchen and was searching through the refrigerator, and Monkey had stripped down to his waist. He had twisted the Zhang's anglepoise lamp around so it shone on the wall and now he was fighting his own shadow to practice a series of razor-sharp roundhouse kicks.

With this new scene unfolding around him, Tiger breathed out and took his seat once again. This was a familiar moment for the Chinese government man: the tension of a half-completed mission heavy in the air, the smell of fear floating like incense. Not for the first time he wondered if he would miss all this when he finally turned his back on it.

But he was a professional and there was work to do. He glanced at his watch: not long now until Agent Dragonfly fluttered into his trap.

*

143

The Boeing 747 rumbled along the tarmac on its way to Runway 24 and Lexi Zhang's eyes watched the clouds gather over Schiphol Airport. Her mind was elsewhere – she couldn't stop thinking about her father. She had always been close to him. He was the one who had made her laugh and comforted her tears away. Memories of her childhood rose in her mind like blossoming orchids – the time they walked around the park; when he taught her to ride a bicycle; helping him in their tiny garden.

Could he really be dying? The sound of her mother's voice told her it was true. She sounded scared, weak, and alone.

As the plane roared up into the sky, she pulled the shutter a little to block the sun and cast two uncaring eyes across the Dutch landscape below. Clouds flashed past her window and the wing bent up and down as they plowed through some turbulence. Glancing at her watch she sighed and closed her eyes. The flight from Amsterdam to Beijing was scheduled to take a little under ten hours.

She was certain it was going to feel a lot longer than that.

\*

The last few hours had lived up to Alex Brooke's greatest expectations and wildest fears. Traveling alongside her father, who was still riding high in the polls back home and even more popular abroad, she had been whisked from one meeting to another and met more dignitaries than she could remember. She was also totally exhausted and missing her friends more than she thought possible.

The Presidential limo was making its way toward Downing Street now, and she was sitting in the back with her father, an advisor named Todd Williams, and two US Secret Service men, including Brandon McGee. Brooke had been on the phone since the journey began and now he ended the call and sighed.

"A problem, sir?" said Todd.

"We're getting some chatter about a terror attack in the UK," her father said with his usual calm tone.

"What's the target?" Alex said.

"Unknown. Our boys and MI5 are just picking up some talk. It happens. Don't worry about it, darling." He tried one of his famous crooked smiles, but it didn't help to calm her nerves.

Under heavy police escort, the Presidential motorcade cruised past the Cenotaph and turned off Whitehall into Downing Street. Up ahead she could see a crowd of international press gathering outside the famous address. "Oh, *God...*"

"You're doing great," Brooke said. "We're going home tomorrow morning, Alex. Hang in there, kid. I'm proud of you."

Alex said nothing. Her thoughts turned inward again, back to Hawke and the team. She hadn't heard from them since she'd said goodbye to Hawke and Kim in the Oval Office, and now she was starting to worry something had gone wrong.

The limo pulled up right outside the world's most famous front door, and as if by magic it swished open to reveal the British Prime Minister.

Brooke clapped his hands together and took a deep breath. "All right, everyone. It's showtime." He leaned over to the advisor. "And Todd, while I'm talking with the PM I want you to get more on this security threat."

"Yes sir, Mr. President."

"We don't want any nasty surprises," Brooke said, and

then climbed out of the limousine.

As he turned and waved to the press pool, Alex shut her eyes to dodge the thousands of high-speed sync flashes now lighting up her father as he greeted the world yet again. He made a casual joke and they all laughed, and then he turned and walked over to the British Prime Minster. When they were shaking hands, McGee leaned over to her. "Time to go, Alex. Only Westminster Hall left on the schedule and then we're done."

"Sure thing, Brandon," she said.

"Problems?"

"Just thinking that I can't stand four years of this."

Todd leaned into the car. "Of course, you can. And it's eight years, you defeatist."

Eight years, she thought, shaking her head. "I've got to get back to ECHO," she mumbled.

"What was that?"

"I said let's get that damned wheelchair, Brandon..."

She returned his smile, but she knew now where her heart lay and that was with ECHO.

And Joe Hawke.

# CHAPTER TWENTY-THREE

Hawke fired into the air to disperse the crowd. With the sound of the gunshot still echoing off the buildings around Stationsplein, hundreds of people scattered in all directions, and a flock of fat pigeons took to the air.

The men holding the girl now released her and hauled Kloos away to the station as fast as they could go. Hawke gave a sigh of relief as the girl ran screaming back to her mother.

"Get out of here!" he yelled at them. "Get as far away as you can!"

Scarlet and Reaper opened fire on Zito and his men, and Zito fired back. Reaper was the target but the bullet found its way into the neck of a man trying to flee while dragging his wheeled luggage behind him. He spun around in the street just as a cloud of blood-mist burst from his jugular and he collapsed like a bar of lead over the tramlines.

His violent death triggered more screaming and hysteria but most people had now scattered, with some going to the sides of the station and others hiding behind the trams. Others were lucky enough to make it down into one of the entrances to the Metro. Their howls of terror boomed up from the tiled steps as they descended underground to escape the madness.

Hawke had taken cover with the rest of the team inside the lobby of the Amsterdam Visitor Centre, but now he stepped out behind one of the entrance pillars and brought his Glock into the aim. He fired – this time not a single shot but a controlled burst of five rounds. The bullets struck Toscano in the chest and abdomen, puncturing his lungs and tearing into his stomach. The Italian gunman staggered backward a few paces and crumpled to the stony ground outside the station's main entrance.

Lea, Ryan, and Scarlet joined Hawke outside the Visitor Centre, and across the square, Reaper led Kim and Devlin forward from the trams to the cover of a Renault van parked closer to the entrance.

"I do hope your man Devlin isn't going to do anything stupid again," Hawke said.

"He's not *my* man," she protested. "And I'm not responsible for what he does."

Hawke reloaded the Glock as Zito and his men continued to make their way to the train station's entrance. They were going slower because two of them had stopped to drag Toscano to safety, but when he died in their arms they lowered him to the ground. His corpse now lay cooling at the head of a long trail of blood where they had hauled his fatally wounded body. Driven by a sense of mad revenge, Bruno fired an entire magazine indiscriminately across the square, wildly swinging his weapon from Hawke's team in the Visitor Centre to Reaper and the others behind the Renault.

The vicious fusillade echoed around the empty square but was drowned out by the sound of approaching sirens. It sounded like they were coming from the east – probably Prins Hendrikkade which was now bereft of all traffic and Hawke presumed sealed off by anti-terror police. It wouldn't be long before the Dutch authorities took control of the situation, and he knew they had to move fast if they were to rescue Kloos; the former SBS man was confident that Zito would use the professor as a human shield if M-Squadron backed him into a corner.

A VW Beetle with police markings skidded into the

scene. The men inside tried to get out and fire on Zito but he and his men overwhelmed them with their firepower and they tried to reverse. Bullets shredded the glass and killed the men inside in seconds as the Beetle spun out of control and veered to the right.

"They're not slowing down," Ryan said.

Hawke knew what was coming next and frowned. "Foot must be wedged on the throttle."

Gaining speed the dead driver slumped forward and pulled the wheel down hard to the right. This caused the car to turn sharply and tip over on its side in a cloud of sparks and burned rubber smoke.

Devlin made a move. Breaking free of the group, he darted across ten meters of open ground. He was heading for the cover of the crashed police car but Bruno chased him down with a spray of gunfire from his machine pistol. Devlin dived for the cover of the upturned Beetle with a second to spare but Bruno continued to pepper the bottom of the car.

Hawke cursed but reacted in a split-second: he put Bruno under heavy fire, emptying his entire magazine at the Italian with the idea of driving him back into cover.

But it was too late: Bruno's rounds had hit the VW's exposed gas tank and caused the battered police car to explode in a monumental fireball. Chunks of contorted, deformed car parts hurtled through the air, transforming the Beetle into a colossal fragmentation grenade. A twisted car door slammed down into the ground a few meters from Reaper and his sub-unit. It was still on fire from the blast and left a trail of black smoke arcing through the sky behind it.

"Where's Danny?" Lea said. "Do you see him?"

Hawke strained to see through the smoke and detritus of the burning Beetle wreckage. Devlin was undoubtedly brave, but he was starting to become too unpredictable. He guessed too many years at Flynn's had taken a toll on the former Commandant and now he was just a shadow of his former self. "I see him," he said. "He's over there behind the wall to the left of the main entrance."

"He must have made a break for it when you were firing on Bruno."

"He's causing more bloody problems than he's solving right now," Hawke said.

"He just risked his life, Joe!"

Hawke said nothing, but reloaded his Glock and swung the gun up for a second go at Bruno. The Italians were now well inside the station and receding into the shadows beneath the Amsterdam Centraal sign hanging above the main entrance.

Hawke heard Reaper's voice in his earpiece. "Are we chasing the rabbits down the hole?"

"We have no choice," the Englishman said. "They still have Kloos."

Thanks to the gun battle outside, the vast station interior was now as empty and silent as the square out the front. With the rest of the team fanning out behind him and taking up an offensive formation, Hawke crossed the beautiful Main Hallway, gun raised into the aim and sweeping it from side to side to cover all angles. Somewhere in here Zito and his men were getting away with Kloos.

"Any sign of them?" Scarlet said through her palm mic.

"Not yet," Hawke said.

A flock of pigeons flew up from the end of the platform and disappeared into the vast roof of the station above their heads. Hawke spun around and aimed the gun in their original location, certain the other men had startled the birds, and he was right.

Zito and his men were at the far end of the southern

platform now. He was leading them off the platform and along the rails leading out to the station's eastern exit. Hawke watched the small group of men through the sights of his Glock as he fired on them once again. The sound of bullets roared in the cavernous space and Zito's response was to dash behind a filthy blue and yellow commuter diesel.

Seconds later they were all hidden by the train except for one straggler. Hawke fired again and struck the man. He collapsed onto the rails while a grisly bloom of brain matter and blood was illuminated by the light flooding into the opening at the eastern end of the station.

Hawke lowered his gun. Zito and his men still had Kloos and now they had cover as well. He heard them as they ran along the rails behind the stationary diesel train. "Sounds like they're trying to get out along the rails."

They hopped off the platform and used the parked train for cover as they closed in on Zito's snatch squad. Approaching the engine at the front of the train, they heard the sound of another kind of engine – a speedboat was roaring into life somewhere to their left.

A look of confusion crossed Hawke's face. "What the hell?"

"The IJ," Ryan said.

"Explain in two seconds, dorkmeister," Scarlet said.

"It's the main body of water in Amsterdam and it runs just north of this station."

They sprinted to the end of the rails and emerged into the daylight to see Zito and his men hauling Dr. Kloos into a speedboat parked up on the south bank of the IJ.

"Where does it go, mate?" Hawke said, squeezing the grip of his Glock out of frustration.

"Right out into the North Sea."

The boat ripped away from the bank, and Zito waved

at them cheerily with his gun hand as they pushed out into the middle of the massive river.

Knowing the chase was over, Ryan fired up a cigarette. "They could rendezvous with anyone at any number of locations in the city or the plan might be to go straight out to sea and hook up with a boat or something."

"This day is just turning into a massive pile of fuckery," Scarlet said, snatching the cigarette from the young man's lips and taking a long drag.

"Hey!" Ryan said.

Hawke sighed as he watched the boat slip away. "You can say that again, Cairo."

# CHAPTER TWENTY-FOUR

Hawke got into the Suburban, slammed the door shut after him, and brought his fist down on the dashboard with a hefty smack. Losing Kloos like this was a major tactical error. Not only had he allowed the professor's life to be put at severe risk but Giancarlo Zito now had the opportunity to get the missing information he needed to track down the sword. Kruger would be beaming at his success, and there was only one antidote to that: take that success away from him and kill him with it.

Everyone else was already in the vehicle, and Devlin had just told a joke but only Lea was laughing. "And do you remember that time when Benny went on leave and we put his car up for sale?"

Lea laughed again and raised her hand to her mouth to cover the laugh. "Oh *God*, I do! Poor bastard had phone calls requesting test drives all through his holiday."

"Back to Kloos and the manuscript people," Hawke said, glancing at Lea. "This isn't a holiday."

Her face dropped. "You don't say? Jeez – we were just talking about old times."

Devlin said nothing.

"We have to get to Wales in a hurry," Hawke said. "It's not going to take long for Zito to get what he wants out of Kloos, and when he does the sword's his for the taking. That will make Kruger happy, and anything that makes that son of a bitch happy makes me unhappy."

"Got that right," Ryan said.

"Can you get us to the sword with what Kloos gave us,

153

mate?"

"Maybe. I'll give it some thought on the plane."

Reaper slammed the SUV into reverse and spun the wheels as he brought the vehicle out of Kloos's side street and onto the main drag. Hawke glanced out the tinted window at the people who were now daring enough to venture back into the city again after the violence around the station.

As if she had read his mind, Lea leaned forward from the middle seats and handed him her iPhone. The day's horror had already made it to the international press, and there was even a picture of the M-Squadron outside the station on the front cover of the New York Times. The headline ran: TERROR COMES TO AMSTERDAM. Looking closely in the rear of the image Hawke saw Reaper behind one of the trams. Luckily the Frenchman's face was obscured by the distance.

"What's going on?" Reaper asked, not taking his eyes off the road.

"You almost got famous," Hawke said without humor. He showed his old friend the front page of the paper and then returned the phone to Lea.

"Fame is fleeting, mon ami," Reaper said. "Those who chase it are fools running toward the end of a rainbow that never appears. It is not real life, non?"

"Nothing wrong with chasing a dream, Reap," Lea said.

"Celui qui court deux lièvres à la fois n'en prend aucun," Reaper said with his best Gallic shrug.

"Huh?" Devlin said.

"He who chases two hares catches neither," the former Legionnaire said by way of explanation. "Old French proverb."

Outside the crowds were growing in number once again as the city slowly came back to life. They were already some distance from the station now, and these people probably had only the vaguest idea about what had happened in the heart of their own city. Amsterdam was a peaceful place, and it wasn't every day that a team of gunmen dragged a kidnapped man across the busiest part of the city, opened fire on anti-terror police, and then fled to safety on a speed boat.

And all on his watch.

Hawke pushed back into his seat and closed his eyes. He knew that there would already be an alert out not only on Zito but also on the men and women of the ECHO team who had fired on them. Normally Lea would call Eden and he would start pulling strings connected to the Dutch authorities, but with the old man in a coma, there was only one thing they could do if they wanted to get out of the Netherlands and reach the Welsh mountains before Zito.

He half-turned in his seat and faced Lea. "Something tells me we're going to need Magnus Lund."

The quiet chatter in the Suburban came to a sudden halt.

"Lund?" Scarlet said. "You mean the walking corpse we met in Miami before the Lost City mission?"

"Know any other people called Magnus Lund?" Hawke said.

"Living dead or not," Lea said. "Lund is the only contact we have with the Eden Consortium. I say we contact him again."

"Me too," Ryan said confidently. "The man proved himself when he sent those rescue helicopters to get us in the jungle."

"Exactly," said Kim. "Getting that sanctioned in a country like Peru would have taken a lot of top-level negotiations. So not only did he prove we could trust him but we know he can make things happen. I say we call him."

"On it," said Lea, and started making the call. She spoke to his Copenhagen office for a few minutes and then disconnected the call. "That was his assistant. She says he's in Tehran on business but she'll pass it on."

Scarlet sighed. "Great. We only find out if he's sorted it when we arrive at the airport and get nicked or not."

"You should have more faith in humanity," Kim said.

Scarlet turned in her seat and looked at her as if she were a fool. "You don't know me at all, darling."

\*

Back in his office, Davis Faulkner twiddled his thumbs as he waited for the video conference to begin. Two of the five large plasma screens on his wall now flickered to life to reveal the faces of Colonel Frank Geary and Karen Conrad, the deputy director of the NSA. Faulkner trusted the NSA more than the CIA. He had more people willing to do his bidding there, not to mention they were military intelligence and more clandestine. He could squeeze much more out of them than the CIA.

"Are we all secure?" Faulkner said.

They confirmed that they were.

"Good. Regarding our earlier conversation, I wanted you both to know that the order has come down to deal with the ECHO team."

"Deal with them how, exactly?" Conrad said.

"They are to be executed."

A brief look of anxiety washed over both their faces, but before either could reply, Faulkner, spoke again. "And soon. Karen, have you ever heard of a man named Edward Kosinski?"

Conrad shifted in her seat. "I know Kosinski. He's very capable. He worked for us for a while, but now he's back with the Company," she said, referring to the CIA.

Faulkner gave her a look as he lit one of his famous Cuban cigars. "He is indeed – both with the CIA *and* very capable." A large cloud of smoke filled the humidified air in front of Faulkner's face. "How quickly can he put a team together?"

Conrad spoke with confidence. "Within hours."

"I mean the *best* team," Faulkner said firmly. "This isn't the first time I've been given the order to kill ECHO. I'm getting some serious pressure to take these guys out so I'm talking about the mother of all wetwork here, Karen."

She nodded. "Maybe a few days if you want the very best. I know Cougar is out of the country right now. She's in Nicaragua."

"Cougar?" Geary failed to subdue a laugh. "Is she particularly dangerous around young men in nightclubs?" He shook his head. "What's her real name?"

"I don't know," Conrad said. "And I don't want to know. She was raised in Chicago's toughest neighborhood, mostly on the streets. She joined the army the first chance she got. Ended up in Delta Force before crashing out and working as a mercenary, mostly in Latin America. Army intelligence tests ranked her IQ in the ninety-eighth percentile, which is one in fifty, and it's a very cunning intelligence, believe me. She is utterly ruthless and as far as we can tell she has pretty much nothing to live for except carrying out hits for large sums of money. Don't laugh at her codename, Frank – you might live to regret it."

Geary didn't look convinced. "If you say so."

"I do," Conrad said. "If Kosinski needs the best to take out ECHO then that means Cougar and her team."

Geary brushed his chin with the back of his fingers. "Is this kill order coming from the President?"

Faulkner locked eyes on him. "No, it is not, Frank. It's coming from a much greater power than that."

Geary looked shocked. "I don't know, sir…"

"You look uncomfortable, Frank. I hope you're not losing your fucking nerve."

"No, sir. It's just that…"

"And we have something a little more delicate to discuss," Faulkner said, cutting him off. "The sort of business you don't do in a video conference, no matter how secure, if you catch my drift. I want you both at my office later today. My assistant will send you the time when I've checked my schedule."

"Yes, sir," they both said.

"And make sure you have a strong drink before you arrive," Faulkner said. "You're going to need it."

# CHAPTER TWENTY-FIVE

## Snowdonia

Lund had pulled through, and now the ECHO Gulfstream was approaching Llanbedr Airport from the south. Lea followed their descent through the small portside window, watching as they punched through the layers of low, gray cloud and eventually emerged in the stormy world beneath them. Looking over the wing she saw the Irish Sea, twisting and turning in the heaving swells caused by the rainstorm. A flash of lightning streaked across the sky and plunged into the sea, followed by the deep animal roar of thunder.

Somewhere over all that water, somewhere through the storm, was the place she had once called her home, but turning back into the small, private jet she realized that had all changed now. Scarlet was talking quietly to her brother in a hushed phone call, Danny Devlin was cheating Ryan out of a few quid in a poker game, Kim was reading the front pages of newspapers now dominated by the news of the attack in Amsterdam; Vincent Reno was sending a text message to his twin sons.

And Joe Hawke was sleeping, arms crossed over his chest, eyes firmly shut against the world.

Wherever these people went was her home now.

Yes, ECHO was her family, and Hawke was something even more than that. She had thought many times about whether or not they would take the next step together and marry, but their lives were so hectic and filled with danger it seemed almost self-indulgent. What if something happened to one of them? She knew only too well what the death of his first wife had done to him. Maybe he had been scared away from marriage forever. She had thought about asking him to marry her, but that just wasn't her. That was something Cairo Sloane would do, not the girl from Galway that she saw when she looked in the mirror.

But if he asked her she would say yes in a heartbeat.

"Ready for the off?"

Startled out of her thoughts, she looked up to see Hawke smiling at her. He had just woken up and looked tired but up for the challenge ahead.

"We've stopped?" she asked. She had been staring out of the window and not even noticed they had parked up and the door was open.

"Yes," Scarlet said. "So get off your arse, you lazy cow. We have a magical giant-slaying sword to find."

Lea flipped Scarlet the bird, got out of her seat, and followed Hawke down the compact airstair and onto the soaking wet tarmac.

The airport was located inside Snowdonia National Park and was originally opened in World War Two as part of the No. 12 Group of RAF Fighter Command. It was small and thanks once again to Magnus Lund, getting out to the car park was fast and easy. Also, thanks to the reclusive Dane was the chunky Toyota Highlander sitting at the end of the parking lot in the pouring rain.

Hawke blipped the locks and after putting their bags and weapons in the back they all piled inside and got out of the wet. The former SBS man fired the engine up and cranked the heaters to full blast as he drove the enormous SUV out of the parking lot and headed south along the coast.

They turned inland at Barmouth and followed the

estuary east, passing through Bontddu and the ancient market town of Dolgellau. Ryan pointed out that long before the Romans, this was the land of the notoriously hardy Ordovices, one of the last Celtic tribes to hold out against the Roman invaders.

Scarlet yawned and closed her eyes. "Thanks for that, boy. I needed something to help me get to sleep."

Steering through a labyrinth of narrow roads and lanes, some almost turned into tunnels by the canopies of overhanging oaks and ashes, Hawke made good progress in the rainstorm. He followed the road south for a moment before it twisted around to the west and brought them along the south side of the mountain range.

They were on a straight road now, lined with ancient dry stone walls and deep in a valley between two impressive mountains. Cadair Idris was on their right – its peak was obscured by the low-hanging rain clouds, and ahead of them they could just make out Llyn Mwyngil, a large lake also known as Tal-y-llyn. Carved by glaciers millions of years ago, there was a route leading up to the peak of the mountain from its shores, but the ECHO team didn't have time for sightseeing.

Hawke turned a hard right at Abergynolwyn and drove the SUV on the final leg, dropping down to third as he crossed the Cader River on a tiny bridge and pushed the SUV up the western slopes of the mountain.

"No sign of Zito," Kim said from the back.

"Plenty of places around here for a rat like that to hide," said Devlin.

Hawke pulled the Highlander up on the side of the track and killed the engine. "I think this is about as far as we can go in this thing. We're on foot from now on."

Lea emerged from the SUV, shivered, and pulled up the collars on her jacket. The others followed and Hawke

161

padded around to the back. He opened the rear door, checked his weapon, and then slung his bag of tricks over his shoulder. Scarlet did the same, followed by the others as they each got tooled up ready for the search ahead: guns, flashlights, rope, and anything else they could fit in.

Ryan sniffed and shoved his hands into his pockets. "We still have time to get to the peak before nightfall and fulfill the legend."

"What do you expect to see?" Kim asked,

"Fuck knows," he said bluntly. "I want a fag."

"Glad you're on board, Ryan," Kim said sarcastically.

"Here." Scarlet tossed him one through the rain.

They followed the track which led up to the peak but its visibility was poor due to the conditions. Like everyone else, Lea scanned as far as the weather would let her for any signs of Giancarlo Zito and his men, but the mountainside was theirs.

"Not much longer to the peak," Ryan said from the back. "His voice was hollowed out by the wind and rain.

"Thank all the fucks for that," Scarlet said. "We have a private beach house in the Caribbean and we're getting our faces blasted off by a howling gale in Snowdonia."

"We have a wrecked headquarters in the Caribbean," Lea corrected her.

"Still better than this."

"Focus on the job," Hawke called out from the front. "As I said – we're not on holiday."

Lea looked back at the Highlander but it was now completely gone, lost inside the veil of mist and drizzle covering everything in the valley.

"Looks like we're in the location that Kloos specified," Ryan said.

They stopped hiking and lowered their bags to the ground. It was bleak. The wind was howling and the fog grew thicker with each minute.

"And we have to spend the night here?" Scarlet said.

"That's what Kloos said," said Lea. "He was very clear about how we had to follow the legend. Whoever spends the night on the top of Cadair Idris becomes either a poet or a madman."

"Sounds like a load of bollocks to me," said Scarlet.

"There's a reason why the manuscript specified this particular cairn," Hawke said. "It must have something to do with the legend, so we're going to spend the night here and see what happens."

Kim looked around at the gloom and frowned. "At least we won't get bothered by anyone, that's for damn sure."

"Unless Zito turns up," Reaper said, and started to set up the first tent. "But that's only going to happen if he breaks Kloos."

They followed his lead and put up the two four-man tents on the leeward side of the peak, tucked in out of the wind and rain. Hawke and Lea shared their tent with Reaper and Devlin, while Scarlet shared hers with Ryan and Kim, and when they were dry they gathered in Hawke's tent and shared out some food. Devlin produced a bottle of whisky and they passed it around.

After eating, they settled down and got ready for a long night, but then in the new quiet, a slightly drunk Devlin started speaking. "So," he said casually. "Three men were trying to join the SAS. One from the Grenadier Guards, one from the Paras, and one from the Royal Marines..."

Lea groaned. "Come on, Danny."

"Heard it anyway," Scarlet said. "It's shit."

Hawke said nothing, and Devlin continued, unmoved. "They're on their last test. The Guardsman goes in and the SAS sergeant gives him a revolver with six rounds and tells him his wife is upstairs. He has to go and kill her if he wants to get in the regiment."

"We've all heard it before, mon ami," Reaper said.

"A minute later the Guard comes downstairs and says that he just couldn't do it. He loved his wife too much. So then they ask the Para to do the same thing, and sure enough, a minute later he comes back down with the revolver and says he can't do it either. He just loves his wife too much."

Lea glanced at Hawke and then back to Devlin. "Leave it, Danny." Her voice was tense and anxious.

Hawke said nothing but just stared at the Irishman from across the room.

"And then the Commando takes the gun and goes upstairs. They all hear him fire the weapon – all six rounds. A few moments later the Commando comes back downstairs, all red in the face and worked up and he says 'You fuckin' assholes coulda told me they were blanks – I had to strangle the bitch!'"

Without a word, Hawke lashed out and pinned Devlin to the ground by his throat. He had respect for the Irish Ranger Wing but they were no match for a former RM Commando and SBS man. If he wanted to he could have killed him on the spot. The Irishman would have been unable to offer any real resistance and Hawke wouldn't have broken a sweat.

The tent was tense as everyone waited for Hawke to do whatever he was going to do next, but then he pushed the Irishman away with a powerful arm and stormed out of the tent into the storm.

"You total fuckin' eejit, Danny! I told you Joe's wife got killed, what the hell were you thinking?"

"It was just a joke, for fuck's sake!"

"You're just a joke," Kim said with disgust. "And put that damned bottle down. You're holding onto it like it's a life jacket."

Devlin looked at the Frenchman for support. "You were in the Foreign Legion, man. A joke's a joke, right?"

"Some things are not funny, mon ami," Reaper said gruffly. "Making jokes about a man killing his wife when his wife was murdered is one of those things. I am surprised you could be so... crass – is that the right word?"

Kim nodded. "It is, Vincent."

Reaper looked at her and smiled. "It's Reaper if we're on a mission. I'm just saying."

Scarlet fixed Devlin in the eye. "Are you a professional arsehole or just an enthusiastic amateur?"

"Now that's just rude, Scarlet."

Her face grew colder. "I took an instant dislike to you, you know."

"Why?"

"Just to save time, I think."

"Ouch," Devlin said, swigging from the bottle. "You're as sharp as an ice pick."

"You're going to apologize to Joe," Lea said flatly.

"I am not."

"You are, Danny," Lea said, moving to the entrance. "What you did was totally out of order."

Before waiting for a response she pushed out into the night in search of Hawke, scanning the horizon for the Englishman. The first thing she noticed was that the storm had blown itself out. She had read that the weather moved fast in this part of the country, and it was no joke. The clouds were blowing away to the east and revealed a sparkling grove of stars in the black sky.

Standing on the next rise, a few hundred meters to the west on another large cairn was Joe Hawke. He was perched on top of an uneven block of granite with his hands in his pockets and staring up at the sky.

*

As Hawke looked up at the constellations he was dimly aware of someone making their way over the rocks toward him. He turned to see Lea Donovan approaching him. She stood beside him and pushed her arm through his arm.

"He's a fool, Joe."

"Forget about it."

"Me and Danny go way back and I'd trust him all the way but he can push things too far."

"He's making a play for you."

She looked shocked. "He is not."

He knew she wanted to talk about it but his mind was elsewhere. The Danny Devlins of this world were nothing to worry about when you were up against the likes of the Oracle and his secret cult.

In his right pocket, he turned over the small box that contained the engagement ring he had bought back in Washington. It never seemed to be the right moment to ask her. Something always came up and kicked it along the track. "Come on," he said at last. "We need to get some sleep if we're going to wake up before dawn and find out what the big surprise is."

# CHAPTER TWENTY-SIX

Hawke woke first. He had never needed an alarm clock to wake up early, and even as a child, he was able to train himself to wake naturally at a precise time and usually got it right. Today was no exception and when he checked his watch he saw it was just before dawn.

Even before he opened his eyes he was aware of Lea beside him, one of her arms over his chest. Reaper and Devlin were enjoying a less intimate arrangement and their two separate sleeping bags were on either side of the entrance.

He yawned and woke Lea. Moments later they were all outside the tent. Ryan and Kim were already outside.

"And what about Cairo?" Hawke said, leaning inside her tent.

"Piss off," Scarlet said. A boot sailed past his head and thudded down in the muddy ground. "I've decided to have breakfast in bed."

"Get up," Hawke said. "Now."

"But it's still night."

"Dawn's about to break, Cairo."

"All right, all right. Let's get this show on the road, fuckers," Scarlet said, clambering out of her tent. "Any sign of Zito?"

"Not yet," Ryan said.

"Maybe Kloos kept his mouth shut," Kim said, but not too convincingly.

"Talking of Kloos," Devlin said. "What did he say about this legend again?"

167

Ryan climbed up on the highest granite slab of them all and looked out across the mountainous horizon. "He said that the son of Arianrhod will reveal where the Sword of Fire rests."

Hawke turned to Ryan. "And who might that be, mate?"

"Arianrhod was an important part of ancient Celtic mythology, and the mother of Llew Llaw Gyffes," Ryan said, lighting up a cigarette and flicking the match into the breeze.

"Give us one of those, will you?" Scarlet said. "Smoked all mine."

He handed her one and took a deep drag on his own.

Hawke watched Ryan's eyes for a moment. A new coldness was moving in, for sure, but he wasn't the boy's father. Maybe when all this was over, he'd have a chat... "Who was that last bloke you just mentioned, mate?"

"He was a major hero in Welsh mythology, tucked away deep in the fourth branch of the Mabinogi." He breathed out another long cloud of smoke and sniffed. "Point is, he was symbolized by Perseus, the slayer of dragons. I was thinking about this all night and now I *posit* that the reference to the heavens in fact means stars. Jesus, I could do with a drink."

Hawke shot a quick sideways glance at the young man but said nothing.

"So we're looking for something in the stars?" Lea said.

"A constellation?" Kim asked.

Scarlet sighed. "No, a Klingon mothership. What do you think?"

"Hey, I was just asking."

"Which one's the Perseus constellation?" Lea said.

"There," Hawke said, raising his arm. "The bright star just there is Mirfak, the brightest star in the Perseus constellation."

"Most of these constellations have an important role to play in traditional Welsh mythology," Ryan said. "The Milky Way was originally called the Fortress of Gwydion. Every one of these stars has a part to play in these ancient legends, including Perseus there."

They followed Perseus down to the horizon and one by one the stars in the constellation began to fade.

"Look!" Lea said. "The Sword of Perseus is pointing precisely to that smaller peak down there."

"Craig y Castell," Ryan said. "The tip of Perseus's sword is pointing to Craig y Castell."

Then it happened.

The sun broke the horizon in the northeast and struck the western slopes of the caldera directly beneath the peak of Craig y Castell. They watched in silence as one particular rock glowed almost as bright as the sun itself.

"It faces the sun at dawn in such a way that it's acting like a mirror," Ryan said, shielding his eyes from the glinting, gleaming piece of smooth granite.

"Looks like we found the tomb," Hawke said.

"So let's get on it, people," Ryan said.

"Look who thinks he's the big boss," Scarlet said sarcastically.

"I could be the big boss," said Ryan, nodding his head firmly. "An apex predator."

Scarlet laughed. "You? You're just the comic-relief sidekick."

Instead of a comeback, Ryan said nothing and headed toward the ridge to the west of them. Hawke thought he looked offended by Scarlet's comment, but let it go.

They walked along the ridge and as the sun slowly climbed in the clear sky it illuminated the valleys on either side of the mountain. Great oceans of emerald green farmland stretched out in every direction. They could see the famous Minffordd Path snaking its way up from a visitors' car park, and Hawke followed its path as it twisted through forests and rushing rivers on its way up the slope.

The massive lake to their right sparkled in the morning sun. The previous night Ryan had regaled them with ancient myths about how it was supposed to be bottomless but the reality was more prosaic: it was the caldera of a volcano that last burned in ancient times not long after the glaciers carved these valleys out of the landscape for eternity.

Hawke looked at his watch. "Still no sign of Zito."

"Or that giant tank of shit, Kruger," Scarlet said.

"Just as well, eh?" Devlin said. No one had spoken about the night before, and Hawke wanted it kept that way. "Maybe we got lucky?"

Hawke shook his head. "No way. Kruger won't mess around with this. For one thing, I think he's working for someone else and that someone else will want results. Failing your boss in Kruger's world means more than a demotion or getting fired – it means your life, so he'll do whatever he has to do to get what he needs out of Kloos. They're here all right. It's just a matter of time."

"You're such a pessimist, Joe," Lea said. "Maybe just this once we got a break?"

"I'll believe it when I see it," he said.

And then, just to prove him right, the destruction unfolded right in front of their eyes.

# CHAPTER TWENTY-SEVEN

The surface-to-air missile screeched down the center of the valley at Mach 3 and smashed into the caldera's western slope. The resulting fireball was of Hollywood proportions, blasting tons of granite and earth out of the side of the mountain and scattering smoking detritus all over the slope. As the deep roar of the explosion echoed back down the valley like thunder, dislodged boulders tumbled down the mountain and crashed through the black surface of the lake far below.

"Holy smokes!" Kim said, unable to take her eyes off the unfolding devastation. "What the hell was that?"

Hawke was already on it, scanning the valley to the north with his binoculars. The deep folds of the pastoral farmland below were still untouched by the rising sun, but it was easy enough to track the smoke trail back to its origin. He was just able to make out a pair of black Jeep Cherokees on a track to the north of a smaller lake just beyond the main one in the caldera. "Around a dozen men," he said. "Looks like the fireworks were provided by an Eryx."

"A what?" Kim said.

Reaper replied. "Eryx – it's a shoulder-launched missile. European. Of all the handheld weapons it has the biggest caliber."

"Right," Hawke said. "And their warheads are easily capable of breaking open a concrete bunker seven or eight feet thick. The granite slab blocking the entrance to the tomb in that mountain would be no match at all – as we all just saw." He watched the Jeeps move along the track toward them.

"So now what?" Kim said.

"We're still much closer to the entrance," Devlin said. "Surely we can get in there and out again with the sword by the time they get up the mountain?"

"No," Hawke said. "Look."

The Jeeps had driven closer now and were pulling up around the northern shores of Llyn y Gader in the bowl of the caldera. Giancarlo Zito climbed out of the leading vehicle and gave them all a cheery wave. The Jeep's other doors opened and then Bruno and another man dragged Henk Kloos out into the new day. He was badly beaten and had to be held up by the two Italians.

The doors of the Jeep in the rear now opened and several more of Zito's men got out. Armed like a militia, they looked out of place in the Welsh countryside, but then things cranked up another notch when a face they all knew and hated emerged from the front passenger seat.

"Dirk Kruger," Hawke said through gritted teeth.

Scarlet dragged on her cigarette, as cool as ice, and stared at the South African. "That, my friends, is a face that invites a massive slap."

"What he needs is a few years in a Russian salt mine," Reaper said.

Another man stepped out behind Kruger and Hawke shook his head with disbelief.

Lea noticed him bristle. "You know him, Joe?"

"Yes. His name's Vermaak. The last time we met was on a joint training exercise in Angola. He was a South African commando, but now it looks like he's a mercenary."

Before anyone could respond, Dirk Kruger cupped his hands on either side of his mouth and called up to them. His voice echoed weirdly as the horseshoe shape of the caldera acted as a giant soundbox and amplified his words.

"How nice to see you all again," he shouted. "Especially you, Mr. Bale."

Hawke took a step forward ahead of the group and called back down. "You want to talk, you talk to me, Kruger."

"Major Hawke, the big hero..." Kruger looked around at Zito and the others and they gave a short laugh. "Listen up then, big hero: throw your guns and weapons into the lake or I'll drown Doctor Kloos in it with my own two hands."

"He's got us," Reaper said.

"Bullshit," said Devlin. "We're not going to roll over that easy now, are we?"

"He's right," Hawke said. "We haven't got a sniper rifle and even if we did we can't take out that many men before they kill Kloos."

Devlin looked at Hawke. "But we've got to try *something*, dammit."

"I'm responsible for the safety of everyone on this mission," Hawke said, "including Kloos. If I say it's over then it's over."

Lea was first to hurl her gun off the edge of the mountain. What was a heavy, chunky weapon in her hands was now a tiny, fragile piece of metal bouncing off the rocks with a light smack until it finally hit the lake and vanished forever.

The others followed her lead until they were all unarmed.

"That was awesome!" Kruger called up in a mocking tone. "Now walk over to the tomb's entrance and wait like the good dogs you are until we come up."

Hawke watched the South African give a series of orders. From the body language, it was clear to see that

173

Kruger was the man in charge, and Zito and his men were just the hired help.

"Looks like we'd better do as he says," Kim said. "We all know he's capable of killing innocent people."

"We should fight," Devlin said.

"You're crazy, Danny," said Lea.

"Just sayin'."

"No," Hawke said. "Kim's right. Any funny business and he'll kill Kloos. We play along with his rules for now and bide our time."

"So what are we waiting for, girls?" Scarlet said. "Let's get this thing over with."

And with that, they started to march toward the smoldering entrance that the Eryx had gouged out of the mountainside. Smoke was still spiraling out of the newly blasted hole, and somewhere behind it was a tomb containing the Sword of Fire.

# CHAPTER TWENTY-EIGHT

With the sun at their backs, the team started along the rim
of the caldera. The howling wind of the previous night
was now a light summer breeze blowing on their faces
from the Irish Sea to the west. With each step they took
toward the newly-blasted entrance, the faces of Kruger
and Zito slowly came into sharper focus until they were
almost face-to-face.

"All right," Hawke said. "We're here and we're
unarmed. Release Kloos."

"Not until we have the sword," Kruger said. "Now get
inside – and no funny business." To clarify the
consequences of any rebellion, Zito and his men moved
forward and raised their guns.

Lea stood defiantly. "Where's Maggie's idol?"

"Shut your mouth and move!" he snarled.

They moved into the hole and quickly found
themselves inside a cold, narrow tunnel, kept secret from
the world for countless centuries by the slab of granite the
Eryx had destroyed moments earlier. Shuffling deeper
now, the hand-carved tunnel was so narrow they had to
move into single-file, and their shoulders brushed against
the rough stone as they moved into the heart of the
mountain.

The tunnel opened out and revealed a small chamber.
Opposite them, an arched entrance was carved into the
rock wall. Hawke shone his flashlight beam at it, and
above the door was a smooth, granite lintel with some
words carved into it.

175

Kruger turned to Kloos. The old man was still being held up by Zito's thugs and was barely conscious.

Kruger poked the professor in the stomach with his gun. "What does it say, old man?"

Kloos mumbled incoherently.

"What about you, Bale?"

Ryan frowned. "It says Annwn. It's the Welsh underworld, but I don't know much about it. It's the Welsh version of the classic otherworld – the Tibetans had Shambhala and the Irish had Tír na nÓg."

"The Land of the Young," Lea said quietly. "My father talked to me about it."

"This stuff is all very pre-Christian," Ryan continued. "All I know about Annwn is that there was endless food there and no death or disease. It morphed into the Christian concept of Paradise, except there's a difference – the word Annwn refers to the great depth of the place, whereas we see heaven as high above us and hell being below."

"That's right," Kloos said, his voice weak and trembling. "The King of Annwn was Gwyn ap Nudd, and he used to hunt for mortal souls with his hell hounds, known in Welsh as Cŵn Annwn. There is an ancient poem called the Spoils of Annwn – a very cryptic and strange piece of text that describes how King Arthur himself made an expedition to Annwn,"

He stopped to cough and spit out some blood. "There are Irish accounts recounting similar details. At this stage, Welsh and Irish myths are closely intertwined. Some say this expedition was nothing more than Arthur's journey to Ireland, but I have always known in my heart he went to the actual underworld... Annwn."

"And you think this damned place is Annwn?" Kruger said.

"Sounds like nonsense to me," Zito added. "All this for

a sword."

Kruger turned on him and raised a blade to his fat throat. "You keep it down, Gianni, or I'll gut you like one of your Italian sardines, right boy?"

Zito was shocked, but Kruger had the power and everyone knew it, including Zito. He gave a hurried nod and tried to smile. "I meant nothing by it, Dirk."

Kruger slid the blade back in his belt, satisfied he had quelled the mutiny, but Hawke noticed a look in Zito's eyes. Something told him Kruger had better watch his back around the Italian from now on.

"I've had enough of all this crap about underworlds and hell hounds," the South African said, and turned to Vermaak. "I was married to a hell hound once."

Vermaak laughed and gave Kruger a hearty slap on the back, but Zito and his men were less impressed, and Hawke wondered if he could exploit the difference of opinion between the two groups of men.

"So let's get inside," the arms dealer said. "I want to get out of this place."

They made their way deep inside the mountain. In the second tunnel, the wind howled and whistled like an army of ghosts disturbed after centuries of silent rest. Moving further forward now, and with Kruger and the others a safe distance behind them, they started to notice the tunnel opening out.

They advanced further until they reached a large cavern: carvings in the rocky walls showed an ancient human presence, and then they saw stone steps carved into the side of the cave. Each step had been hewn from granite into a perfectly smooth slab, and they descended away from the ledge until disappearing into unsettling darkness deep in the earth.

Hawke looked at the steps doubtingly. "I don't like the

177

look of that."

Scarlet appeared at his arm and peered down the steps into the damp gloom. "I used to go to a nightclub with an entrance like that."

"No doubt the sort where you need a password to get in," Hawke said.

"As a matter of fact, yes," she replied.

"And a safeword when you're in there," Ryan said with a smirk.

Scarlet leaned in and whispered in Ryan's ear, but loud enough for all to hear. "As a matter of fact *yes*. Where do you think I get my fighting techniques from?"

The young man's response took a second too long to come, and then Kruger filled the silence. "What are you waiting for, Hawke? Get down the steps. If you think there might be a booby-trap then send one of your team first."

"I go first, Kruger," Hawke replied. "We don't all think like you."

The Englishman took the first step with the same level of trepidation he imagined Neil Armstrong must have felt, but his boot landed on solid granite and slowly he led the others down the stone steps into the darkness with only his flashlight to guide him safely and stop a lethal fall off the side.

They reached the bottom of the steps and found themselves facing a decrepit rope suspension bridge that spanned a narrow gorge. Hawke pointed his beam down and it disappeared into blackness.

"Afraid, Hawke?"

He turned and saw Kruger moving through his men.

"Why don't you go ahead of me, Dirk?" Hawke said. "Ladies first, after all."

Kruger leaned into Hawke, making sure he had a tight grip on his gun. He pushed the muzzle into the

Englishman's stomach. "Get over the fucking bridge, cuiter."

Hawke stared back into his eyes and never blinked or flinched. His team was looking to him for leadership, and getting shot in the stomach and left to bleed out inside a mountain wasn't what they needed right now.

"Take care, Joe!" Lea said.

He cautiously crossed the bridge, his hands gripping the frayed rope cables on either side as he made his way to the far ledge. It swayed violently as he passed the middle, but came under control again when he drew closer to the other side.

The others followed and when they reached the other side they followed a crumbling tunnel until they pulled up at another set of stone steps. "Christ," Kruger cursed. "This is like Lord of the fucking Rings. Move on, you bastards!"

They obeyed, and at the bottom of the second staircase was a running river. They were hundreds of feet inside the mountain now, and the sight of the sparkling water surprised them all. Looming behind it was an enormous door, built into the rock and firmly closed. Dust and cobwebs obscured much of it and it was clear it hadn't been opened for hundreds of years.

Kruger greedily pushed his men out of the way, including Giancarlo Zito whom he nearly knocked into the river. "Looks like we're in business." He turned to Kloos who was still being held up by Bruno, one eye badly swollen. The professor was mumbling to himself through a mouth frothing with blood. "Looks like Teach here isn't going to be much use." His men shared a low, humorless chuckle. "But you all remember what that insane crackpot told us – get the sword at all costs. Prepare the Eryx."

"Wait – what?" Lea said.

"Are you crazy?" said Scarlet.

Kim said, "Crazy? This dude is weapons-grade crazy."

"You've beaten Kloos so hard you now have to fire the world's biggest shoulder-launched missile to open a door," Hawke said. "That's not just crazy, it's stupid, ignorant, and short-sighted."

Kruger snapped, and raising the stock of his rifle he smashed Hawke in the face and knocked him into the dust beside the river bank. "Any more fucking shit out of you and your bones are staying down here forever. Got it, you stupid bastard?"

Lea ran to him, and with Reaper's help, they hauled him to his feet. It took a second to get his balance back and after he spat a wad of blood into the river he was back again. His mind was buzzing with the pain of the blow, but also with the off-hand comment, Kruger had just made about working for an insane crackpot.

As the South African surveyed the door and watched his men load the Eryx, Hawke turned to Lea. "Did you hear what he just said?"

"About you being a stupid bastard?" Scarlet said. "We all heard that, yes."

Hawke gave her a look and then returned to Lea. "No – about him having a boss – he's working for someone else. He described him as a crackpot."

"That hardly narrows things down these days," Scarlet said.

Kruger raised his eyebrows. "Yes, I'm working for someone, and yes, the man I work for is definitely crazy, but what do I care? I'm just a greedy bastard from Cape Town. Now shut the fuck up and let my men break this door down. Somewhere in here is my destiny. I will be a great man!"

"You'll never be the man your mom is, Dirk," Kim

said.

Kruger ignored her comment, now fully occupied with the progress the men were making with the Eryx. There was a grim silence in the chamber as Bruno loaded the shoulder launcher.

"Everyone take cover!" Kruger yelled, and seconds later, they fired the missile into the arched doorway. A massive explosion tore through the chamber and blasted smoke, dust, and flames in every direction.

When the smoke cleared and the doors were blown off their ancient iron hinges, Lea Donovan gasped. The explosion had revealed a second, larger chamber that reminded her of a cathedral's nave.

At the far end of the chamber, there was something still partially obscured by the remnants of the smoke. With the smell of the detonated warhead lingering in the damp, musty air, they moved forward into the cavernous nave.

As they walked through the chamber they saw the object could only be one thing: a sarcophagus, and it was surrounded by other, smaller cadaver tombs. They gathered around it in solemn silence, and for a moment even Dirk Kruger looked awestruck as his eyes danced over the ancient stone coffin.

Neatly carved into the slate tomb lid was a dragon with two wings behind it and a snarling face, all fangs and forked tongue. Below the dragon were the words: HIC IACET SEPULTUS INCLITUS REX ARTURIUS.

"Oh my God," Kloos said. "This is unbelievable."

"What is it?" Kruger said.

Ryan saw the words and knew at once. "King Arthur's tomb."

Kruger's eyes sparkled like two solitaire diamonds. "Are you fucking with me, Kloos?"

"No, he's not," Ryan said. "It says Here Lies Buried

the Glorious King Arthur."

"So the legends were true after all," Kloos said. "Not only was Arthur real, but the Sword of Fire was Excalibur."

"I thought the legend says that King Arthur never died?" Kim asked.

"Not by the looks of this coffin," said Devlin.

"If he's inside it," Hawke said.

"Does that make this place Avalon?" Ryan asked the professor.

The old man shook his head. He looked confused. "Legend says Arthur was buried in Avalon, but it also says he will come back to lead the Britons to freedom, so..." he shrugged his shoulders and gave Ryan an apologetic look. "The problem is that all of this happened so long ago the records are very vague and sometimes totally contradictory."

"I thought Glastonbury was Avalon," Scarlet said. "That's what they said when I got stoned there back in ninety-four."

"Some say Bardsey Island, just off the coast not far from here," Kloos said. "But it's entirely possible the area above us right here is Avalon, and this mountain leads to Annwn. This is... I don't know what to say. My entire life has been for this moment."

"You got that right," Kruger said and fired his hunting rifle into the Dutch professor's chest.

# CHAPTER TWENTY-NINE

Tiger listened to the sound of the ringing phone up against his ear. The gentle electronic tone reminded him in a strange sort of way of his songbirds back in his garden. He was making a call to Zhou Yang, his boss and the second in command of the General Office of the Central Investigation Department, but as usual, Zhou was making him wait.

What was it his mother used to tell him about patience? *Young plants can't be forced to grow by stretching them.*

Yes, that was it; and mother was always right.

A watched pot never boils, as the Westerners put it.

The phone continued to ring, but he could not hang up. He had already spoken with Zhou's stern personal assistant who had put him through, so the boss knew he was on the line. He closed his eyes and turned the ringing tone back into his songbirds – the ones he kept in the little bamboo cages hanging from his plum tree.

Pig dreamed of retirement in the south, but not Tiger. For him, the perfect retirement away from all this deceit and killing was simply to be among his plum trees and Sichuan Bush Warblers. His wife and daughter laughed in the kitchen as they made dinner together; the evening sun sliding through the blinds and scattering on his living room wall. He could atone for past sins right there among the small domestic comforts of his Shunyi home.

"Report."

It was Zhou, and his voice sounded harder and colder

than usual.

"We have the parents under arrest."

"Where?"

"At their apartment."

"And the rogue agent?"

Zhou was talking about Agent Dragonfly, although in this small apartment she was probably better known as Zhang Xiaoli. "I had the mother contact her. She was told her father is gravely ill. She said she was to fly home at once to see him before he died."

"Good."

"Am I still to execute her?"

Zhou paused before replying. Tiger had long given up trying to read his boss's mind. He had never been able to predict him or his moods, and today was no exception.

"No. I have been given new orders. She is to be kept alive and taken for interrogation. We can use her as a pawn in a much bigger game. The ECHO team is up to something and I want to know what it is."

"I understand," Tiger said, drawing a long breath. "And the parents?"

"Kill them, of course. They are witnesses and can identify you and your men."

"Understood." Tiger spoke casually as if he had been asked to do nothing more than file a report. To him, it was all just bureaucracy.

"Report when you have the rogue."

"Yes, sir," Tiger said. He was already screwing a suppressor into the muzzle of his pistol as the line went dead and the disconnect tone rang out. Tiger heard his songbirds once again in the electronic bleeping, but they flew away when he hung up the phone and slid a round into the chamber of his gun.

"What did the old bastard have to say this time?" Pig said, looking at the newly-suppressed pistol with interest

184

but no fear.

"Dragonfly is to be taken alive. The parents must be killed."

"You want me to do it?" Pig asked, moving to get up from his chair. The legs squeaked on the linoleum tiles. Monkey was sleeping on the couch with a folded newspaper over his face.

"No," Tiger said calmly. "It's my job." And it was his job. Zhou had ordered him to lead the team, and asking one of the others to do it would make him look weak. "Where are they now?"

"I put them in the bedroom," Pig said. "They are tied up and gagged. Quite safe, and Rat's outside their door."

Tiger stepped along the small apartment's narrow central corridor and made his way toward the bedroom. On the walls hung family pictures of happy times spent together – a black and white photo of smiling people on a beach, a laugh around a picnic table. He saw Dragonfly as a child, standing between her parents. Her father's hands were on her shoulders. They all looked so happy.

Tiger moved on. He had no such memories. His childhood was no picnic. He was raised by a hateful uncle who used him as a punching bag during his frequent drinking binges. He had fled domestic beatings for the wilder violence of the streets before finally being sucked up by the Ministry. Such was life, he thought with a shoulder shrug as he reached Rat and the bedroom door.

Rat saw the electric light glint on the barrel of the suppressor and knew at once why Tiger had visited the old couple. He pushed his chair out of the way and took a few steps back. He yawned. "I'm going to get more of those noodles," he said and walked back down along the corridor. "Hungry?"

"No."

185

Tiger heard Rat shuffle down the corridor and then he opened the bedroom door. It was dark inside. The curtains were drawn but the light from the hall stretched across the carpet and lit up the end of the bed. The old couple was under the sheets. It sounded like they were sleeping.

He raised his gun and without emotion, he fired at the bed. The first few shots triggered quick, sharp jolts as the Zhangs reacted to the bullets, but by the time he had emptied the magazine they were still and the room was silent; the only movement was the smoke drifting from the tip of the suppressor.

He closed the door and walked back along to the kitchen. As he gently unscrewed the suppressor and slipped it in his suit pocket he smelled the noodles and decided he was hungry after all. Dragonfly would be here soon and who knew when he would get to eat again.

\*

As Davis Faulkner walked into the dark, smoke-filled office, he had to remind himself he was the Vice President of the United States, and this was his turf. A telephone call with Otmar Wolff had an unsettling effect on him, but things were different in here, and everyone at the conference table knew it.

He walked to his seat with a confident swagger and occupied the leather swivel chair at the head of the table with all the gravitas his office endowed upon him. Among a handful of trusted, administrative lackeys, seated around the table were Colonel Frank Geary and Karen Conrad, both of whom had changed their schedules to be here as per the Vice President's earlier instructions.

"There's a war raging, people," he began pompously. Faulkner was tall and tanned and despite never having served, he moved with the easy, commanding grace of a senior military officer. The parting in his silver hair ran along the left-hand side of his head with laser-guided precision. It all came together to tell the world: I am a man you had better not fuck with.

"A war, Mr. Vice President?" Conrad asked.

His eyes sparkled. "A war like we have never seen before and using ancient forces none of us know how to control."

"Like what?" Geary said.

"Like Poseidon's trident, for one thing."

A heavy silence occupied the room. They had read Faulkner's Top Secret briefing on the weapon but hearing words like this was still shocking.

Faulkner reveled in the power his words held over his underlings. He knew how they felt; he felt that way in the presence of the Oracle. "We're going to need that trident. Not now, but soon."

"And where is it?" Conrad said. She crossed her legs and Faulkner fought the urge to stare as the low-lighting shone on the sheen of her pantyhose.

"In the Smithsonian," Geary said, shifting his eyes from Conrad to Faulkner to let the Vice President know he was part of the loop.

"Wrong," Faulkner said bluntly. "The trident *was* in the Smithsonian, in a special section referred to as Archive 7. Now it's in a highly restricted black site along with all the other treasures we've gotten our hands on these past few years. You wouldn't believe the stuff they were hiding in Archive 7. Some of it surprised even me. Poseidon's goddam trident is like a water pistol compared to some of that ancient stuff, believe me, and a great deal of it is still undiscovered all over the world."

"I still find this very hard to accept," Geary said.

Conrad broke in. "It was *moved*, sir?"

187

A shallow nod was just visible behind the cloud of cigar smoke. "There was some trouble over in Archive 7 and an item of vital strategic interest to the United States was stolen."

"Medusa's head?" Conrad said.

Faulkner gave a brief nod. "It was retrieved by the Alphabet Boys over in Langley, headed up by our friend Edward Kosinski under somewhat notorious circumstances."

"We all remember when the President was kidnapped." Geary spoke as if he had personally known him. "Just terrible."

"But back to business," Faulkner said, cutting him off. "The meat and potatoes of why we're here... what I couldn't talk about on the video conference."

"Sir?" Geary asked.

"Operation Crossbow, Frank," Faulkner said, his voice almost a whisper.

"I never heard of that," Conrad said.

"You wouldn't have," said Faulkner. "It doesn't exist – not officially, at least. It's my own little baby. I cooked it up to save this country. Someone has to give the American people the leadership they deserve, Frank."

"My God," Geary's face paled. "You can't be talking about..."

"President Brooke is a disaster for the United States, Frank. We all know he has to go."

Geary looked around at the small number of people in the room with growing concern.

"Relax, Colonel," Faulkner said. "These are all my people. Good people. People who know that Brooke has to go."

"We're talking about *treason*, Mr. Vice President."

"Wrong. *I'm* talking about treason. You're just listening." Faulkner flicked through a manila folder on the desk. "It says in here that your career is just about washed up, Colonel Geary. Something about embezzling army funds."

An unexpected rush of anger flooded into Geary's voice. "That was a set-up!"

"Hush, Colonel," Faulkner said. "And tell me, how do you like the sound of *General* Geary?"

"Well, I…"

"Because when I'm president that's what your new title will be."

Geary settled down. Faulkner knew he had no cards left to play. "Count me in."

"I thought as much," Faulkner said.

"When?" Conrad asked.

"Sooner than you think," said Faulkner.

"Is it an assassination?" Geary asked.

"No," said Faulkner. "We don't want to make a goddam martyr out of him."

"So, what then?"

"That's above your paygrade, Frank," Faulkner said icily. He looked over at Karen Conrad. "Leave the fine details to us, right?"

"Yes, sir."

"Now, you'll have to excuse me. I have a meeting at the Pentagon."

"Of course."

"It's going to be a piece of cake," Faulkner said. "We just have to hold our nerve."

Conrad nodded. "We'll have to work hard to keep it from turning into a serious three-ring circus."

"We can do it, Karen," Faulkner boomed as he got up from his chair. "I know we can. You, me, Kosinski, Cougar, and the soon-to-be *General* Geary right here are going to work together, take out ECHO, and put me in the

White House. Then things are going to change."

Two men in black coats started to speak into their palm mics as the Vice President strode over to the door. Another man opened it but Faulkner stopped and turned around to address the room one last time. "And when I say change, I mean Big Time."

And then he was gone.

# CHAPTER THIRTY

"No!" Lea screamed.

Devlin was closest to the professor and leaped into the line of fire but it was too late; he crashed into the ground beside the now dead Henk Kloos.

"You bastard, Kruger!" Lea yelled. "He was innocent."

Hawke saw Zito rub his jaw and cast an anxious glance at Bruno and his other men. The look on his face said: this guy's unpredictable and Bruno seemed to share the opinion.

"Innocent!" Kruger scoffed.

Devlin clambered to his knees and checked Kloos's pulse. He turned to the others and shook his head and then got to his feet. He dusted himself off and looked Kruger in the eye. "Where I come from, shooting an unarmed man makes you a proper fucking coward."

"He was completely dispensable," Kruger said. "As will you be when you get the lid off this tomb." He swung the gun up. "Get moving you vermin."

Hawke rolled up his sleeves and grabbed the edge of the slate lid. The others joined him while Kruger, Zito, and the gunmen kept a safe distance away from the action.

At first, there was no movement, but then they all felt something click and the slate began to move. Hawke improved his grip on the heavy lid and pushed harder. He thought for a moment he had caught a glimpse of some kind of blue glowing light emanating from the inside of the sarcophagus. Its strange, unique glow reminded him of something, but he couldn't remember what it was...

191

Atlantis.

It reminded him of Atlantis – specifically the buzzing, neon color the sunken city had glowed when it had started to rupture and the entire underwater metropolis had exploded in a giant fireball.

He tipped his head and peered beneath the slate cap. It was halfway open now, and he saw that he'd imagined nothing – something inside the sarcophagus was glowing the same soft, fuzzy lambent blue he had witnessed on the terrible day of the Seastead battle. He realized that the alluring light wasn't the only thing linking that day to this – Dirk Kruger was another common factor.

"Stop dawdling, you lazy bastards," Kruger yelled. "And hurry the fuck up." The South African slid the bolt back on his rifle to underline the seriousness of his mood.

With one final push, the team managed to heave the lid off the top of the sarcophagus. It crashed to the stone floor and broke in two, producing a large cloud of dust in the air around the stone coffin. When it cleared they all moved a step closer and peered into the light and what they saw amazed them all.

They were looking at a stone carving of a corpse.

The stonemason's work was intricate. It was holding its hands together over its chest as if in prayer, and at its side was a yellowed, ragged cloth stretching from its waist down to its boots.

"What the hell is it?"

"It's a gisant," Ryan said.

Hawke shot him a glance. "Eh?"

"A cadaver tomb, or a memento mori tomb," he said. "We call them effigy tombs. What we're looking at here is a depiction of Arthur's rotting corpse. It means the real thing is underneath, almost certainly."

"Who gives a damn about his corpse?" Kruger said. He took a step back and raised his rifle. When the stock was neatly in his shoulder he pointed the barrel in Ryan's face. "Open up that cloth. I want to see the glow more clearly."

Kruger and his men took a cautious step back. They were expecting another booby trap, but when Ryan carefully opened the cloth they knew at once it was no trap. As he pulled it open, the dark, neon glow covered his hands and forearms, and then the young man's face was the same ghostly hue.

There, at Arthur's side was a long, wide blade, and its gentle blue glow almost seemed to hum and buzz in the dark chamber.

They were looking at the Sword of Fire.

# CHAPTER THIRTY-ONE

Mesmerized by the mellow glow, Lea stared at the sword and noticed a line of tiny symbols carved into the hilt. "You see those symbols, Ry?"

He nodded. "They have a strong resemblance to those on the idols."

"For fuck's sake, is this thing Excalibur or not?" Scarlet asked.

"Maybe, maybe not," Ryan said. He cast his eyes down to Professor Kloos's dead body and then he looked at Kruger with utter contempt. "The one man who would know for sure is dead."

Kruger lowered his rifle and laughed. "If you idiots knew the first thing about this game you're playing you'd know it doesn't matter if you call the damned thing Excalibur, the Sword of Fire, or anything else. This sword is a gateway."

As Kruger's word echoed in the cavern, Hawke looked at him sharply. "What do you mean a *gateway*?"

Kruger jabbed the Englishman's chest. "You mind your own damned business, cuiter."

Hawke resisted the impulse to grab Kruger's finger and snap it off before landing the punch of his life on the arms dealer's leathery face. Vermaak was loitering somewhere behind him with an MP5 in his hands, and Zito and Bruno and the other men were still armed and maintaining a good distance.

In normal circumstances he would take Kruger by the neck and use him as a human shield; buy some time, barter his way out using the boss's life as currency, but these were not normal circumstances. He had seen the look in Zito's eyes when Kruger pushed him around, and if he used the South African as a human shield he was one hundred percent certain Zito would use them both for target practice. The only question was why Zito hadn't already killed them all now the sword had been found. He guessed the ancient relic didn't mean much to the Italian mobster and that he was waiting for a large cash payment.

"Now get out of my way, you fools," Kruger snarled.

With the danger of any booby trap now gone, Kruger pushed his way forward through the small collection of people gathered around the sarcophagus and leaned inside to get the sword, but before he did he was careful to wrap it up again.

He moved away from the sarcophagus and carefully placed the covered sword inside a leather bag. "You," he said, pointing a commanding finger at Bruno. "Take this bag, and guard it with your life. It's the most precious thing on this whole fucking planet, you understand?"

Bruno stayed calm. He glanced at Zito who gave a shallow nod. After the nod, Bruno casually strolled over to the bag and lifted it over his shoulder, never once taking his eyes off Kruger and Vermaak.

Hawke guessed the South African would have preferred to give the sword to Vermaak but knew he wanted the commando's arms free in case any trouble kicked off with Zito's crew.

"It's time for me to bid you farewell, Hawke," Kruger said. "You have been a worthy adversary, but I won in the end." He turned to Vermaak. "Get the men out of here!"

Vermaak ordered the others out of the tomb and they began to file out with Bruno and the sword at the front of the line.

Kruger raised the rifle and pointed it at Hawke's face.

He started to leave the tomb, walking backward and never breaking the gun's aim. "When I seal this tomb you'll die in the dark, you bastards. All of you – like desperate, starving rats. They eat each other to stay alive, you know. I wonder what starvation and fear will drive all of *you* too?"

One of Zito's men was last, moving slowly past Hawke and the others, but he wasn't as careful as Kruger and came too close – close enough to strike.

Kruger saw it first and cried out: "Look out you fool!"

But it was too late.

Hawke struck his hand out with the speed and accuracy of a Cobra attacking a mouse. In one fluid movement, he grabbed the man's gun, twisted it from his hand, broke his wrist, and powered his other fist into his jaw. Before anyone knew what was happening, Hawke was diving through the air to the cover of the sarcophagus and firing the weapon at Kruger, yelling at his friends to get down.

Kruger stayed cool, crouching down behind a boulder and tracking Hawke with his rifle. Hawke guessed years hunting big game on illegal safaris had trained the South African to hold his nerve in dangerous situations.

From the cover of the sarcophagus, Hawke craned his neck to check if the others were safe. Lea slid in beside him, and Ryan arrived a second later. Scarlet and Reaper were taking cover behind one of the other cadaver tombs, while Kim and Danny Devlin were safely behind one of the stone support pillars.

That was the good news. The bad news was that Bruno had left the tomb with the sword and Kruger and Vermaak were now jogging out of sight in the tunnel right behind him. Giancarlo Zito and the rest of the Italians were forming a barrier between the ECHO team and the sword.

"We have to stop them, Joe!" said Lea.

"Gotta get past these fucknuts first," Scarlet said.

196

"Cairo's right," Hawke said. "And it looks like Reaper's made a start."

The former French legionnaire was able to exploit his position on the far west of the chamber and was using the support stone columns as cover to inch closer to the Italians. When he was close enough to do some damage, Hawke put down some more cover fire and distracted the enemy, and then the Frenchman attacked.

Lunging forward from the final column, his attack was obscured by the shadows until the last second. He grabbed the nearest man around the neck and Lea winced when he roughly twisted his head and snapped his neck. The terrible sound was covered by the noise of the gunfire, and now Reaper had his weapon – a Heckler & Koch VP9 – and he used it without mercy.

Using Reaper's attack for cover, Hawke and Lea moved forward now until they were in the thick of the battle. They both watched as one of Zito's men turned and fled, but they did not need to take him down: Giancarlo Zito himself raised his gun and fired three times, cutting his own man down.

Hawke seized the moment. He grabbed Zito's arm and leaned into him as he twisted the SIG from his gun hand and brought his elbow up into his face. The Englishman kicked the SIG to Lea who snatched it up while he spun around and smashed his fist into the Italian's face and exploded his nose.

Two men came to their boss's aid, dragging Hawke off and piling punches into him. Hawke fought back, but a bloodied Zito was already staggering to his feet and lurching toward the entrance tunnel. He greedily snatched a submachine gun from the hands of one of his men and turned it on Hawke. He fired at the Englishman, even though it meant hitting the two men who had just saved him.

Hawke saw it coming, hit the dust, and rolled to cover as fast as he could, while above him Zito's insane desire for revenge on the former SBS man peppered his own men with lead and tore them to shreds.

*

Scarlet, Ryan, and Devlin charged forward to the entrance tunnel but Zito was ready and met them with another savage hail of gunfire. They dived for cover as Zito now retreated in the tunnel and fired warning bursts of automatic fire from his submachine gun. The rounds traced through the cave, lit by the gun's muzzle flash in a macabre strobe effect that flashed white up the sides of the rocky walls.

As Zito slowly retreated, most of his men followed, but the last of them decided to have another go, and one of them had Scarlet in his sights. He fired at her, but his gun jammed and that gave the English woman the only chance she ever needed.

She lunged at him and moved into the fighting stance. The man laughed, but his mirth was cut savagely short by a brutal palm strike that smacked into his chin and fired his head back so hard it nearly broke his neck.

"You people are really starting to get on my nerves, fucksqueak," she said.

The man made no reply but took a swing at her.

She dodged the blow and sighed. "I can't decide whether to kill him or date him."

"Why not do both?" Ryan called over. "If it's good enough for the Black Widow, what's stopping you?"

"Really, darling," she purred. "Sexual cannibalism is hardly my thing."

He swung another punch and she twisted as she ducked

backward and avoided it by millimeters. She regained her balance and fired a no-nonsense tiger punch into the man's throat. He pulled his arms up and blocked her punch with his right hand which he now squeezed into a fist in a bid to break her fingers.

Anyone else would have screamed, but Scarlet brought her left leg up into the man's balls and delivered a hefty whack where it hurt most.

The man grunted in pain and released her hand, giving her enough time to grab his hand and turn it around one-eighty, breaking it right out of his wrist socket. The grunt turned into a howl and he fell to his knees to nurse his broken wrist.

"Please," Scarlet said. "Let me help you with your pain."

She snapped out a vicious scissor kick and belted him down into the dirt. She knew he was out cold without even having to look at him. She could tell by the level of resistance she felt when her boot struck the side of his head.

She heard a scream of rage.

She turned to see Lea swinging a piece of rock at arm's length in a wide arc and bringing it crashing down on the side of a goon's head. He grunted and crumpled to the floor, knocked out cold.

Across the chamber, Hawke was struggling in his own battle. She watched as he punched his opponent's jaw, sending him stumbling back over the rubble of the shattered sarcophagus lid and falling onto the floor.

"Had enough yet, dickhead?" he yelled and punched him several more times before picking up one of the slate fragments of the lid and slamming it into his temple. The impact split the skin open and blood gushed out over the rock, but the man was out like a light. Hawke tossed the rock down and pulled himself up to his full height, scanning the chamber for another fight. He locked eyes on Scarlet as he heaved his breath back.

"I think we're done and dusted, darling," she said.

The two of them high-fived and then turned to see the rest of the team waiting at the entrance.

"That's quite a show you two put on," Kim said. "But are you coming or not?"

"Kruger's getting away, Cairo," Ryan shouted. "Have you finished your foreplay or not?"

Scarlet walked casually over to them and dusted her hands off. As she passed Ryan she said, "If I didn't know it would turn you on I'd put you in a nose hold for that."

Ryan laughed and they too shared a high-five. "You're an arsehole, Cairo."

"And I love you too."

Hawke looked at them both as if they were his brother and sister. "Can we move on now, please?"

"After you, darling."

# CHAPTER THIRTY-TWO

Leaving the chaos and carnage of the tomb behind them, they emerged into the bright daylight and for a moment it was just like any other peaceful day. The wind blew through the valley and in the distance they heard the shriek of a red kite cutting through the sunny sky.

"Any sign of the bastards?" Devlin said.

"Right there," said Hawke, pointing at the fleeing party. They were sprinting down a rocky path toward an open field to the west of the main lake. Some men Kruger had ordered to stay with the Jeeps had driven the vehicles around to the field and were waiting there with their engines idling.

Bruno was already at the Jeeps and was clambering into one of them with the sword. When he reached the safety of the vehicles, Kruger looked back, and then leaning on the hood he aimed his hunting rifle and took a few more pot shots.

Hawke and the others scrambled for cover. Even if they'd had their handguns they would have been like peashooters compared with the South African's high-powered hunting rifle and they had no chance against him. The attack came to an end and they peered down to see Kruger had leaned his rifle against the Jeep and was now screaming at someone on his phone.

"Looks like something hasn't gone to plan," Kim said.

Lea sighed. "By the time we get down there, they'll be long gone."

"Horsecrap," Scarlet said. "We can still get them if we

get back to the Highlander, plus we've got more guns there as well. How far are they going to get on these roads?"

They sprinted along the ridge of the caldera and then down the southern slope, past where they had slept the night before. Rounding the side of a low rise, their Highlander was still parked up on the side of the track. They jumped in and Hawke stamped on the throttle, hammering the hybrid SUV up the side of the mountain.

"What the hell are you doing?" Ryan yelled, pointing in the opposite direction. "The road is that way!"

"We're not going on the road."

"What?" Kim said.

"We're going over the top of that ridge and then down the other side," Hawke said. "It's the only way we're going to catch up with Kruger."

Devlin laughed. "And you say I'm the one who's crazy!"

Lea gasped. "But it's almost a vertical drop on the other side, Joe!"

"They weren't kidding when they said whoever sleeps on this mountain either ends up a madman or a poet," Scarlet said. "And you're no poet, darling."

Hawke slammed the Toyota down into third, sighed, and struck the tone of a disappointed father. "Didn't any of you survey the terrain on the way up?"

"Well..." Devlin said.

"Christ," Hawke said. "What about you, SAS?"

"I was too busy filing my nails," Scarlet purred.

"If you *had* you would have seen that to the west of the caldera the mountain begins to recede into a more gradual incline. If we drive along the ridge for a few hundred meters we can turn north and drive down one of the shallower slopes. We'll save fifteen minutes."

Suitably chastened, the team sat in silence while the

former SBS man moved down through the gears and pushed the powerful SUV up the steep southern slope. After some slipping and sliding around on mud and rogue patches of scree, he made the ridge and they were met by a breathtaking view of Dolgellau and the Mawddach River valley stretching away to the west.

"Anyone see Kruger's jeeps yet?" Kim said.

"Not yet," said Lea.

Hawke changed gear. "We need to get further along."

He navigated the Highlander along the ridge of the mountain, but a few minutes into their journey a low rumbling sound started to come from the back of the SUV.

"You hear that?" Kim said.

Hawke checked the rear view. "I hear it."

"What is it?" Ryan asked.

"Is it something wrong with the SUV?" Kim asked.

Reaper shook his head. "It's a chopper."

Devlin turned and looked over his shoulder. "Nothing this side."

"I see it," Kim said. "But don't ask me what it is. They all look the same to me."

Reaper leaned over her and stared into the sky. The wrinkles around his eyes creased up as he squinted into the sun. "Sikorsky Super Stallion."

Hawke glanced over his shoulder to Reaper. "A Super Sta... what the hell?"

"What's one of those?" Kim asked.

"It's usually a military chopper. Heavy cargo lifter."

"Not the sort of hardware you'd think Kruger would pack on his vacation then?" Kim said.

"No," Hawke said with a scowl. "It has kevlar armor plating and the engines are so powerful it can fly nearly two hundred miles per hour despite its colossal size and weight. I'm starting to think Dirk Kruger has a very powerful employer."

"I guess now we know what Kruger was so miffed about back in the field," Scarlet said. "He was expecting the chopper to be there when he came off the mountain."

"So we're in trouble?" Kim asked.

"Oui," Reaper said, but with his usual air of nonchalant indifference. "The Super Stallion has window-mounted fifty cal machine guns and a Gau-21 machine gun on the cargo ramp, and looking at this one..." he leaned over Kim again and looked up. "Oui... c'est exactement ce que je pensais... il y a – sorry – there are some missiles on this bird also."

"What you seeing, Reap?" Scarlet said.

"Maybe Stingers, mais..."

"Looks like we're about to find out, friends," Devlin said. "She's moved over to my side and she's coming down. Looks like she means business."

The Stallion swooped down behind the Highlander as they raced along the ridge of the mountain. Hawke dropped down from fourth to third to increase torque but even over the chunky roar of the Highlander's 3.3-liter V6, the cab of the SUV was now filled with the chilling growl of the Super Stallion's General Electric three free-turbine turboshaft engines.

"Anyone still see Krugs?" Ryan said.

"*Krugs?*" Scarlet said.

"It's my new name for him."

"He's past the town and heading out to the fields beside the river over there. Looks like a rendezvous to meet the chopper after we've been dealt with."

"They're firing!" Scarlet yelled.

Hawke said nothing, but spun the wheel hard to the right and sent the Highlander swerving down the slope. The Stinger screeched past them at the head of a grim, billowing smoke trail. Lea watched with fear as the

204

missile ripped into the ridge and exploded in a massive
fireball, blasting chunks of mud and rock in all directions.
One fist-sized rock slammed into the Highlander's
windshield and left a thick spider-web fracture in the
middle of the glass.

Lea gasped and shielded her eyes.

Hawke turned his head but kept his eyes on the slope.
The slope's incline was too steep here and was sucking
them down into the valley again. He doubted he could
keep them safe if the SUV started to head straight down
the slope. As they gathered speed he would be unable to
brake or turn without flipping them over. That would
make them easier for the Stallion to hunt, so he decided
to turn the Highlander to the left and head back up to the
ridge.

He slammed down into third again and the engine
roared. "Some cover fire would be nice."

"You think this Glock is going to take down a Super
Stallion?" Scarlet said.

"I think the pilot is human and your firing on him will
force a reaction."

Scarlet sighed and pushed down her window. She
pulled the gun from her holster and climbed out of the rear
window of the SUV until her entire upper body was
outside and the wind was whipping her hair across her
face. She cursed Hawke and started to fire at the cargo
chopper.

Reaper pushed down Kim's window and followed suit,
firing his weapon up at the chopper. Kim jumped and
lifted her hands to her ears as the Frenchman discharged
the firearm right next to her face.

Hawke was right, and the Super Stallion took evasive
action, flying up and to the left. Swinging out over the
valley now it went full circle and prepared to make

another run on the Highlander.

Lea leaned her head to look past the smashed windshield. "We're running out of ridge, Joe!"

"I'm on it!"

The Stallion was behind them again, but this time keeping its distance. "They're staying out of the range of the handguns, Joe!" Scarlet said.

"Incoming!" Reaper yelled. He pulled his head back in the window.

Scarlet climbed back inside. "Five seconds, Josiah, and we're a thousand pieces!"

Hawke checked the mirror and saw this time they were firing the missile to their right to stop them from taking cover down on the slope.

But the left was a steep drop down to the bottom of the mountain.

And then the Stinger was on them.

Hawke spun the wheel to the left to avoid a direct hit and sent the Highlander scrambling over to the edge of the ridge. His plan was to try and keep the SUV from tumbling over by constantly steering the vehicle to the right and fighting gravity until the danger was past, but it struck much closer than he'd anticipated and he had underestimated the awesome power of the Stinger.

The Highlander tipped onto its two left wheels and they all knew that their lives were now in the hands of the gods.

"Put your windows down!" Hawke yelled.

As they tipped over onto their side, Lea screamed and held onto the sides of her seat. In the rear seats the rest of the team clung on for their lives, and up front, Hawke struggled against hope to get the steering wheel lined up in the right place for when the Highlander finally crashed back down on its wheels.

It turned over and over, partially crumpling the

reinforced roof in over their heads and throwing them about as if they were in an industrial washing machine. The glass in the windshield exploded into their faces like a grenade as the roof collapsed, but thanks to Hawke's quick thinking the other windows were open, and the glass was safely inside the doors. After what seemed like forever the wrecked Toyota came to a stop on the shores of the lake.

The ECHO team immediately crawled from the smoking wreckage of the trashed Highlander and checked for injuries. They had gotten away lightly, with only a few bruises and cuts among them. Worse was the damage to their professional pride as they watched Kruger's Jeep Cherokee screech to a halt in an open field down by the Mawddach River. The Super Stallion swooped down and landed a few dozen yards further west, its powerful rotors blasting the surrounding grass flat as the South African ran to it and disappeared inside its side door with Zito and the other men following a few paces behind. This time none of them looked back.

"So now they have the Sword of Fire," Ryan said.

"And they murdered Kloos in cold blood," said Kim.

Lea sighed. "We're going to need Lund again. We need to trace that chopper in a hurry." She pulled her phone out and made a call to the enigmatic Dane.

Scarlet leaned against the wrecked Highlander and lit a cigarette. "Look on the bright side," she said.

"And what would that be?" Hawke asked.

"You've broken a new record, Joe."

"Have I?"

She nodded and blew out a cloud of smoke. "Not even Jeremy Clarkson could inflict this much carnage on a Toyota."

"Funny," he said.

"So what now, Batman?" Kim said, looking at Hawke.

"We wait for this," he said, pointing his chin over at Lea, who was still on the phone. She ended the call and walked over to them.

"What's the deal?" Hawke said.

"The Stallion is owned by a man named Pavel Horak, and the scheduled flight path takes it back to a mansion he owns just outside of London."

"So that's who's pulling Krugsie's strings," Ryan said.

"A mansion?" said Kim.

Lea nodded. "Uh-huh. Apparently, it's called Woodrow House. This Horak guy has owned it for years. Lund says he's an eccentric Czech billionaire. He also says there's some kind of terror threat going on in London. This has to be linked."

"Wait a minute – you mean *the* Pavel Horak?" Ryan said. "As in *Sir* Pavel Horak?"

Lea shrugged her shoulders. "I never heard of him so he's just like any other Pavel Horak to me."

Ryan sighed. "Pavel Horak is one of the country's leading software magnates and to say he's eccentric is the understatement of the century. He's totally crazy."

Another shrug from Lea. "I don't care if he's the Easter buggering Bunny. Looks like Dirk Kruger is staying at his place before he flies out of the UK so that makes him a legitimate target."

"What the hell does a man like Pavel Horak want with the idol?" Reaper said.

Hawke said, "That's just what I was thinking."

"Wait a minute," Ryan said. "I remember now – Pavel Horak was in the news recently because they're about to take his knighthood away over some kind of financial scandal."

Kim frowned. "You think that's enough to drive him to commit some kind of terrorist atrocity in London?"

"That's a strategic concern," Hawke said. "We're in the field, focussing on the tactical. Lea, is Lund going to get us some back-up?"

Lea shook her head and sighed. "As far as getting the authorities involved, Lund says it's a big no. He says there's no way he can run security checks before we get there. If we alert the police or anti-terror units we might be alerting the enemy. Horak has deep pockets and long arms."

"Fuck that," Scarlet said. She whipped out her phone and punched some numbers into the pad. "We need back-up and I know just the man to call." She walked away from the group as she started to speak into the phone.

"Does Lund know how Horak and Kruger are planning on getting the sword out of the country?" Hawke asked.

"Horak does a lot of business in London and his preferred method of travel is a helicopter. He has a hangar at the property with a small collection of choppers there. Lund says there's only one flight scheduled for today and that's an AgustaWestland belonging to Horak himself."

"Sounds like that's the escape plan then," Ryan said.

"When?" Hawke asked.

"Just after midday," Lea said.

Scarlet returned and slipped her phone into her pocket. "Sorted. An old mate of mine from the Regiment has agreed to join our madness. Hope he doesn't make you feel like some sort of big girl, Joe."

Hawke opened his mouth to reply, but Scarlet cut him off: "So what's the plan?"

"We think our arms dealer friend is going to try and leave the country with this Horak bloke. They have an AgustaWestland," Lea said.

"When?"

"Midday."

Reaper glanced at his watch and shrugged. "We can do it if we hurry."

Kim laughed. "When do you crazies ever do anything that isn't in a hurry?"

"True," Scarlet said. "And that includes Ryan in bed... so Lea says," she added hastily.

Hawke rolled his eyes and looked at the Toyota. "Looks like we're going to need some new wheels to get back to the airport though."

# CHAPTER THIRTY-THREE

## Berkshire

Scarlet was up front in the Lexus LX. They had hired it after landing at London Heathrow Airport and even kept a straight face when they had signed the form promising to bring it back in one piece.

Following a round of jokes about Hawke's driving back in Snowdonia, Vincent Reno was at the wheel, and now they were turning off the M4 and heading into the Berkshire countryside. If the Google Earth images were anything to go by, Woodrow House was a large Georgian mansion nestled in around twelve acres of prime Home Counties real estate and just a stone's throw from Windsor Castle.

For Scarlet, this was as close to home as she could get. Not only was Richard Eden's country house close by, but so was her own family home. She closed her eyes and the darkness took her back there once again. The sunlight shining on the bricks on the side of their sixteenth-century manor house, her father's smile as he walked a tray of drinks out to the shade of an ash tree, her mother cursing as she dropped one of her beloved books and lost the page. Her brother Spencer playing with his toys on the croquet lawn.

All of that was rubbed out in less than a minute by unknown gunmen.

They had stormed into the peace of their house and cut Sir Roger and Lady Phillipa Sloane dead like stray dogs

211

while Scarlet hid in the wardrobe like the terrified little girl she was at the time. Now her parents were in their graves and her brother was Sir Spencer Sloane after inheriting his father's title and the manor.

She realized her eyes were squeezed shut so hard they nearly hurt and she opened them to relieve the tension. She felt a tear running from her left eye and turned to look out at the countryside as she dried it away. She didn't want anyone else to see it. She would kill the bastards who murdered her parents if it took her entire life to find out who did it and why, but she would do it alone. The bloodlust she felt coursing through her heart could only be slaked if she kept this personal and avenged her parents herself.

"Everything okay, Cairo?"

It was Hawke. She felt his hand on her shoulder. Relegated to the back seat after the mountain fiasco, he was sitting directly behind her. She knew he had seen the tear, but he had kept it vague. Just between them.

"I'm righter than rain, darling – et toi?"

Hawke smiled. "Keen to get on, you know how it is."

"What about you, Donovan?" Scarlet asked.

"Just about ready to ram that Sword of Fire right up Dirk Kruger's arse, to be honest."

"Amen to that," Ryan said. "I still owe that bastard for kidnapping me."

She gazed out the window as Reaper raced the Lexus SUV along the narrow country lanes. It was the same unspoiled countryside she remembered from her childhood – chestnut trees, shire ponies, gentle hills.

She was knocked from her memories by the gruff nicotine-streaked voice of Vincent Reno. "We're here."

Ahead of them, parked in the entrance to a field was a battered Land Rover with dried mud caked over the wheel arches and up the doors. As they pulled up in front of it, a lean, tanned man with his arms covered in tattoos casually slid out of the four-wheel-drive and tossed the stub of a roll-up cigarette into a puddle.

"Bugger me," Hawke said. "If it ain't Eddie Donald!"

"Who's he?" Ryan asked.

"He's our back-up," Scarlet said. "And an old friend of mine."

Hawke laughed. "And mine. Good call, Cairo."

"Anything we should know about him?" Kim said.

"Call him Mack and don't get on the wrong side of him," Scarlet said. "He's the most experienced soldier I've ever known. I met him on Operation Dagger Strike a long time ago. He's solid gold, darling – but you wouldn't like him when he's angry."

Hawke pushed down the window as Mack sidled over to the Lexus. The Scotsman leaned his head inside and gave them all a toothy grin. The stink of stale tobacco wafted into the SUV on his breath as he spoke. "Was wondering when you big Jessies was gonnae turn up."

Hawke shook his hand and Scarlet blew him a kiss. "Your presence is appreciated, Mack," she said.

"Ah, fuck off," he said. "Anything for an old friend."

Hawke made the introductions and then got straight to business. "Anything to report, Mack?"

The tough Glaswegian shrugged his shoulders as he rolled up another cigarette. "No traffic in or out since the chopper landed. They're all up at the big house having a high-old time."

"Let's get in there then," Hawke said. "Word is there's increased chatter about a terror attack and my money's on this Horak."

"We're pretty close to Windsor Castle as well," Lea said.

Mack stepped up on the running board on Hawke's

213

side of the Lexus and banged the roof. "Come on then, bawbags – let's do this."

Unable to translate the Glaswegian, Reaper gave Hawke and Scarlet a confused look but hit the throttle all the same, and moments later they were driving along another narrow country lane that formed the estate's western perimeter. It was marked by an old six-foot-high stone wall with trespass warning signs pinned here and there along the way. Approaching the gatehouse, Reaper slowed the vehicle while Scarlet pulled out her gun and lowered it out of sight down by the handbrake.

Reaper pulled up at the gatehouse and a rotund man with mousy hair and a loosened tie around his neck strolled over to the Lexus. In his right hand was a two-way radio, and he didn't seem to like the look of the tattooed man hanging onto the side of the vehicle.

"Can I help?" he said. He was looking at Mack, but then Scarlet pushed down her window, winked at him, and pulled the gun into his face. "Drop the radio and put your hands up, darling."

\*

Lexi Zhang's flight landed at Beijing Capital Airport just before dusk. She had watched the mountains north of the city melt into the sprawling capital with total disinterest as the aircraft banked and prepared to land. She dealt with the customs officials with the same detached attitude and when she climbed into the cab she was just about ready to fly away again.

Tonight her heart was like the setting sun. It knew the day had passed and the night was beginning, but for the sun, the new dawn was just hours away. Lexi had a feeling her own night would last much longer. The dying rays lit the busy freeways in rosy reds and glowing ambers, and above it, all the stark steel and glass skyscrapers of her home city stretched up into the purple twilight.

Black and white. Yin and yang. Darkness and light. Her mind was built to see the world this way, and it tortured her. Her father was good. He had never harmed anyone, working hard his whole life for a pittance. He had gone without any comfort to send her to Oxford – but what had she done with it?

An assassin for the Chinese Government. A hired killer who lied to her parents every day about her true nature. A woman who seemed to betray everyone she ever loved and who ever loved her. Even Hawke... perhaps that betrayal had been the worst of all. She shook it from her mind. A problem like that wouldn't be resolved while crawling in a cab through Wangjing Park. That would require some special attention in the future.

But she could settle things with her parents right now. Before the sun rose again she could make things right with both of them. Come clean; start again with a blank slate. These thoughts did not come easily after so many years of deceit, but she had always known it was something she had to do while there was still time. When her mother told her that her father was dying she knew what she had to do.

The cab crawled on. She looked at her watch and sighed. She was tired, and she wanted to rest. Her mind wandered to the ECHO team again. She had said goodbye to them in the Netherlands just a few hours ago but it seemed like an eternity.

At least she would be home soon, she thought.

Home and safe.

*

When President Jack Brooke turned to the crowd gathered outside Westminster Hall and waved goodbye, everyone knew he had pulled off a successful state visit. Alex watched him as he ducked his head and climbed inside the Presidential limo, took off his jacket, and loosened his tie.

"You did a great job, Dad."

"Thanks, Darling, but the people will be the judge of that. We still have a whole bucket of crap to sort out in North Korea."

Todd sat down opposite him, followed by Agent McGee and the other agent. "Wheels up in less than an hour."

"Thanks, Todd," Brooke said and turned to his daughter. "We'll be home before you know it."

But Alex knew that Washington DC was no longer her home and that she had to break the news to her father that she wanted to rejoin ECHO. She knew that meant a Category Five Shitstorm heading her way, but there was nothing she could do about it.

As soon as they got back, she would tell him she wanted to leave DC and go back to the life she had started to carve out for herself with her friends.

Brooke scratched his jaw and yawned. "What's the flight time, Todd?"

"A little of over eight hours, Mr. President, and if we're lucky..."

Todd stopped talking to take an urgent call. Alex and her father both saw the young man's face visibly pale. When he cut the call he spoke in a rapid but measured way. "That was my contact in the CIA. She just heard from MI5 that there's new chatter pointing to a terror target somewhere in London, sir. The Houses of Parliament, Buckingham Palace, and Windsor Castle are all named as potential targets and on lockdown. We're on full alert and the British authorities have increased our protection as well."

"All right," the senior Secret Service man said bluntly. "We're out of here." Without discussing anything with the President, he leaned forward and spoke to the driver. "Get us to Cowpuncher as fast as possible." Cowpuncher was their codename for Air Force One.

"Dammit all," Brooke said. "Any idea who's behind it?"

"No, sir, Mr. President."

"All right, let's go."

The motorcade pulled away from the ancient building and made its way back to the airport, flanked either side by a host of British police officers on motorbikes.

# CHAPTER THIRTY-FOUR

With Mack still hanging onto the side, Reaper cruised the Lexus up the winding drive and slowly the mansion came into view. It was a large honey-colored stone building covered in ivy and flanked by various outbuildings and what looked like stables.

"All right, earpieces in everyone," Hawke said. "If we get split up we need to stay in contact." He pulled his out of his pocket and set it up under his shirt and the others followed suit.

"Are you sure you sorted the security guard?" Kim asked Scarlet.

"I know how to incapacitate a man, darling."

Ryan turned and looked at Kim. "True story. Just ask Jack Camacho – his dick's still in a sling as we.... ow!"

Scarlet tweaked Ryan's ear and pulled his head down so she could whisper in his ear, but she did it loud enough for all to hear. "I already told you, Jackie Boy's on a covert CIA mission. Now be a good boy and stop being so silly before I put your dick in a sling, and in the nastiest possible way."

The car erupted into howls of laughter, but then Reaper brought everyone around with a sobering observation. "We have company."

Hawke looked up and saw several off-road bikes were now racing across the airfield in their direction.

Kim sighed. "I thought you said you handled the guard?"

"And I thought I told you that I did?"

"It's just a protocol failure," Hawke said. "I'm

guessing the gatehouse guard has to radio through all approaching vehicles to on-site security, so now they want to know just who the hell we are. Let's keep this under control."

"I think that ship has sailed," Lea said. "They've got guns."

"Looks like Kruger's not taking any chances," said Devlin.

Ryan nodded sagely. "Either that or this Horak dude doesn't pay his TV license and thinks we're BBC inspectors."

Lea rolled her eyes, but it was good to hear Ryan relaxing and making his usual idiotic comments. Camacho's absence had given him plenty of room to make gags at Scarlet's expense, and now this let her see that there was still some light in there.

"You need pump-action shotguns for those license guys?" Kim said with a smirk.

"Here they come," Reaper said.

Hawke frowned and reached into his bag for his handgun. "And the guy in the lead has just chambered a cartridge on that pump-action."

The first rider fired at the Lexus and Reaper swerved to dodge the impact but part of the shot sprayed up the front-left side of the windshield and instantly shattered half of it.

He spun the SUV off the drive and plowed across the lavish lawns to the south of the house while the bike turned back in a wide circle, chewing up chunks of mud and spitting it out in a high arc in its wake.

"One o' you tadgers give me a gun?" Mack yelled.

Hawke pushed his window down, handed a gun to the Scotsman, and returned fire, but the rider took evasive action and dodged the incoming fire.

"Would you like me to do that?" Scarlet said.

Before Hawke could reply, Cairo Sloane climbed halfway out of her window and loosed a savage volley of sidearm fire from her weapon.

"No, thank you," Hawke muttered. "I've got it covered."

Swerving to avoid Scarlet's rounds, the rider slid another cartridge in the pump-action with a one-handed slide while still deftly steering the bike back to them.

Hawke was impressed by it, so too bad he'd probably have to kill him to stop him. He raised his gun and fired again, and again he missed and so did Scarlet. As he cursed another two bikes zoomed into view, ridden by more armed men. They raced ahead of the SUV and flanked the leading rider.

"Bloody fantastic," Hawke said. "Now there's three of them."

Reaper was in hot pursuit, and they were racing toward what looked like a giant hedgerow. "Look out for the hedge, Reap!" Lea yelled.

"It's not a hedge," Ryan said.

"Damn fuckin' right, it ain't!" yelled Mack, and peeled off another few rounds.

"Well, it sure ain't no goddam wall, Ryan!" Kim said.

"It's a maze," he said casually. "It's the biggest maze in Europe."

"Goodness me, isn't that something?" The sarcasm in Scarlet's voice was heavy.

"Yes, it is. The central part of the maze is hundreds of years old," Ryan said. "It was built in the late seventeenth century. Over the years various owners added to it but it was Horak who bloated it up to the current monster when he bought the place in the mid-eighties."

"You really are a mine of totally useless information," Scarlet said, turning to look over her shoulders at the riders. "Where do you get all this crap?"

"It's called *reading*," he said, stretching the last word out as long as he could. "Ever heard of it?"

"Sorry, did you say something Ryan?" she said. "It's just that all I could hear was the whine of a wasp. Or was that your voice?"

"Man," Kim said. "To think you guys saved the United States..."

"It's worrying, no?" Reaper said with a broad, toothy grin.

"Oh yeah," Kim said. "Especially if you're a sane person who's trapped in some freaking English manor with them."

"Don't be like that, darling," Scarlet said. "Not everyone was born with a pole up their arse."

Kim turned on Scarlet. "I'm sorry?"

"Let's face it," the former SAS captain continued, "you are rather serious."

"How is that a problem?" Kim said, astonished.

"No problem," Scarlet said. "Just that the only serious thing about all the Special Forces I've ever known has been their sense of humor."

"Forgive me if I don't get your *humor*," Kim said.

"You're forgiven," said Scarlet.

"There is one funny British joke," Kim said.

"And what's that?"

"Your navy. What was it now – one aircraft carrier without any aircraft. Oh my."

Scarlet smirked, determined not to be baited. "You're quite right, we're not in the same league as you Yanks. I especially admire your writers. What was it Mark Twain said – God invented war so Americans could learn geography?"

Ryan laughed out loud and confirmed the quotation.

# ROB JONES

"This is true," Reaper said.

"All right," Hawke said. "Enough of the nationalist dick-waving."

Scarlet and Kim turned on him. "Kinda hard for either of us to do *that*, wouldn't you say, Hawke?"

"You know what I mean, *ladies*. We're all on the same side here, remember that."

The riders broke away like a fighter jet display team and came back around the Lexus in three giant arcs.

"They're coming in again, Joe," Lea said.

"What are we going to do?" Kim said.

Devlin grinned. "We're going to lose them."

"In the middle of the world's most expansive croquet lawn?" Ryan said.

"Nope," the Irishman drawled. "In the middle of the world's biggest maze, right, Mr. Reaper?"

"We draw them in, and then we hunt them down," the Frenchman said.

"You could have told me!" Mack said and leaped off the Lexus with seconds to spare.

Reaper smashed the massive Lexus through the outer hedge of the maze. The weight and momentum of the heavy-duty SUV were enough to easily rip through the outer wall, but then the next few hedges gave too much resistance and they ground to a halt halfway to the center of the maze.

"Everyone out!" Hawke yelled.

Behind them, the riders were now racing over to the hole in the maze wall as fast as they could go. The sun flashed on their helmets and shotgun barrels as they drew closer.

Mack jogged over to them and laughed. "Not had this much fun in years."

"Into the maze!" Hawke said.

The maze was billed as the country's biggest, but no

222

one ever got to enjoy it because it was closed to the general public. The entire thing was nothing more than a monumental folly maintained by the eccentric Horak to entertain his high-powered friends when they visited the house. The only way it could be viewed was by looking on Google Earth, which is what Lea was trying to access right now as they sprinted through the crazy labyrinth.

They turned left and cut down a winding passageway that took them ever deeper into the maze. "I hope this ends better than it did for Jack Nicholson in The Shining," Ryan said.

"At least it's not snowing," Kim said. "But yeah..."

"Maybe," Hawke said. Like the others, the high summer sun was making him sweat through his shirt as he pounded his way along the path. "If we had snow we could follow their tracks."

Kim frowned as she loaded her gun. "Or they could follow ours."

They heard the bikes' engines a few meters to the right, but there was no way through. The hedge was a meter thick and full of dense thorns. "Maybe we should leave them," Ryan said. "Just go up to the house."

To Hawke, this was the worse thing they could do. "No – never let the enemy get behind you. We don't want them on our tail when we go up to the house. We'll just end up fighting on two fronts. We're on these guys now and we don't stop till we take them down."

The passageway arrived at a central junction where several other paths came together. "We're at a vortex," Ryan said. "This is where the spiral we were following was leading. This damned place must have been created by Daedalus himself!"

"Just what I was thinking," Scarlet said.

"Piss off, Cairo."

"By the way, is there going to be any loot coming our way for doing this?" Scarlet asked, totally ignoring Ryan. "I mean, how much is this sword worth on the black market?"

"You and your bank account," Kim said.

"Hey, I like a bit of OA as much as the next gal," Scarlet said. "I'm not doing this bollocks for shits and grins, baby."

"OA?" Ryan said.

"Offensive action," Mack said.

"Keep it down," Hawke said. "I hear something."

"Me too," said Devlin. The Irishman silently raised his arm and pointed to the hedge right behind him.

Hawke nodded. "They're backtracking."

"This way," Lea said, staring at her phone. "This leads to the center of the maze."

They walked along another long pathway and then they turned a corner to arrive in the heart of the maze.

"Oh, you have to be *kidding* me," Scarlet said.

She had her hands on her hips and now raised an arm to point at the vast array of statues of various Greek and Roman goddesses that populated the center of the maze. "Are these guys trying to tell us something or what?"

Mack frowned. "What's the big joke?"

"And there's Poseidon," Hawke said with a grin. The tall marble statue was in the dead center of the display beside a giant koi pond, and his metal trident shone in the sun. Hawke sprinted over and stood next to it.

"I'm sorry, Joe Hawke," Lea said. "But if you think this is the right time for a photo then you're crazier than I thought."

"No," Hawke said patiently. "I don't want a photo of me and old Poseidon here, I want his trident."

Hawke pulled the trident out of the statue's grip and weighed it in his hands. "Poor old Zaugg," he muttered to

224

himself.

"What the buggering fuck are you pissing about with that thing for?" Scarlet said.

Kim gave her a look and rolled her eyes. "Language, dear."

Scarlet slowly raised her middle finger and waved it in the American's face. "Bite me."

"Hey!"

"I know what he wants it for," Ryan said.

"Moi aussi," Reaper said.

The bikes were closer now. It sounded like two were to the south and a lone rider was to the north but closer. Hawke carefully tracked the progress of the lone rider and then jogged over to the hedge wall that corresponded closest with the sound of the bike's raspy engine. He got down on his knees and stared through the base of the hedge and then climbed back up to his feet. "He's coming along here."

"I told you he wants to be Indiana Jones," Devlin said.

Hawke's response was to hold his nerve and then plunge the trident through the hedge, ramming the end of the metal bar into the bike's front wheel.

No one saw what happened, but they all heard the desperate whine of the engine as the bike flew through the air and then a deep, metallic crunching sound as it smashed back to earth. Hawke peered through the hedge again and confirmed the rider was dead. "Broken neck," was all he said.

"Two down and one to go," Reaper said.

Their celebrations were cut short when they heard the other two bikes turn around and head in their direction again. Worse, a Viking Side-by-Side vehicle filled with armed men was now racing down the slope up at the house and heading toward the maze.

225

"Looks like we're surrounded," Kim said. "What do we do now?"

Mack checked his gun. "Aye, the lassie asks a good question."

"What we always do," Lea said. "We fight for survival."

# CHAPTER THIRTY-FIVE

The first of the riders burst into the center of the maze and opened fire with his shotgun. The round blasted a chunk out of Poseidon's shoulder and showered Hawke and Lea with a cloud of dust.

"He's keen as mustard, this bloke," Hawke said.

Lea rolled her eyes. "He's a proper arsehole, is what he is."

"You can say that again," Mack said.

The rider also knew a thing or two about how to handle a bike, and he deftly spun it around in the grass. Turning it south, he aimed for the cover of a trellis that was connecting some of the Roman statues at the other end of the maze's heart.

Devlin was closest, hidden behind a statue of Venus. As the bike flashed past him, the Irishman acted in a heartbeat and launched himself at the rider and knocked him clean off the bike. The machine revved wildly and slammed into the koi pond, and then the two men rolled to a stop at the base of one of the hedge walls, engaged in a bitter fist fight.

Reaper moved to help him, but Devlin handled things fast. He raised the man's head off the ground by gripping his helmet and then twisted it hard to the right, breaking his neck. The rider's lifeless body slumped down to the concrete paving as Devlin dusted his hands and ran back over to the others.

"Two down and one to go," he said.

"Plus the Goonies over there in the Viking," Hawke

said.

"Plus the Goonies, sure," Devlin repeated.

The Viking SSV was almost at the maze, but now the final rider appeared. Seeing his dead associate he turned and disappeared into another maze pathway, but Scarlet saw a way to head him off.

She grabbed the trident and sprinted to the far corner of the central section where she slipped out into the pathway. She waited for a second until the man turned the corner, and when he did he was met with the trident's prongs hard in his chest.

Knocked clean off his bike, he hit the grass with the trident still sticking out of his body. He howled and grunted as he wrenched the metal spikes from his chest, but Scarlet was in no mood for mercy.

He got to his knees and raised two palms of surrender, but she lashed out, kicking the wounded man in the stomach and sending him flying into the hedge. He howled again in triple agony at the force of the kick, the trident wound, and the thorns now tearing into his back. Another kick to the face sent him off to dreamland and she headed back to the others.

When she got there, she found the Viking was parked up in the trail of destruction just behind the Lexus and the goons inside were engaged in a full-scale brawl with the ECHO team. Worse, smoke was spiraling up from the Lexus's engine compartment and the tires were all blown out.

Lea was fighting a woman, and expertly blocking a rapid succession of strikes from her. She was good, but Lea was better and for several seconds the two of them took each other's blows and bobbed and weaved in the chaos of the maze. Their macabre dance of death was brought to a swift conclusion when Devlin threw a knife into the woman's back.

It thudded into the muscle, hard and deep and it was obvious that the blade had pierced her heart when she fell onto her knees with blood frothing around her mouth.

"I had her, Danny!" Lea said angrily.

"Just lending a hand, Lea."

One of the men rushed Scarlet, hooking her foot out from under her and making her tumble backward. She reached out for something to grab but he finished the job by powering a palm strike into her solar plexus.

She hit the dirt floor of the maze with a thud. She was on her back and vulnerable to attack, but just as the man lunged toward her, the tall broad figure of Reaper appeared behind him. His shovel-like hands gripped the man by his shoulders and spun him around as if he was a child.

"Ça va?" he said and rounded the question off with an eye-watering uppercut punch. It crashed into his face, immediately dislocating his jaw and shattering several of his teeth.

Scarlet winced. "Ouch. That's gotta be like getting hit in the face by a massive French legionnaire – oh, wait..."

The man was on all fours now, spitting teeth and foamy blood from his mouth. He began to stagger to his feet but Scarlet leaped up and kicked him in the face. She pulled her leg back just as the now-unconscious man's body slumped into the side of the hedge. He slid down to the dirt, the thorns scratching deep lines into his back as he went.

She got herself back together and saw Hawke and Lea crossing the center of the maze, they were followed moments later by Ryan, Devlin, and Kim. Across the other side of the maze's heart, Mack had wrenched a club from the statue of Heracles and was screaming at one of the men from the Viking. "You asked for it, ya tadger, so you're gonnae get it!" He swung the club and knocked the man out with one blow, then strolled over to the others with his hands in his pockets.

"Aww, the family's all together again," Scarlet said. "The Viking crew?"

Hawke smiled. "You and Mack just knocked the last ones out."

"Good job," Kim said.

"Always a pleasure," Scarlet said, kicking one of the unconscious men in the balls.

Devlin winced. "He's gonna love waking up to that."

Hawke and the other men shared a look of understanding, then Scarlet turned to the other unconscious man and gave him the same treatment. "There," she said, dusting her hands off. "They can share the pain, and you know what they say: a problem shared is a problem halved."

"You are literally unbelievable," Kim said.

"Oh, she's real, all right," Ryan muttered. "Just ask that bloke there when he wakes up to find a couple of watermelons in his pants."

"Just not funny," Kim said. "It's a British thing, right?"

They climbed into the Viking SSV, and with Hawke at the wheel they raced up the smooth slope leading away from England's largest maze. Up ahead was Horak's enormous ivy-clad Georgian mansion.

And Dirk Kruger.

"So how are we going to play this?" said Lea.

"We initiate Secret Plan A," Hawke said.

"You mean to burst in and just start shooting and punching with minimum finesse and zero tactics?" Scarlet said.

Devlin chuckled and Ryan rolled his eyes.

Hawke sighed. "That was the *secret* plan. How did you know about it?"

She shrugged. "Just a lucky guess."

Up close, the property was even more impressive than it had looked from the western edge of the estate. There was a main house with two large wings and jumbled around them were several outbuildings, including what they now saw was definitely a stable block and also what looked like some kind of studio. The honey-colored Cotswold stone reflected the heat of the summer's day and the sun flashed on the lead-lined windows.

Hawke pulled the Viking up on the gravel drive and killed the engine. "So this is how the other half lives!"

"Sadly yes," Scarlet said. "This house has only got three stories. Spence's has five."

Hawke gave her a look but made no reply. After everything she had gone through as a girl, it was good she could joke about her family. Holding onto one of the roll bars he pulled himself out of the Viking and his boots crunched on the gravel. The others joined him and they stared up at the house.

"Doesn't look like the fracas back at the maze caused too much consternation," Scarlet said.

Devlin looked at her. "Fracas?"

"The bunfight back there."

"Don't count on it," Hawke said. He stepped in the flower bed running around the base of the main house and cupped his hands against a window. "If they're around the back they wouldn't have heard a little upset like that."

"A little upset!" Kim said. "You guys are crazy."

Cupping their hands against the lead-lined windows they saw the typical English country house with oak-paneled doors and a wall of library books.

"I keep expecting Lara Croft to swing into the picture on one of those chandeliers," Ryan said, staring up at the ceiling.

"Expecting, or fantasizing?" Scarlet purred, giving him a seedy wink.

"Give it a rest, Cairo," he said. "But yeah, fantasizing."

Suddenly they all saw a blue flash emanating from one of the downstairs windows in the west wing.

"Holy shit – the sword!" Kim said.

"All right," Hawke said. "Time for us to crash this party. Kruger and Zito and the rest of their baboons are in this house, and so is Horak. They may be coercing him, or he may be complicit. We also know they're planning on escaping using the chopper, so we're going to need to split up. One team goes into the house, gets Kruger and the sword, and the other heads over to the hangar compound and makes damned sure none of the helos are taking off today."

"Great plan," Scarlet said. "Except when was the last time anything we ever did went to plan?"

Hawke gave her a look and said, "Lea, Reaper, and Mack with me, and Scarlet can lead Kim, Ryan, and Danny on the sabotage mission."

"Let's go smash some skulls!" Scarlet said.

"Did anyone ever tell you that you have a serious attitude problem?" Devlin said.

"Not more than once, honey."

The Irishman laughed and shook his head.

It was time to smash skulls.

# CHAPTER THIRTY-SIX

As Hawke led Lea, Reaper, and Mack into the ground floor of the mansion, they all heard a strange, electrical crackling sound and then another bright blue flash. It was followed by the sound of a man's terrified screams.

"Through here!" Hawke said, darting toward a door on their left.

They entered the room they had seen from the outside but there was no sign of any flashing light or sword. Then, a section of the wall containing the bookshelves slid to the right and revealed Vermaak and an Italian. The bookshelves were on a fake wall and now both men stood in an open doorway leading into another previously hidden section of the drawing-room. The South African was holding a commando knife in his hand and the Italian was armed with two pistols.

"Well, howdy Tex!" Lea said.

Vermaak scowled at her. "Shut the fuck up, bitch."

Everyone stared at Hawke, looking for his leadership, but there was nothing he could do so he turned to Lea and gave her an apologetic smile.

"Guns out of holsters and on the floor," Vermaak said. "And then raise your hands to whatever god you choose."

Hawke pulled his Glock from the holster and lowered it down to the large Persian rug on the floor, and Lea and the others followed a second later. "You really are starting to get on my tits, Vermaak," he said.

"I'm glad to hear it, you bastard," Vermaak sneered. He lifted the blade and pointed its tip at Hawke's face.

"You and this knife have a date with destiny, Pom. I was going to retire this week – make this my last job. But now I know you're on the guest list I've decided to stick it out a bit longer."

"Please, not in front of my girlfriend," Hawke said.

Vermaak scowled. "You think you're so damned funny, Hawke. You always did, even back in the day when you were just an ordinary soldier. But now you've met your match." He tossed the knife into the air. It spun around and he snatched it back with a commanding swipe. "I'd kill you right now, but unfortunately Mr. Kruger has other plans for you and the rest of these losers."

"How kind."

"If it was up to me I'd gut you with this blade and let you bleed out on the floor before shooting your friends down like the stray dogs they are."

"I'd pay good money to see you try," Mack growled.

"I think I'd plump for meeting your Mr. Kruger if that's the alternative," Lea said.

"Keep the hands high and get over here, bitch," the South African commando said. He walked to Lea and pushed the gun in her face. "You want to die today?"

Lea kept her mouth shut, and Hawke used the moment while Vermaak was distracted to remove his earpiece and slide it down into his shirt. Reaper and Mack saw him and did the same.

Vermaak walked away from Lea, smiled coldly at them, and raised the pistol in their faces. "For you, the war is over."

*

Scarlet Sloane led Kim, Ryan, and Danny Devlin around the back of the stables and over toward the hangar compound. They followed a narrow trail cutting through a small copse of chestnut trees and then emerged once again much nearer the site. Now she could see a low jumble of red-brick buildings and a small helicopter hangar beside them. Inside the hangar was a Bell 204 and outside were the AgustaWestland and a Eurocopter.

"That'll be our place then," Devlin said, rubbing his hands together.

"And that looks like Kruger's escape plan," said Ryan. He pointed at the AgustaWestland on the tarmac outside the hangar. Its engine was idling and some men were milling around it. A few meters behind a man was servicing the Bell 204 helicopter just inside the hangar.

"Let's get on it," Scarlet said. "Then we can get back to Hawke."

They made their way to the hangar but then everything changed. One of the men in an office saw them and ordered an attack. The next thing they knew someone was firing grenades at them from a handheld launcher. The first went wide but the second caught them before they could take cover and blasted all four of them into the air.

Ryan landed on the grass at the side of the airfield, but Scarlet, Kim, and Devlin had been too close to the blast and were now sprawled out in the sun, as lifeless as three corpses. With more incoming grenades Ryan scrambled over to them. They were all alive but out cold. The shock wave had knocked them for six, and now another grenade exploded right beside him and nearly dealt him the same hand.

He realized he wasn't just putting his own life in danger by not taking cover – he was endangering the lives of Scarlet, Kim, and Devlin too. The men attacking them were unlikely to waste ammunition on unconscious combatants.

He leaped to his feet and sprinted for the cover of the

235

hangar. Bursting through a side door, he found himself in a long corridor that was lined on either side with several windowless doors. A line of three strip lights lit the dreary, gray breeze block walls as he made his way toward an internal entrance that led through into the main hangar.

With the rest of his team out of the game, it was up to him to sabotage the helicopter, but when he turned into the hangar he was faced with the terrifying sight of two men staring back at him. One of them was a giant with a shaved head. He was wearing mechanic's overalls and gripping a heavy wrench in his hand. The other was Bruno, and now the Italian spoke.

"Well, look who it is... get him!"

*

Inside the drawing-room, Kruger and Zito were leaning against a substantial mahogany desk while the other men lounged around on various chairs. The bodies of two dead men were still sizzling on the floor. They looked like they had been seriously burned.

Mack saw them first. "Run out of sausages for the barbecue, Dirk?"

Kruger looked up at his prisoners. "Ah – Josiah Hawke and some other key members of the Red Hand Gang, and all right here in my new house." He was holding a large tumbler of what looked like vodka filled to the brim with ice. He smiled at them and took a sip of the drink.

"*Your* house?" Lea said.

Kruger gently pushed the leather swivel chair around with his snakeskin boot to reveal the dead body of Pavel Horak. A single bullet hole was drilled into his forehead and a look of terrified surprise was etched on his face for eternity. "Sadly, Mr. Horak tried to modify the agreement he had struck with the Oracle. As you will know, he is not a man to trifle with."

"The Oracle?" Lea said, taking a step back.

"Bugger me," said Hawke. "I thought you were working for him," he nodded in the direction of Horak's corpse. "But I can see now how such a working relationship would have its limitations."

"So you gave the Tinia idol to the Oracle?" Lea said.

"You catch on quick."

"How could you?"

"Only the Oracle knows the purpose of the idols."

"If you're involved with Wolff then you're a bigger fool than I imagined, Kruger," Hawke said. His eyes were drawn to the bag containing the sword. It was parked innocuously on a long leather couch running under one of the bay windows.

Kruger saw him looking at the bag and his smile grew wider. "You want it, don't you? You want to know what it really is, and what it does! You want to know about the gateway."

"You're a bastard, Kruger," Lea said defiantly. "How could you work for a man like the Oracle?"

Kruger took more of the vodka while he and Vermaak shared a glance for a few seconds. "He has taught me a great deal. For a long time, I thought diamonds and gold were the most precious things in this world. How wrong I was... how wrong I was." His voice started to trail away, but then he came back sharp and loud. "The question you have to ask yourself, young Miss Donovan, is whether or not the Oracle really is a man."

"There's an obvious joke there," Lea said, never taking her eyes off Kruger. "But I'll leave it till the company's better."

"I'm not interested in your pithy one-liners, Donovan," Kruger said, rounding on her. "Tell me, any luck working out who killed your daddy?"

Lea lunged for him, cursing his name as she rushed forward but Hawke grabbed her arm and stopped her. "Leave it, Lea. He's baiting you and you should know better."

Kruger laughed and finished his drink. "Quite the temper on that one, indeed. Quite the temper..." he tutted. "Very sharp."

Lea scowled at him. "You join me in a fair fight and you'll find out just how fucking sharp."

Kruger ignored her comment. "When the Oracle has this sword, he will be able to open the gateway to the king's tomb. After that, your fight will be over."

"What do you mean gateway?" Reaper asked.

"Yeah," Lea said. "And what king's tomb?"

Kruger cackled. "I'm loving this. The great ECHO team begging *me* for information. It doesn't get any better than this."

"Oh, it does," Lea said. "Like when the Oracle works out he's used you for all he needs and then has you snuffed out. I just hope I'm there to see it."

Reaper nodded. "Et moi, aussi."

"The Oracle is very generous to loyal servants," Kruger said. "And as for the second part of your little fantasy – you'll all be dead within the hour, and about fucking time too."

"People have threatened that before, mon ami," Reaper said. "And yet here we all are."

Hawke pointed at the dead men on the floor. "What happened to these men, Kruger?"

"Ah – yes, very sad... they tried to wield the sword, but unfortunately it turns out the legend is true."

"What legend?" Lea said.

Hawke sighed. "Where the hell is Ryan when you need him?"

"The legend of the Sword of Fire states that only a person of innate goodness can wield it. Those with an evil lurking within are, apparently, char-grilled. It has something to do with negative and positive ions."

"And you haven't given it a try yet, ya lavvy heid?" Mack said. "Good to see you rate yourself as highly as the rest of us do."

Kruger looked at him with disgust. "No, I haven't tried it. What I need is someone new to try it for me." His eyes crawled up to Lea and a second later a grin spread on his tanned face. "That is why you're going to wield the sword next, Lea Donovan."

# CHAPTER THIRTY-SEVEN

Ryan faced the two men. The mechanic was closer to him and swung the wrench, but he remembered everything the others had taught him and he ducked out of the way and sidestepped the blow. Still in the moment, he powered his left fist up into the man's ribs and winded him hard, forcing him to drop the wrench.

The only thing faster than Ryan snatching up the wrench was the smile dropping from Bruno's smug face, but it was too late to save his friend. Ryan spun around three-sixty to gather speed and momentum and then smashed the mechanic in the temple with the wrench, knocking him clean out.

Bruno cursed in Italian and rushed the young man, swinging a chunky punch at him. He was faster than the mechanic and this time Ryan's only evasive maneuver failed and the blow hit the target.

He felt the strike on the side of his head and then a boot curled around the front of his ankle and hooked his foot out from under him. He lost his balance and fell backward, helped on his way by another colossal punch on the side of his head.

The young hacker hit the smooth hard floor and nearly got knocked out with the impact. Hearing the Italian's boots as they slapped down on the polished concrete, he scrambled up to his feet and reached out for anything he could get his hands on. The closest thing with any value as a weapon was a countersink cutter perched on the edge of a workbench.

Ryan snatched it up and swung it at Bruno. The Italian

240

flicked his head back to dodge the two-kilo rivet shaver and both men realized at the same time that the saw was still connected to the mains.

Ryan pulled the trigger and the business end of the tool whirred around at over twenty thousand revs per minute.

Bruno desperately scanned the workshop for something he could use to fight back, and the answer came in the form of a high-speed panel saw down on the floor beside the unconscious aviation mechanic. The Italian snatched it up and gave his opponent a fiendish grin as he pulled the trigger. The diamond cutting wheel spun around at twelve thousand revs per minute.

Ryan took a sidestep and evaluated the situation. Both tools would kill the other man in an instant and make a damned bloody job of it too, but he knew that the Italian had a massive physical advantage. Since Maria's death he had been working out but he was nowhere near ready to take on an ex-military man like Bruno.

At least he had the rivet shaver, and he revved it in his hands as he scanned around to see if anyone else on the team was near, but there was no one. This was a fight to the death, and if he made one mistake it would be his own, but Bruno was nothing like the overweight mechanic.

The Italian moved like lightning, and before Ryan knew what had happened he had kicked the rivet shaver out of his hand and punched him to the floor. He tried to roll away but Bruno jumped on top of him, pinning him down with his knees, and then the man from Naples revved the diamond cutter. "This is going to hurt you a lot more than me."

\*

Lea looked at Kruger with nothing but contempt. She

thought she had hated him enough after what he had done to Ryan on the Seastead, but now she had learned about his teaming up with the Oracle as some kind of lackey she realized there was a whole new level of hate in her heart.

Kruger grinned like an old crocodile. "Take the sword to Miss Donovan, Adem!"

Lea watched Vermaak pick up the old leather bag and walk it over to her as if it contained nothing more than some tennis rackets. He set it down beside her and after giving Hawke a scowl he padded back over to the space behind his boss.

Kruger sniffed and shifted in his seat. "So there it is."

Zito took a step back and moved around behind the desk.

"Why is it glowing like this?" Lea said.

Kruger shrugged. "I don't know, but I know a man who does." He laughed, and then the gang of men around him joined in for a moment. They hushed up when he spoke again. "It has something to do with the way static electricity becomes current electricity in a thunderstorm, only this sword magnifies the process like a motherfucker."

"You mean like a Van de Graaff generator?" Hawke said.

Kruger gave Vermaak a nod and the South African commando piled a machine pistol into Hawke's stomach and sent him to the floor, gasping for air. "If I'd meant that I would have said so, you bastard."

"Thanks for clearing that up," Hawke coughed and clambered to his feet.

"You bastards know *nothing*," Kruger snapped. "All around us in the air, water vapor is hanging on tiny, microscopic pieces of dust, and in that water is where the static electricity is stored. Imagine that – as much electrical power as you could ever want, right in front of

242

your face. It's one of the holy grails of the environmentalist lobbies – trying to turn the static electricity into a live, usable current."

"And that's what you think this sword does?" Reaper said.

"So I'm told, yes... and in a big fucking way."

Lea and Hawke shared a look, and then she said, "So what do you want me to do?"

"I want you to pick it up – by the grip."

"She's not doing it," Hawke said. His hand involuntarily brushed against the engagement ring box and his mind turned to the proposal. Watching Lea get electrocuted to death wasn't part of the plan.

"Hush now, Hawke. Don't be a silly boy." Another sniff. "She opens the bag and wields the sword or Vermaak here cuts you all down with the MP5."

To underscore the point, the commando slid a round into the chamber and raised the muzzle in their direction. He wedged the weapon's stock in his hip and gave them a grin and a wink. "Go on, please give me just one chance and I'll spray your insides all over that pretty bookcase."

"I hope you don't kiss your mother with that mouth," Mack said.

"Just one chance – I beg you."

"Enough, Vermaak! Enough of this bullshit. Donovan – open the bag and lift the sword or you die right here, right now and I find some other little angel to do it for me... and if you try anything funny you'll be dead before that thing farts a single thunderbolt, got it?"

Lea ignored him but dropped her eyes down to the bag. The sword was partly wrapped in the cloth they had seen when it was back in the tomb, and it was still glowing. Hawke had been right – it was the same sort of light they had seen back in Atlantis and her heart began to quicken as she wondered what the connection might be.

Her speculation was ended abruptly by Kruger barking at her to hurry up, and then her eyes turned to the two dead men on the floor just a few meters away – stone-cold corpses because they had attempted to lift the sword.

Hawke moved closer to her and held her arm, but she brushed him away. "You know how electricity works, ya eejit."

Reaper gave her a look of serious respect and admiration as she put her hand in the bag and wrapped her hand around the grip.

She felt a jolt, but it was gentle, like when she was a kid in Galway and they dared each other to touch the low-voltage electric fences holding the cows back. A warmth crept up her arm and she squeezed her hand around the grip, and she gasped gently as the blue glow from the sword began to creep into her hand and turn it the same shade of neon blue.

She released the sword and jumped back, but Kruger wasn't satisfied. His eyes were sparkling like black diamonds. "Do it again, and this time wield the sword properly."

She glanced at the machine pistol in Vermaak's hands and obeyed, wrapping her hand around the sword's grip. It was easier the second time, and she watched the blue creep over her hand and up her forearm not with fear, but with fascination. "It feels so *warm*."

Kruger took a step back. "Wield it! In the air."

"Maybe I should wait outside," Zito said.

"You'll wait where I fucking tell you!" Kruger snapped. "Now – do it, Donovan!"

Lea obeyed again and lifted the sword. It was heavy, but she could just about manage to hold it aloft. It began to vibrate in her hand and she got scared. "Joe..."

"Just let go!"

"Don't you fucking dare!" Kruger said.

Suddenly a bolt of lightning shot up from the tip of the sword and crawled all over the ceiling like blue fire. They could all feel the power, a strange sort of static crackling in the air and now the sword began to judder more severely.

"None of my men got this far," said Kruger, glancing at the corpses strewn on the floor. "Maybe you'll survive it."

Then an immense burst of power shot along the blade of the sword and forked out into two bolts. The first reached out to Reaper and Mack who were now standing closest to her and knocked them both for six, and the second snaked up in a loop and raced back down the blade, blasting Lea off her feet. She lost her grip on the sword as she flew backward and the ancient weapon fell to the floor with a chunky smack.

"Pick that thing up, Adem," Kruger said. "The Oracle wants it before nightfall."

Lea was dazed and stared up at the blackened, smoldering ceiling as if she was on drugs. She was dimly aware of Hawke running to her and helping her up, but she felt numb and sick.

Kruger looked at the unconscious Reaper and Mack and then kicked the Scotsman in the ribs. He looked over at Hawke and Lea. "And bring those two pricks as well."

"Where are we going?" Hawke asked, helping Lea to her feet.

Kruger took a deep breath and stared at them. "We have a world to shock with the greatest terror attack in history."

# CHAPTER THIRTY-EIGHT

Ryan stretched his arm and extended his fingers as far as he could in a bid to reach the rivet shaver. It was millimeters beyond his grasp and Bruno's knee was pushing down into his throat.

"Now we see what happens when a diamond blade goes through a human skull, no?"

Ryan watched, helpless as the stronger man lowered the panel saw toward his face. The blade reflected the LED work lights strung beneath the two and a half-ton Bell and the terrible whining sound was a hundred times worse than anything he had heard in any dentist's room.

The Italian laughed and nodded his head up and down with enjoyment as the whirring blade neared the young man's face. He waved it back and forth to prolong the agony and increase the pleasure he was taking in torturing the young man.

"Now, for your skull!"

Ryan heaved against the man's weight, but he was just too heavy. He still had his arms pinned down and a knee in his throat... and the blade was a millimeter from the skin on his forehead. He screamed in terror but the sound of the cutter drowned out his desperate pleas for help. Ryan imagined the blade biting into the front of his skull and wondered how long he would be conscious; how long until he finally passed out from the fear and the pain.

Worse, now Bruno had him pinned down, a large man emerged from the office to the rear of the hangar and walked casually over to the fight. "You want some help, Bruno?"

"No, this bastard's mine. You get Mr. Zito and Kruger out of here."

"Roger that. Enjoy!"

The man laughed, walked across the tarmac, and climbed up into the Agusta's cockpit. The engine whirred faster and then the helicopter lifted into the air and started to fly toward the main house.

Ryan cursed. Not only was he going to die, but he had failed his one mission – to sabotage the Agusta. He clamped his eyes shut as the blade drew closer to his face and prayed for a miracle.

*

They were walking back down the slope toward the maze, but Kruger pulled up a few dozen meters short of it and set the leather bag on the smooth, clipped lawn. Vermaak was covering Hawke and Lea with a Milkor BXO submachine gun and their hands were tied behind their backs. Zito kept well back from everyone, and now Kruger scanned the sky for a few moments before taking a few seconds to look at his watch.

"This should just about do it."

Hawke took a step forward. "What's going on, Kruger?"

"I already told you – we're going to change the world today, and we're going to see what this sword can do when you open her up. People will talk about this moment for the rest of their lives, believe me. There's not a man or woman alive who won't remember exactly where they were at this precise moment."

Hawke saw the same skepticism in Lea's eyes that he felt in his own heart. Except for the carnage caused in the maze, the scene around them was the archetypal English country garden: birds sung in the chestnuts and ash trees, a gentle breeze combed through the acers lining the croquet lawn, and the scent of freshly cut grass drifted in the warm air.

Then the silence was broken. They both heard a chopper approaching and moments later the Agusta appeared over the top of the mansion and slowly descended onto the lawn. "Oh no, Joe! Scarlet's team must have failed."

"Maybe," he said calmly. "But don't write them off just yet." He turned to Kruger. "I thought you were going to attack Buckingham Palace?"

Kruger looked at him sharply. "Whoever told you that?"

"I have my sources."

"Then you should get new sources. The target is right here."

"Oh my God," Lea said. "They're attacking Windsor Castle!"

Kruger and the others shared a laugh. "No, the target is right here in this garden."

Lea looked confused. "I don't understand."

Kruger and Vermaak shared another short, sneering laugh and the arms dealer checked his watch one more time. "Or more precisely, *above* this garden."

And then they heard the sound of an approaching aircraft. Hawke recognized the sound at once; it was a wide-body jet with four engines. Moments later this was confirmed when he saw it in the distant eastern sky.

"Oh my God," Lea said. "You're going to use that thing to shoot an airliner out of the sky!"

"And not just any old airliner," Kruger said. "That's Air Force One."

"Oh my God!" Lea cried out.

"Alex is on that aircraft!" said Hawke.

Lea took a step forward but Vermaak tutted and raised

the gun to her face.

"You bastard, Kruger."

Kruger gave the order and Vermaak raised the Milkor to Hawke's temple. Kruger pulled Lea away from the Englishman and cut the cable tie holding her hands behind her back. "The sword, Donovan. Raise the sword, or Adem here will blow your man's brains out all over this pretty lawn."

"Don't do it, Lea," Hawke said quietly.

"Joe... I can't let them kill you."

"Now!" Kruger screamed, and Vermaak pushed the gun harder into Hawke's temple. "And you try and turn that thing on us and you're both dead before you move an inch."

Lea's world started to spin. She was in an impossible position. She had to commit a terrorist atrocity with the sword's ancient power, or watch the man she loved shot dead in front of her.

When it came down to it, there was no choice.

She picked up the sword and raised it to the sky. They all instantly felt the same intense crackling and buzzing all around them. She gripped the sword tighter now as it drew static electricity from the air and began to glow a wilder, brighter blue. The buzzing increased as it started to convert the energy into a live current. Her mind raced to think of a way out of this nightmare, but one look at Hawke with the gun at his head was all it took to keep holding the sword.

Through all of this, Kruger was nodding with approval. "Say goodbye to the President."

*

Ryan's eyes were still shut when the miracle happened:

249

the panel saw motor cut out and the blade stopped whirring.

He opened his eyes and looked up to see Bruno as he stared at the tool with uncomprehending eyes, but Ryan knew what had happened – when the Italian had pulled the saw down to his forehead he had pulled the power lead out of the mains and cut the power.

Bruno pulled his other hand up to study the saw and the young lad from London seized the moment. With his new free hand, he swung his arm like never before in his life and piled a haymaker into the Italian's left temple.

The blow knocked Bruno over and he tumbled away from Ryan, allowing the younger man to scramble to his feet and do whatever it took to save his own life. Using what he had at hand, Ryan snatched up the saw's loose power lead and wrapped it around Bruno's neck, pulling it as tight as he could around the soft flesh of his throat and choking him.

Bruno coughed and spluttered as he tried to push his fingers under the black cable and pull it away but Ryan had wound it around twice so there was zero chance of that. He was red in the face and the veins on his temple and neck were bulging like blocked fire hoses.

Bruno stared up with terror at the chunky skids of the Bell, suspended a foot or so above the floor by an aviation jack. The mechanic had been working on the chopper, and now Ryan was dragging him over towards it.

He tried to scream and beg for mercy through the cable that was still choking him. "No!"

Ryan was unmoved and dragged him along the floor with the power cable. As soon as Bruno was directly under the skid he knew what he had to do. When the Italian was in place Ryan had a second to act before he would be able to wriggle free, so the instant he had him in place he released the tension on the cable and hit the release on the jack.

Bruno's screams lasted for the full half-second it took for the enormous chopper to crush him, and then they stopped. Ryan looked away at the moment of death, but the sound of the man's body bursting open and his head flying off would stay with him forever. He knew that much.

Without looking back, Ryan Bale sprinted from the hangar and headed back over to the field outside. As terrible and violent as it was, he knew those few minutes fighting with Bruno would change the rest of his life, and now, as he moved into the battle to fight beside his friends one more time, his change was complete.

He was a stronger man now, mentally and physically, hardened like steel by the bitter experiences he had suffered: the deaths of Sophie Durand and Maria Kurikova and now the brutal murder of Bruno. Yes, it had been self-defense, but nothing was stopping him from running from the hanger when the Italian was choking on the floor. He had stayed and finished the job the way Hawke or Scarlet or Devlin would do – because that was what you did when you had a mortal enemy: you fought to the death or they would rise and kill you later. He understood that now.

He sprinted around to the rear of the hangar to find Scarlet and Devlin helping Kim to her feet. He knew they had to get back to Hawke and reunite the team but then they all saw something that stopped them dead in their tracks. A wide-bodied jet was flying to the north of the property, around three or four thousand feet high and a bolt of strange blue lightning was crawling all over its aluminum skin.

"My God," Devlin said. "That maniac Kruger must be testing the sword out on a jet!"

251

"It's a 747," Ryan said, holding his hand up to shield his eyes from the sun's glare. "There could be four hundred people on board!" He rubbed a shaking hand over his face. "And if it's under attack that means Joe failed."

"We have to get over there!" Scarlet cried out.

"Wait... that's not any old 747," Kim said grimly. "That's Air Force One!"

# CHAPTER THIRTY-NINE

Colonel James Scott fought with everything he had to control Air Force One as the blue fire streaked across the 747's metallic fuselage.

Sitting beside him in the first officer's seat, Lieutenant Colonel Matt Jennings was also fighting hard to keep the aircraft level. "We're going down, sir!"

"I know, dammit! We're losing power!" Scott said.

President Jack Brooke burst into the cockpit, followed closely by his terrified advisor, Todd Williams. "What the hell is going on?"

"We don't know," said the Colonel. The yoke was vibrating wildly in his hands and a series of various warning alarms were sounding out in the small cockpit. "It's some kind of electrical attack!"

"I thought this plane could defend against an EMP?" Todd said.

Scott shook his head. "Sure, but this ain't no EMP!"

They all heard the grim sound of the four General Electric turbofans powering down as the terrifying neon-blue electrical fire leaped and crackled over the aircraft. Brooke shielded his eyes from the blinding flashes sparking across the windshield.

"Five thousand feet and going down fast!" Jennings said.

With wheels up only a few moments ago, London Heathrow's Runway 27R was only seven or eight miles behind them and the gear was barely retracted inside the plane.

"Can she stay in the air?" Brooke said.

Scott shook his head again as he desperately scanned the instrument panel. "We have a vertical speed of five hundred feet per minute, Mr. President. At this rate, we're on the floor in less than five minutes."

"Can we do anything?"

"We've already deployed all countermeasures, sir, but they're designed to deal with incoming missiles or fighter jets, not whatever the hell this is."

Scott slammed his hand on the chunky throttle quadrant and pushed it forward again, this time to the max. The normal response would have been a mighty, bass roar as the engines spooled up to full power, but the blue lightning was interfering too much with not only the electrical systems but also the turbofans themselves. The response to the Colonel's action was the sound of the engines continuing to lose power.

"RAF jets have been scrambled," Jennings said.

"It's too late," Scott said. "We're going down! Everyone into crash positions!"

*

"She's coming down!" Kruger said. 'We're actually going to knock Air Force One right out of the sky!"

Hawke and Lea exchanged a look of horror before returning to the terrible sight of the President's aircraft as its flight crew desperately struggled to keep the wounded bird in the air. Lea felt the sword's power in her hands more acutely now, and it was starting to burn and sizzle.

"Bring that bastard down!" Vermaak yelled.

"I've never seen anything like this before," Zito said. "It's like we have the power of the gods!"

The intensity of blue light produced by the Sword of Fire was terrifying, and Hawke was forced to look away.

"Jesus Christ!" Vermaak said. "The fucking thing's going down in that field."

Hawke watched helplessly and was consumed with rage as he watched the world-famous Boeing fighting against the ancient power of the sword. Its engines whined and moaned as the lethal blue lightning flashed and leaped all over the wings and onto the main fuselage. He had never seen anything like it in his entire life and never wanted to again.

"This will kill them all, Kruger!" Lea shouted.

"That's sort of the point," Vermaak said.

Lea felt herself passing out, and as her head swam she heard another sound now: fighter jets screeching through the air to the north. Hawke saw them first – two typhoons, and they weren't messing about. When they got closer he saw the RAF insignia, and then he saw they were armed to the hilt with Brimstone air-to-surface missiles.

"They've fucking found us, Dirk," Vermaak said.

The typhoons banked hard either side of Air Force One to avoid the same fate, and then swooping around toward the house, Hawke saw them both fire.

"Incoming!" he yelled.

Hawke saw in Kruger's eyes that he wanted more than anything in the world to be the man who blew up Air Force One and killed the President, but he knew the game was up.

Exhausted now, Lea dropped the sword and collapsed into the grass. With the sword on the ground, it had stopped drawing the energy from the air and the blue lightning was dissipating as fast as it had arrived.

Two Brimstone missiles scorched a path of death across the sky before slamming into the upper stories of Horak's manor house and sending a colossal fireball shooting into the air. The shockwave blasted everyone to the ground.

Hawke rolled to a stop and watched as the neon fire finally released its grip on the presidential plane. The aircraft was seconds away from a devastating impact in a wheat field, but now they all heard the power of the engines as the wounded bird pulled up out of an imminent stall.

Lea started to come around again. "Thank God!" she mumbled.

With fire and smoke billowing from the mansion, and Air Force One racing away into the blue sky, Kruger cursed and passed a gnarled hand over his chin stubble. "Damn it all."

"We'd better make tracks, Dirk," Vermaak said. "This place will be crawling with anti-terror cops in minutes."

"Get to the chopper!" Kruger said. "We have the sword, and that's all that matters. And don't forget the parachutes."

With Reaper and Mack still unconscious in the house behind them, Vermaak marched Hawke and Lea toward the AgustaWestland.

"Parachutes, Kruger?" Hawke said. "Nervous flyer?"

"We have a boat waiting for us in the North Sea. Me, Vermaak, and Gianni parachute onto it while the chopper drags your boys in blue on a wild goose chase all over France. We get safely away with the sword and your anti-terror idiots are being sent in the opposite direction."

"And what about us?"

"You're going to find out what it feels like to hit the ground at terminal velocity, and so is your girlfriend. Get on the chopper."

Hawke watched Vermaak as he loaded the bag on the plane and then threw the three parachutes in behind it. Lea was still too dazed to fight, but the former SBS operative decided it was now or never and made his move when the commando's back was turned. With his hands still tied behind his back, he lashed out and headbutted Kruger in the face and then turned and delivered the same punishment to Zito.

Kruger cried out for Vermaak who pirouetted back out of the aircraft and scrambled to contain the situation. He raised his MP5 and screamed at Hawke to get back. He obeyed, but it was too late for Zito. Hawke's hefty headbutt had knocked the Italian hard and now he was staggering backward toward the Agusta's tail rotor propeller blades.

Even Kruger turned away as the speeding metal blades ripped into the Italian mobster and sprayed what was left of him all over the helicopter and tarmac.

"Jesus Christ!" Vermaak said and raised his gun at Hawke. "Try that with me and see what happens, Englishman."

Kruger looked up and saw the fighter jets had been joined by two more and all four were now flying toward Air Force One to escort it out of British airspace. "Get us in the air!" he snapped at the pilot.

Hawke's last stand had failed, and now Vermaak forced them to get on the chopper at gunpoint.

\*

Scott and Jennings shared a glance that spoke a thousand words as the blue fire streaked away from Air Force One and released its deadly grip on the aircraft. From the jumpseat just behind them, President Brooke shared their relief as the Colonel slammed the throttles forward. This time the engines responded correctly, and a deep, satisfying roar filled the cabin as Scott rammed them up to N1 and pushed the turbofans to full capacity.

"Good flying, Colonel," Brooke said.

"I wish I could say it was, sir," he said.

Brooke had no response. He knew things had gotten too close today, and a very dark chapter in American history had been narrowly avoided thanks to the RAF jets that had ripped the hell out of the terrorists' ground position.

Now escorted by no less than four Eurofighter Typhoons, the VC-25 shredded its way into the western sky leaving a no-nonsense roar of power in its wake. It burned noisily away from the attack site and headed to cruising altitude.

With the danger behind them, Scott ordered an immediate check on all systems while Jennings got busy on the radio. Brooke rose to his feet, gave the Colonel a solid pat on his shoulder, and headed back into the cabin.

"Dad?"

Alex was sitting down beside Agent McGee. Both looked pale.

"It's fine, darling. We're through it."

"What the hell was it?"

"We don't know, but I'll tell you one thing – whatever sons of bitches just tried to bring me, my plane and my girl down are going to wish they'd never been born."

# CHAPTER FORTY

Lea looked at Hawke and saw he was watching Vermaak closely as the aircraft's Pratt & Whitney turboshaft engine pulled them up to altitude. Kruger was upfront with the pilot, and the only trace of what was left of Giancarlo Zito was smeared over the tail boom at the rear of the chopper.

Hawke turned to her and smiled, but she didn't return it.

"What's the matter?" he asked.

"Kruger's going to throw us out this frigging helo in about five minutes. That's what's wrong."

"Don't be silly," he said, giving her shoulder a reassuring squeeze. "We've never been beaten yet and it's not going to start now."

Lea peered out at England, thousands of feet below. "If it starts now it's going to bloody stop now too. Listen... about the letter I got in Dublin."

"You said you weren't ready, Lea."

"I'm not, but I can't die not knowing what it says, Joe!"

He was silent for a long time, then he said, "This is your decision."

"I've made up my mind. I'm going to read it, but I want to be alone."

"What about Smiler over there?" Hawke said, indicating Vermaak.

"I mean it, Joe."

Hawke understood. He kissed her on the cheek and moved to the next seat. Vermaak gave him a suspicious glance. "View's better this side," the Englishman said with a cheery grin.

Vermaak sniffed and slumped back down in his seat.

Lea reached inside her jacket pocket and pulled out the letter she had found in the box of Maggie Donovan's things back at her brother's house in Dublin. She stared at the handwriting on the front of the envelope and whispered: *Maggie, I'm so scared of what I might find inside...*

With the chopper rumbling through some light turbulence, she ran her finger under the envelope seal and pulled the letter from the inside. She held in her hands a piece of small, neatly folded notepaper and could see through the paper that it was written in the same shaky handwriting that was on the front of the envelope. Now, her hands started to shake as she gently opened the note and began to read Maggie's words, scrawled in blue ink on the delicate white paper.

*

Halfway to the main house, Ryan could hardly believe what they had all just witnessed in the sky above their heads. Air Force One had narrowly escaped total destruction and a good part of the mansion was nothing more than burning ruins. Before flying away to escort the President's plane, the typhoons had blasted the top half of the mansion with SAMs, and now they helplessly watched as an AgustaWestland chopper powered up into the air and turned to the east.

They saw two men moving toward them across the airfield.

"Holy shit!" Kim cried out. "That's Vincent and Mack!"

They sprinted over to them.

"Holy crap," Ryan said. "What happened to you two?"

"I'm not sure..." Mack rubbed his head. "I was standing there listening to this proper tadger going on about the end of the world and then Lea did the whole 'hold-aloft-your-magic-sword' thing and then the next minute it felt like I was shagging a toaster."

Reaper looked confused. "We got electrocuted."

"Ah," Kim said. "Now I understand."

"What about Joe and Lea?" Scarlet said, staring over Reaper's shoulder for any sign of them.

The Frenchman shook his head. "I regained consciousness just in time to see Kruger piling them both into the Agusta."

"Aye," Mack said. "Fuckers were airborne before either of us could do a thing."

"Bastards!" Devlin said.

Sheer desperation forced Ryan to run his hand over his face. Everything had gone wrong. They had failed to stop Kruger and Zito from leaving the country and now it looked like Hawke and Lea were hostages.

"So what do we do now?" Kim said.

"We go after our fuckin' mates, is what," Mack said. The Scot gave the young Londoner a stern look. "Right, Ryan?"

Ryan took a deep breath, unable to keep his eyes away from the hangar where he had killed the man. "You got it," he said at last. "Let's end this."

\*

Reaper led the others to a parking lot at the side of the hangar where a man was pulling into a space marked AVIONIC TECHNICIAN. The Frenchman padded over to him and tapped him on the shoulder.

"Excusez-moi, Monsieur."

"Eh?"

Reaper's shovel-fist smashed into the man's face and knocked him to the ground. "Where are the keys to that shiny helicopter over there?" He pointed to the blue and white Eurocopter EC130 parked outside.

"Oh, *God* no," Ryan said.

Kim looked worried. "What's the problem?"

"The last time Reap flew us in a chopper was in Peru and we all vowed never again."

"Keys," Reaper repeated, ignoring Ryan's comment. "Where?"

"In the office," the technician said, his voice quivering.

"Take us there."

The man led them to the office and handed the keys over. He started to speak but Reaper punched him again, and this time hard enough to end the debate.

"Bon... let's get after them!"

"You can't be serious?" Kim said.

"He's always serious," said Ryan.

"True story," Scarlet said.

Reaper fired the chopper up and raised the collective, slowly lifting the machine off the ground and pushing up into the sky. "What was the AgustaWestland's registration number, Ryan?"

Ryan gave the number, burned into his eidetic memory during the fight with Bruno.

"Scarlet, start tracing the number and see if the flight path is on a live tracker website," Reaper said.

"All over it like a donkey on a waffle, Reap."

"Bon." He swooped the chopper over the top of Horak's burning mansion and turned it to the east in pursuit of the fleeing Agusta Westland.

"They would never let themselves be tracked that way!" Kim protested.

"No, he's right," Devlin said. "They have to have the

transponder switched on for safety reasons. If they turn it off they're inviting a mid-air collision."

Reaper spoke through the headset, "In the meantime, everyone else try and keep an eye on it, non? If Hawke gets control of that chopper he's going to need back-up when he brings it down."

Reaper looked into the sky and saw the AgustaWestland slowly vanishing in the sky to the east. Things had looked better for the ECHO team, but he took a deep breath and raised the collective.

# CHAPTER FORTY-ONE

With the letter held tightly in her hands, Lea closed her eyes and tried to work up enough courage to read it. She had kept it in the pocket next to her heart since Dublin but now it was time. When she opened her eyes again, she saw her hands were trembling. She fought against it and started to read the letter.

*My Dearest Lea,*

*I'm writing this letter to you because I'm feeling tired and I'm not sure how much longer I have. There is no easy way to say what I must say, so I'll just write it down – I know you'll be strong enough to handle it. You're a Donovan.*

*I am your sister, Lea, and our father was not like other men. He was born at the end of the nineteenth century and was well over 120 years old when he died. I know this is hard for you to understand, but there it is.*

*He wasn't born this way. He often told me he wasn't one of 'them', whatever that means. He never explained. He told me they were a kind of cult and used some strange Greek word to describe them. He said if I knew more it would frighten me too much.*

*As a young man, our father travelled on a medical research expedition to find a cure for malaria but he found something else –water that kept him young. He drank some and it extended his life. You ask why he never shared it? He said it was too dangerous. Too much or too little brought not youth, but an even faster death. He told me he wished he'd never tasted it. He regretted it his whole life. I felt so sad for him.*

*You have probably seen the little gold statue I left behind. Father called it an idol. He gave it to me many years ago for safekeeping. He said the cult didn't know about me so they would never find it. He told me he found it in Italy during an expedition there in the 1920s. He spent his life searching for more but never found any.*

*He told me the idols were the key to everything but they don't belong to the cult. They belong to something much more ancient and deadly that the cult doesn't understand. He refused to tell me more because the knowledge was too dangerous.*

*Don't think badly of me, sister. I wanted to tell you about these things, but Father made me promise to keep it to myself and let him tell you in his own time when you were a grown woman. Now you are grown, he is dead and I am dying. Now is the time for me to tell you.*

*You need to understand that our father was not a bad man. He kept these things from you only because you were too young to understand. He wanted to keep you safe. He loved you. I know he intended to tell you everything he knew when you grew up, but then they murdered him, as I think you know in your heart.*

*Only you can continue the search that cost him his life.*

*With love, my dear sister,*

*Maggie*

Lea Donovan was not expecting to cry, and it came even harder for the lack of expectation. Overwhelmed by what she had just read, she began to sob but quickly stuffed the letter back inside her jacket and dabbed her eyes with the cuff of her sleeve.

Hawke moved over to her. "Are you all right? What did it say?"

"It said...wait." Lea leaned her head over to look past Hawke's shoulder. "Kruger's coming. Vermaak too."

Hawke turned to see the men walking down the short aisle from the cockpit, and both Kruger and Vermaak were holding guns. No one, including Lea, had noticed that when she was reading the letter he had pulled his tied wrists under his backside, and now his arms were in front of his body, instead of behind it. They were still held together with the cable ties, but at least this way he had a fighting chance.

"All right," the arms dealer said. "This is your stop. Get over to the door."

"You can't be serious."

"Orders are orders. You're going to die this way because the Oracle wants it this way. He wants a message sent to your top brass, and he wants to see your demise on the news this evening while he dines."

Kruger opened the side door while Vermaak kept his gun on them. "By the time you're splattered all over the streets of London, I'll be well on my way." He turned a devilish grin on them. "Who wants to go first?"

Hawke stepped to the door. Lea pulled at his arm but he brushed her away and peered outside at the city so far below. He knew people *had* survived falls from this height after parachute failures, but it was a one in a million hope.

Then he saw something that gave him much more hope, and it was right in Dirk Kruger's hands.

The South African arms dealer had left the safety catch up on the HK USP pistol he was gripping.

Hawke was familiar with the weapon and knew Kruger

266

would have to reach up with his right thumb and click it down into fire mode if he wanted to shoot a round, and that was going to give him time.

As the wind buffeted his hair and he got closer to the open door, his mind made a speedy calculation: three seconds for Kruger to fire at him and realize the catch was on, another two seconds for him to release the catch and take the shot. Two more seconds for Vermaak to work out what had happened and turn his own gun on him.

Seven seconds.

Hawke turned on Kruger and stepped toward him.

Kruger grinned fiendishly as he raised the gun and prepared to fire. "I knew you'd do something stupid," he said and fired.

Nothing happened, and now the South African's eyes widened as he realized the mistake he had made. As he fumbled with the catch he suddenly looked like a man thrown into a tiger cage.

Hawke piled into him, elbowing him in the face, grabbing his gun, and twisting it in the direction of Vermaak. Kruger had released the catch and the weapon was now on fire mode. With the gun still in the arms dealer's hands, Hawke fired at Vermaak.

Lea screamed and Vermaak dived for cover behind a leather seat, causing Hawke's rounds to rip through the cockpit cabin wall and drill into the pilot's back. The dead man slumped forward in his shredded seat and the helicopter immediately started spinning around like a sycamore seed.

Kruger grunted as he struggled against the former commando. Blood poured out of his nose as he fought hard to regain control of the gun, and now Vermaak was firing a volley of shots from behind the front row seats. The rounds missed Hawke, raked the rear bulkhead, and then snaked their way through the starboard side of the chopper. Everyone watched in horror as the rounds blasted chunks from the speeding rotors.

With the chopper now angled down and speeding toward the ground in a spin, and with his hands still tied, Hawke twisted the gun from Kruger's hands and pushed the muzzle into his neck. "Tell him to drop the gun, Kruger – or I'll put a hole through your head."

Kruger needed no time to consider the choice. "Lower your weapon, Adem!"

Vermaak obeyed.

Hawke yelled over the sound of the wounded aircraft. "Now get two of those parachutes."

Vermaak hurriedly obeyed once again and brought two parachutes down from the front of the helicopter, struggling against the angle as he went. Hawke watched as Kruger's eyes crawled over to the bag containing the Sword of Fire.

"Put a chute on, Lea," Hawke said. "We're getting out of here and we're taking the sword with us." He pushed Kruger toward Vermaak but kept the gun trained on them both. "You two scumbags can argue about who gets the third parachute."

"Ready, Joe!"

Hawke lifted the bag. "All right, take this, and..."

Without warning, the AgustaWestland spun uncontrollably the other way and caught Hawke off-guard. The sudden change in direction knocked everyone into the side of the aircraft, which was now tipping over dangerously and about to lose its lift. Hawke dropped the bag and gun, and Vermaak moved like a hyena, snatching up the weapon.

"Time to die, Hawke!" Vermaak yelled and pointed the weapon at him.

"No!" Lea cried out.

"Say hello to the devil for me!" Vermaak said and fired the gun at his chest.

# CHAPTER FORTY-TWO

The bullet missed Hawke by an inch and blasted through the seat behind him. He ducked down and yelled at Lea.

"Jump!"

"I'm not leaving without..."

Hawke coiled his leg back and kicked her from the chopper. She screamed on her way out but he knew she'd survive. She was an experienced skydiver and now she was safe.

He knew the helicopter had no more than three or four minutes before it was nothing more than a fireball somewhere down in London. If it landed in a built-up area it meant more innocent deaths, and more blood on Kruger's hands but there was nothing he could do to control the beleaguered AgustaWestland now.

It would be a miracle if he could save himself.

Kruger ordered Vermaak to kill him while he strapped himself into one of the parachutes. Vermaak fired again and emptied the USP's mag but Hawke dodged the rounds, leaving nothing for it but to go mano-a-mano. Now the commando from Joburg was crawling along the angled floor on his way to Hawke.

As Vermaak lunged at him. Hawke knew if he wanted a parachute then he was going to have to fight him for it, and now he was struggling against the man's incredible strength. Unlike the former SBS man, Vermaak had been a serving commando until a few weeks ago and it showed. His stamina was impressive and he was using it to force Hawke toward the open helicopter door. When they reached it, Vermaak hooked his feet out from under him

THE SWORD OF FIRE

and Hawke slammed down on his back with his head hanging out the open door.

The Englishman strained with all his might to push the man's hand up away from his throat and managed to elbow him in the face. Vermaak recoiled and this bought Hawke a few seconds to get his breath back. He sucked the air into his lungs as the howling air whipped his hair around and buffeted against his ears.

Vermaak's response was aggressive and fast. He slammed his fist down into Hawke's stomach and punched every last breath of air from him.

Hawke's eyes bulged as he strained to draw some air into his lungs. In the corner of his eye, he saw Dirk Kruger pulling himself up the aisle of the luxury business chopper. He was safely strapped into his parachute and holding the other one in his hand. In his other hand, he held the bag containing the sword. They must have lost at least ten thousand feet by now, and time was running out fast.

"I must bid you farewell, Mr. Hawke," he said, his thick Afrikaans accent cutting through the howling wind like a serrated dagger. "Adem here has orders to kill you and then join me on the ground."

Vermaak's hand was now wrapped around Hawke's throat, stopping him sucking the air back into his empty lungs and slowly Hawke felt the life draining out of him.

\*

Reaper navigated the chopper over the buzzing London metropolis as he tried to handle the various ATC demands to identify themselves. They could still see the AgustaWestland in the sky ahead of them and now it looked like it was in serious trouble.

Reaper pulled the chopper closer to the other helicopter but kept a safe distance. "We're almost there now. Look – the chopper's in a lot of trouble. Mon Dieu... I hope they're all right."

"How the hell can they survive that?" Kim said.

Scarlet shot her a stern glance. "Hush, darling. We don't talk like that in ECHO. If there are two people in this world who can get out of a situation like that then it's Joe and Lea. Never say die."

Kim looked suitable chastened. "I'm sorry."

"I see a parachute!" Ryan said.

"That's the way!" said Mack.

Reaper shook his head and gave a low whistle. "Only one though. That's not good. That helicopter can't have more than a couple of minutes to live and soon there won't be enough time to make a safe jump."

"Maybe that's the second parachute and the other one is already safely on the ground?" Devlin said. "Chin up!"

"Whatever the hell is going on," Scarlet said, "you can guarantee Hawke is on top of things. Every time."

"If you say so," Kim said.

*

Kruger stepped over Hawke and crouched down so they were face to face. "Please allow me to say fuck you very much for all the trouble you have caused." He punched Hawke in the face and laughed.

The Englishman felt a tooth break and spat it in Kruger's face in a spray of blood from his split lip. "You're very welcome, Dirk."

Kruger pulled a machine pistol from his bag and put it in Hawke's mouth. "So this is how you want to go out? Knowing that I can catch up with your girlfriend and do what I want with her because you'll be underground?"

Vermaak took the other parachute and slid inside the harness. While he was tightening the straps Kruger pulled the gun out of Hawke's mouth, leaned out of the door, and fired it at the Agusta Westland's tail boom. The bullets shredded through the rotors and punched a line of holes all over the rest of the boom. "Just to make sure you go out the hard way," he said with a sneer.

The Agusta responded immediately, lurching even more violently to the right and going into another steep inverted dive.

"Enjoy the ride, you bastard," Kruger yelled. He grinned at Hawke and leaped over him and through the small door.

Hawke was still on his back on the chopper's floor with his head hanging out the door. He watched as Dirk Kruger tumbled over a few times before stabilizing himself and settling into a controlled skydive over London.

As he watched him fade from sight, Hawke's head spun with the beating he had just received at the hands of Adem Vermaak. He was aware that his throat was filling up with blood. The muzzle of Kruger's gun had gouged a deep cut in the roof of his mouth, and now he leaned over and spat more blood out on the carpet.

Vermaak drew his boot back and powered it into his stomach, and then again in his face before leaning forward and drawing a hunting knife. "Nighty, night."

Hawke raised his arms to protect himself and used the blade to slash open the cable ties. Vermaak leaped back and readied himself for a third kick when the AgustaWestland stalled and dropped back into a steep dive, throwing him against the bulkhead at the rear of the aircraft.

Hawke saw a chance and climbed up to his knees, but

Vermaak was too fast. He pushed past him and jumped out of the aircraft, taking the last parachute with him.

Hawke saw Vermaak's move coming and made a split-second decision. Grabbing the man's legs as he exited the chopper he was sucked out into the air without a parachute of his own, but it was his only play. Kruger had utterly annihilated all of the AgustaWestland's control surfaces and there was no way to stop it smashing into the ground at hundreds of miles per hour. It was no more than a flying coffin, so Vermaak was the only way out now.

Two men, one parachute.

Hawke knew they had been cruising at around twenty-five thousand feet, and he estimated that thanks to the dive they had left the AgustaWestland at around ten thousand feet. He also knew terminal velocity was one hundred and seventy-six feet per second. It didn't take Albert Einstein to know that without the parachute he was hitting the ground in fifty-six seconds. He didn't know what kind of chute Vermaak was using, so he had to allow around a thousand feet of free fall for the chute to open. That gave him nine thousand feet or fifty-one seconds.

Fifty seconds.

These were all serious concerns, but the main problem was that Adem Vermaak also wanted the parachute.

Then Vermaak lashed out with his leg in a bid to smash his boot into Hawke's face.

The wind howled around them as Hawke pulled his head back but maintained a cast-iron grip on Vermaak's khaki cargo pants. The South African kicked out with his legs as he desperately tried to kick Hawke away, but the Englishman wasn't letting go for anything and took the blows as he unclipped the other man's harness and wrenched it from his body.

Vermaak's eyes widened with terror as Hawke coiled up his legs and wedged his boots in the South African's stomach before kicking away from him with the parachute firmly in his grip.

Hawke knew there and then he'd be able to hear the South African's screams for the rest of his life, but he shook the thought from his mind and strapped himself into the harness. When it was safely on, he pulled the cord to open the chute but nothing happened.

London was racing toward him at over one hundred miles per hour so he had to operate the reserve chute and pray to all that was holy that it was packed right. He was too low now to fix another problem, and as he reached for the reserve parachute's cord he remembered an old Paras joke Eden had told him over drinks one night.

*Never worry about it if anything goes wrong with your parachute – you've got the rest of your life to sort it out.*

He smiled and pulled the cord.

The pilot chute deployed and the speeding air stream around him caught hold of it and pulled the sleeve and main canopy from the pack tray.

As the suspension lines tightened up he watched the reserve chute flare out into the blue sky above him.

He was safe.

# CHAPTER FORTY-THREE

## London

Hawke made a hook-turn and carefully guided the parachute with the steering lines as he descended into London. He'd passed a thousand feet by the time he got the chute on his back and now as he drifted over the capital city he remembered the earpiece and palm mic he'd stuffed into his pocket back at Horak's place. He pulled it out of his pocket and shoved it in his ear.

"Anyone around?"

After a few seconds, he heard it crackle to life.

"Earth calling Joe Hawke. Everything all right, darling?"

Hawke grinned as he heard Scarlet's voice. "Not too bad, thanks."

"What about the Agusta, Joe?" she asked. "Can you see where it went down?"

Hawke scanned the horizon and saw a column of smoke spiraling up from the ground. "Looks like it crashed in Hyde Park."

"Thank God," she said.

"And where are you?" he asked.

"Monsieur Reno landed our chopper in Trafalgar Square. Can you see us yet?"

"I can't see *you*, no, but I *can* see your ego."

"Touché, Josiah. What happened to Vermaak?"

"I'm sorry to say that we fell out with each other – permanently."

"Oh, for fuck's sake," she said. "Why don't you give

this lark up and head over to the Comedy Store?"

"I might just do that."

"Talk about taking idiotic risks," she said.

"I think on my feet, Cairo. You know that."

"Fucking good job you watch James Bond films is all I can say, Hawke."

"Hey! Less of that! I just like to complete missions with a certain *élan*, that's all."

She laughed and he saw them now. They were standing around the bottom of Nelson's Column a few yards from a parked up Eurocopter. He saw Lea's parachute but there was no sign of her or Devlin. He glided the parachute down into the square and executed a perfect landing right in front of Scarlet and the rest of the team. As he unfastened the parachute he realized that dozens of tourists were now forming a circle around him and filming him on various devices.

"You always did like to make an entrance, darling," Scarlet said.

The rest of the team joined them, and Hawke gave her a withering look, but then his face grew more serious. "Kruger got away with the sword."

"You're kidding?" Kim said, taking a step back and looking him up and down. "You mean you haven't got the sword stuffed down your pants?"

"No," Hawke said. "And its *trousers*. We're in London."

She winked at him. "No, I meant pants in the English sense."

"Ah," Hawke said mischievously. "In that case then yes, I do have a powerful sword stuffed in my pa-."

"Do not finish that sentence," Ryan said. "I'm trying to eat a hot dog."

"When we get back to Elysium," Scarlet drawled

277

sarcastically. "Can we please call this Operation Fuckup?"

Mack gave a wheezy chortle. "I like that. You always could make me laugh, Sloane."

"Hey, what happened to Bruno?" Hawke said.

Scarlet shrugged her shoulders. "Ryan, any idea?"

Ryan shoved his hands in his pockets and shook his head. "None at all."

"Maybe he's still out there," Kim said.

Reaper lit one of his roll-ups, totally ignoring the banter. "Tell me, Joe – what happened to Kruger?"

Hawke sighed. "He jumped out somewhere over West London. He'll be long gone by now."

"Either way," Scarlet said. "I'm glad you're safe." She kissed him on the cheek.

"Steady on, girl."

"Twat. By the way – great news."

"You finally worked out how to use a corkscrew?"

"No."

"You've figured out why the wave function collapses when you measure it?" Ryan said.

Scarlet cocked her head and scowled at them. "Funnily enough – no to both of those asinine comments. Rich is out of his coma. The hospital just called Lea when you were playing Roger Moore's stunt double a few seconds ago."

He peered over her shoulder and saw Lea and Danny embracing each other on the other side of the square. "What's going on there?" he asked.

Scarlet bit her lip and looked away for a moment. "Joe... Lea just told Danny about the letter..."

But he had gone. He was storming toward them with the blood pounding in his ears. The adrenalin from the mid-air fight and the parachute jump was still pulsing through his veins. He knew he was being irrational but he was powerless to stop himself.

He pulled Devlin away from Lea and landed a punch on his jaw, knocking him over onto the ground. The Irishman crumpled under the hefty blow but managed to stagger back to his feet in time to save his pride.

"Joe!" Lea yelled. "What the *hell* do you think you're doing?"

"He's been asking for it since the start of the mission – all over you, laughing, joking, taking the piss, taking stupid risks!"

Lea looked genuinely confused, tears still in her eyes. "What? What are you blathering about? Danny's an old friend and he was just trying to calm me down because I was upset."

"Upset?"

Devlin rubbed his grazed jaw. "After reading the letter up there in the chopper, you fool."

"But still..." Hawke stopped mid-sentence, already knowing he had gone too far.

Lea looked distraught. "I can't believe you'd do something like this."

"And I can't believe you'd tell him about the letter before me. I still don't know what it says!"

Lea sighed and pulled her hair back behind her ears. "I was upset and he asked me why I was crying. I've known Danny longer than anyone here, Joe – including you!"

"But still..." He felt the adrenalin from the jump still coursing through his veins.

"But still nothing!" Lea cried. "Why would you do this, Joe?"

"I thought..."

"You thought what?"

"He thought we were enthralled in a mad passionate embrace," Devlin said sarcastically.

Hawke jabbed a finger at him. "You keep out of it.

279

You've been pushing me since the start of the mission."

With tears in her eyes, Lea raised her hands to her face and turned in a circle of desperation. "I don't believe I'm hearing this."

Hawke felt the ring box in his pocket. It had been there since Washington when he picked Alex up from the hospital, awkward, out of place. He felt the anger rise in him.

"If you don't trust me then we can't be together," she said, her eyes flashing with defiance.

"If you didn't give me a reason to doubt you then there wouldn't be any reason not to trust you."

She gasped. "So you don't trust me? Is that what you're saying?"

"I don't know what I'm saying."

"And what about *you*," Lea said, lowering her voice and trying to mimic Hawke back on the Aurora in Italy. "I thought you were reminiscing about our little romance in Zambia...for *fuck's* sake!"

"Eh? That was just me and Lex pissing about."

"But you still don't trust me," she said sadly.

"I..."

"In that case, maybe we should just go on a break!" Lea cried out, loud enough for all to hear.

"Maybe we should!" Hawke knew he couldn't back down now, but he also knew Lea well enough to know she wouldn't either. It turned out they were the immovable object and the irresistible force of relationships.

"If that's what you want, ya stupid eejit!"

"If that's what *you* want."

"Come on, Danny," Lea said. "Let's get out of here."

Hawke watched Lea and Danny walk across the square and after a few seconds, they were gone, melted into the bustling London crowd. He carried on staring long after they had slipped out of sight, almost unable to believe what had just happened: he had lost not only the Tinia idol to the Oracle, but now Kruger would hand him the Sword of Fire too and he would use them in his quest for the mysterious king's tomb.

And now he had lost Lea Donovan, the person he cared about more than anyone else in the world. The woman he loved and wanted to marry.

He saw a group of tourists watching him now, and some even had their phones out to film him, but he turned his back on them all. He saw the rest of the ECHO team across the other side of the square watching him, but he turned his back on them too. His heart was racing and he was consumed with anger and confusion as his mind processed what to do next. All he knew was that he needed to be alone.

He turned on his heel and started to walk in the opposite direction Lea had taken with Danny. Ahead of him was his hometown, but he was just a stranger here now.

"What's happening, Joe?"

It was Scarlet's voice in his earpiece.

"Joe, are you there?"

He knew the rest of the ECHO team wanted to know what had happened, but he couldn't face them – not after this. His mind was in turmoil as he tried to get a grip on what had just happened. He tore out the earpiece, tossed it on the filthy ground, and walked away until he was lost in the crowd.

\*

Lexi Zhang took the elevator to her parents' apartment. So this was it. Maybe her father would pull through, but that wasn't what it had sounded like when she spoke with her mother. This was probably the last time she would ever see her father alive, and she felt shame wash over her when she thought about all the times she had decided to call him, and then lowered the phone down. Life had a way of punishing things like that, and she knew this was punishment time.

The elevator hit the tenth floor and she heard the same, sad metallic ping that had marked so much of her childhood. The door slid open and she saw the dimly lit hall where she had played as a child, lonely and full of dreams.

Mr. Liu was playing his music too loud in No. 3 again. Some things never got old. Maybe later she would go around and tell him his fortune, but now it was time to see her father. She hoped her mother was holding things together, at least. She was a very capable and strong woman and right now they needed each other more than ever.

She fumbled through her bag for the key and then slid it into the lock.

Nothing happened.

She tried it again and realized something was jamming it, so she rang the intercom and called out to her mother.

"Mama?"

No response.

"It's Xiaoli."

She heard her mother fumbling with the lock. She imagined her frail hands struggling with the thing, her mind distracted by her dying husband. A wave of sadness came over her. She was not expecting it to feel like this and worked hard to control herself.

The door clicked open an inch but stayed ajar.

"Mama?" Lexi pushed the door open halfway and peered down into the unlit hall. This was strange. Her mother always kept the hall light on at this time of night. Then again, these were very different times, she considered with a sad shrug.

"Mama?"

She stepped inside, and she saw it a second too late to react.

The man was somehow above the door, holding himself in place with the sheer power of his arm and leg muscles.

He powered an aggressive leopard punch into her throat and then a split second later he delivered a savage thunderclap strike to her right ear. The first blow nearly crushed her windpipe and the second one knocked her off her feet and ruptured the tympanic membrane in her ear. She was confused, disoriented, and now struggling to breathe and unable to maintain her balance.

Lexi Zhang collapsed to the floor in her parent's hall and looked up just in time to see Monkey leap down from the position he had wedged himself in above the door. He landed beside her with the agility and terrifying power of a panther and then cocked his head as he leaned in to deliver a Shaolin horn punch that slammed her into cold, silent darkness.

# EPILOGUE

Dirk Kruger couldn't help noticing how the bravado he had felt back in Horak's mansion when he'd lectured Hawke about the Oracle seemed much harder to muster when standing right in front of the man himself. Now, in the study of one of Wolff's opulent residences his main impulse was to crawl away into a hole and never share his company again.

"You got the sword, Dirk. Very good."

Kruger started to relax as he watched Wolff caressing the long, ancient blade; his face now reflecting the deep, blue glow that emanated from its hardened steel. "Yes, sir. It was a piece of cake."

The Oracle had a file marked KRUGER on his desk. He thumbed through some of the pages, but the effort was perfunctory; only a fool would presume he hadn't already studied the man standing opposite him. "I was impressed with you when you found the Lost City, and you have certainly shown me that you can deal with the ECHO team as well. This plus your successful retrieval of the Tinia idol has pleased me greatly. I have decided to keep you alive."

Kruger swallowed hard and took a step away from the desk. He hadn't realized the price of failure on this mission would have been his life, and now he hardly knew what to say, except: "Thank you, sir."

Wolff nodded casually, but he had returned his obsessive gaze to the sword. "You know what this sword means to me?"

"You said it would open a gateway?" Something about

the way Wolff was staring at the blade had upset Kruger. He was an arms dealer – a thug at heart – and now his insatiable greed had led him into the service of this depraved monster. He thought of Faust with a shudder and started to wonder what he had done.

"You pay attention to my words. Also very good."

A long silence followed, and Kruger worked hard to stay calm and keep his breathing soft and level.

"The Sword of Fire... Dyrnwyn, Excalibur – they're all the same thing. This blade in my hands did not come from the western lands where you found it. Originally it came from the east. Did you know that?"

"No, I did not, Mr. Wolff."

"You address me as Oracle or sir."

"Yes, Oracle."

"That is if you want to be part of all this."

"Of course, Oracle."

"This blade in my hands, *arms dealer*," he said these last two words with contempt, "has the power I need to locate and open the gateway to the king's tomb. Inside that tomb is something very critical to me and my mission... this *pilgrimage* I am on."

"Yes, sir."

"Very critical indeed..."

The Oracle stared at the Tanit idol on the shelf behind his desk. Beside it were two new additions – Tinia and then Viracocha, the primordial deity of the Incan culture. Kruger recognized the idol of Viracocha. He had found it in the treasure haul he had stolen from Paititi back in Peru while Saqqal was obsessing over his Utopia plague. The second he saw it he'd known who to go to for a quick sale.

"I see, sir."

He let out a long, satisfied sigh. "Oh, these idols! If you only knew what they meant, you would break down

285

and cry right now, down on your knees like a man humbled before the very presence of the divine."

"What do they mean, sir? Gold? Treasure?"

The Oracle laughed, but it quickly turned sour. "Treasure? You sad little man, is that all you can think of?"

"I'm sorry, Oracle."

"You're forgetting yourself, arms dealer."

"Yes, sir – but why are the idols so important?"

The Oracle studied Kruger's face for a few moments, and the South African wasn't sure if asking him that question had angered him or pleased him. "The idols are not just golden likenesses of gods and goddesses, arms dealer. The idols are a pathway to a brand new future for mankind, but they will also unlock something terrible that will shake this world to its core."

"I don't understand, sir."

"No, I know you don't, and I doubt you have the intellectual capacity to process what I am talking about."

Kruger felt a wave of anger rise in him. How dare this man talk to him like that? But then, was he a man? Before he could formulate something to say that might save face, the Oracle spoke again.

"You will use the Sword of Fire to locate and open the king's tomb. Is that clear?"

"Yes, sir."

"And you will work with *athanatoi*, is that understood?"

Kruger didn't know what to say. He was used to working with his own men – former soldiers, arms dealers, mercenaries, and thugs. Now, Otmar Wolff was ordering him to complete a difficult mission with a bunch of idiot cultists who all thought they were Mr. Anderson from the Matrix.

"Well?" The Oracle's tone was severe.

Kruger knew immediately what to say in response. "Of course, sir."

"Good... *good*." The Oracle's voice sounded as dry as deadwood on a salt flat as he turned the word over in his mouth. "A mighty battle is racing toward humanity, Arms Dealer. The fog of war will choke every last person in this world when the fighting starts, and it's going to start soon. Very soon."

## THE END

# AUTHOR'S NOTE

The next Joe Hawke novel will be released later in 2017 and will tie up the loose ends in this novel in what will be the fastest, hardest Hawke book to date. Aside from being a supercharged bloodbath, it will also mark a pivotal, climactic point in the current arc and the start of a new one, bringing fresh challenges, victories, and tragedies for the ECHO team. On the series in general, I wanted to say that I'm blown away by how successful it has been and want to thank every reader who has enjoyed the books and made it possible.

The next release is my so-called 'Mystery Project', which is a fast-paced and exciting new series. Similar to Hawke and the ECHO team (and in the same universe), this new series is based on Hawke-style adventure mysteries and features a new band of really exciting tearaways (and some truly hideous villainy). I hope you enjoy the new characters and their adventures, and if you do I'll write more. I'm particularly looking forward to seeing how the new team will handle ECHO, and I think Cairo is about to meet her match at last.

Finally, please consider leaving a review if you enjoyed this novel or any of my other stories. Without reviews, a series loses visibility and disappears faster than a bottle of vodka in Scarlet Sloane's fridge.

So long for now, Rob

Printed in Great Britain
by Amazon

26926654R00169